MOUNTAIN OF FANGS

CARLO HART

Edited by <u>Sara Kelly</u>

Cover design by <u>100 Covers</u>

1

THE BARN

The barn felt haunted. But Kevin was probably just being paranoid.

He would have found something to cover the glassless windows with, but he didn't want to touch anything. The old barn was disgusting. If Kevin moved too much, rats or giant spiders would jump out and run over his shoes. There was garbage everywhere.

He sat on a soft, rotten couch that slumped in a corner. There was one working lamp, and it must have been an 8-watt bulb. It was more like a practical joke of a light. Did anyone make gag light bulbs? The barn was mostly dark.

Kevin was furious. He clenched his jaw until his teeth ached. His green eyes flashed, contrasting with his reddish brown hair and freckles.

Wait, was this even a barn? Kevin didn't see any hay, horses, or stalls. But it had barn doors, so he guessed it narrowly averted being labeled a hobo stink box.

He was stuck there for the night. Even if he wanted to leave, he couldn't. The plan had seemed like the perfect option in the daylight. He couldn't pick up the key to the new rental house until the next day. Kevin had all his stuff in the car and no place to stay. So, Todd offered his barn as a one-night stop, even though he would be out of town.

The problem was, his girlfriend, Faith, needed the car to work her shift at the hospital. He smiled at the thought of her. She was tall, raven-haired and very curvy. Her southern drawl made her sound as sexy as she looked.

He didn't realize the barn had one barely dim light. Or how far the nearest neighbor was.

It reminded Kevin of the *Friends* episode where Monica has a secret closet where she keeps all her random junk. That's what this barn was, Monica's secret closet. That's how Todd kept his house so clean. He threw all his crap in the barn.

Fine, thought Kevin, *it's one night. I'll hunker down and watch something on YouTube.*

He looked at his phone; it had 20 percent battery left. He felt in his pocket for the charger.

Oh, goddammit.

Faith had driven away with it.

So, the only thing separating me from a caveman is this 3-watt bulb? Kevin's heart sped up.

He exhaled slowly; smashing his fist through a wall would help nothing. He should try to find a book or maga-zine before the sun disappeared and the barn went totally dark. Kevin looked along the edges of piles, trying not to disturb too much. He used the light on his phone as little as possible. After ten minutes, he was unsuccessful and annoyed.

I guess Todd's not a big reader, he thought.

Kevin stopped searching. He walked away from a wall of trash bags and tripped over an ancient plank. It looked like part of a door. Underneath it, his eye glimpsed white. It was an old paperback. The cover said *Night Shift* by Stephen King.

Wonderful, a horror book. Just what I need in this creepy ass barn, he thought. He jammed it in his back pocket.

Besides, time to go upstairs and check on the secret babies.

The whole reason he was in this barn was the babies, so he'd better watch them. He could have left his stuff on the porch and come back the next day to unlock the new house. But he couldn't leave the babies out for all the neighbors to see.

He walked up the shaky steps to an unfinished loft. There was no furniture, just floor. Not even any trash. Against the wall was a pile of lights, pumps, buckets, plant food. Kevin's equipment. In the corner, in a little pool of fluorescent light, under a plastic dome, were his tiny baby plants. Medical cannabis clones, to be exact. The last remnants of his hellish time up north, in Merced.

Of the plants he had grown, these were the big yielders. These were the supermodels. They grew gorgeous, enormous flowers that sparkled with swollen THC crystals. The dispensaries in L.A. were going to love them.

He lifted the lid to check the temperature. Warm, but not too hot. Perfect. He took a water bottle from the pile of equipment. Carefully, he fed each plant. Too much water and they would get root rot and stop growing and die. Too little, they withered up and died too. But if you got it just right, then these babies became big, tall trees. All from these tiny clones. It was a balance. Which was why Kevin enjoyed growing.

Keep things in balance and you have a beautiful garden that makes patients happy and pays your rent. If you slip up, if you neglect them, all you end up with is dead plants and a thousand-dollar light bill. It was always a big gamble, but like his friend Todd loved to say, "Those who dare, win."

Kevin wanted to avoid the dump downstairs, but there was no furniture in the loft, and he would go blind in five minutes trying to read by the fluorescent light. Back down he went.

The sun was gone. The downstairs was dark except for the joke light next to the rotten couch. Kevin made his way across the trash minefield. He plopped down and pulled out a joint.

He finished all his work. Time for a smoke and an episode of *The Honeymooners* on YouTube, before the battery on his phone ran down. He watched an episode where Ralph and Ed were trying to sell household appliances on TV. Kevin shook his head. *Everyone is a hustler.* This thought made him laugh.

Kevin looked at the battery. He stopped laughing. Ten percent left. Kevin shut it off. He pulled the paperback out of his pocket. It was a collection of short stories. Kevin could live with that. Short stories were like a fling: there was no commitment, and they could be over in an hour.

The first story, called "Jerusalem's Lot," started off slowly. Kevin was thinking it wasn't very scary until halfway through he realized, with electricity running up his back, that it was about vampires. He fucking hated vampires. He told no one, but vampires were a recurring childhood nightmare.

Really, Stephen King? Really? All alone in this horror movie barn and you throw vampires at me? Kevin was angry. But he wasn't about to stop reading.

When he finished with the story, he put the book down. He listened. The forest was quiet. He looked at his phone. It was ten. And his battery was down to 9 percent.

Ten o'clock? No way he could fall asleep yet. Might as well read another story. This one was about giant mutated rats. Considering Kevin had heard scurrying feet five minutes ago, he was not happy about this story either. It was getting cold, so he zipped up his jacket and pulled the hood on. Soon he was warm. His eyes closed. The book fell out of his hand, and he was snoring.

He slept for hours. His body was tired from the driving and the moving. Hauling all his equipment up the stairs to the loft seemed easy at first. By the tenth trip, he was sore and hated stairs, lofts, and barns. A noise woke him up. Kevin looked around. The entire first floor was dark, except for the pool of dull yellow light from the joke bulb. He looked at his phone. It was midnight.

God, this night will never end.

He heard the noise again. It was like a quiet shuffling. He looked in the far corner—a man was standing there watching him.

He had red eyes and long fangs.

The adrenaline hit Kevin so hard; he jumped off the couch and kicked the lamp over. The bulb shattered and the room went immediately dark.

2

BAD CHUCKLING

Kevin stumbled and pulled his phone out before he tripped and hit the floor. He pushed a button, and the phone lit up the darkness. Kevin whipped it around to the far corner. There was nothing there. He looked around. The room was empty.

What the hell?

He was positive there had been someone right there. That's when the howling started. Kevin jumped straight up. He cursed profusely when he realized it was just a pack of coyotes. He looked at his phone. It was now at 5 percent.

Stupid idiot phone. I would smash you if I could afford it.

Maybe he could find some candles. He would have to be fast. His phone was almost dead. The howling was getting louder. More howls joined the chorus. Now it sounded like a big gang. He stopped and listened. They were screaming, not howling. Kevin could feel goosebumps popping up. It seemed like the screams were coming from all sides. They surrounded the cabin. Kevin was happy for the big barn doors. Nothing was getting through that.

Oh, no. The windows have no glass. Could they jump through?

He picked up the dusty plank he had fallen over earlier. The screaming continued, but he could hear them running around the house now. Like they were all circling. Something hit the enormous doors.

That's when Kevin decided it was time to go. He ran up the stairs to the loft. Something inside told him to turn off the little fluorescent light. So, Kevin stood in the darkness, humiliated. One hand on his phone, the other holding the plank.

This whole staying-in-the-barn-for-one-night plan is working out real frickin' well.

The howling died down. At first, he thought he was imagining their howls getting farther away. But then they faded in the distance; the coyotes were moving on. Kevin's body relaxed. He wouldn't have to kill coyotes with his bare hands after all. He moved to turn the light back on when he heard a new sound. Someone was walking around downstairs.

Kevin felt cold fire race through his body. More adrenaline. He heard it clearly. Footsteps. He could even hear when they were stepping over piles of garbage. He froze and held his breath. Maybe they didn't know he was up there. The steps came closer, as if answering him. He could hear them pause at the bottom of the stairs. Kevin whipped his head around. There was nowhere to run. He was trapped.

Kevin blurted out, "I've got a big gun! Come up here and I will shoot you in the face." He smacked the wooden plank against the door frame for emphasis—even though it sounded nothing like a gun.

He heard a foot on the first step. And then, he wasn't sure why, he yelled, "I've got silver bullets!" His heart was running, his breathing quick. The footsteps stopped. Kevin thought maybe he heard another softer sound. Chuckling?

Kevin suddenly felt a bone-deep cold. He stood still, waiting for the footsteps to come up the stairs. He waited. And waited. He looked at his phone. He was standing there for over an hour. Kevin finally sat down. He was stiff, and his joints hurt.

Was the person still downstairs? He heard no more footsteps. But the big creaky doors downstairs never opened. Could someone crawl out of a window silently? They must still be there, waiting for him to fall asleep. He would not let that happen. Kevin backed himself up against a corner. He pulled his knees up. He held on to the plank with both hands. He would not fall asleep.

When Kevin woke up, the sun was blasting through the windows. He blinked; he was in the same position. The plank was still in his hands. He cursed himself and stood up. Kevin went down the stairs, cautiously, plank raised. In the daylight, the barn transformed from a terrifying cave to a plain old junk shed. How much of last night was his imagination? He had been hungry, tired, cold, bored.

It was that damn Stephen King book.

Combined with the weed, it had activated his paranoia. A couple of coyotes and a few shadows had turned him into a big baby. He was glad that there had been no one around to witness his impressive stupidity. He was stepping over a pile of old coffee cans when he froze. In the corner, in the dust, he could clearly see footprints. They were way bigger than his shoes. And they looked brand new.

Someone had been there last night.

He scanned the room. Kevin realized he was no longer holding the plank.

BAM, BAM, BAM!

He jumped backwards and fell over a bag.

"Babe, are you in there? Did you survive?" It was his girlfriend, Faith. She was banging on the barn door.

He got up, angry at himself. "Yeah, I'm in here." His voice cracked. He cleared his throat. "Hold on, let me unlock it."

He pushed the heavy doors open; they squealed. Faith hugged him around the neck and kissed his face. He could see his dog Inky, the blackest Labrador anyone ever saw, wagging her tail inside the car. The gang was all there.

"Missed you," she said. "How was your first night on the mountain?"

Kevin looked around. "It was boring. Super quiet. Nothing happened. Did some writing and then I fell asleep."

"Cool, so you wouldn't mind staying another night," she teased.

"No, thanks. Let's pack the equipment and get the hell out."

"You hear that?" Faith asked.

Howling.

"Coyotes," he said. *Welcome to Frazier Mountain. I'm going to need a big gun*, he thought.

3

A COZY CABIN

Kevin and Faith moved all of his stuff into the new house that afternoon. It was actually a cabin with a lot of windows and a small deck. It sat back a good thirty yards from the road, surrounded by trees so you could barely see the house until you walked down the driveway.

The inside of the house was cozy but a little old. The walls were wood paneling and there was a fireplace in the corner. There were three bedrooms and a loft upstairs. Enough room for Kevin to have a small but efficient growing operation.

The appliances were ancient relics. They were avocado green and looked like they came from the 70s. They were unusable. But the rent was awesome: seven hundred and fifty dollars for an entire house. And the surroundings were perfect. It was quiet, remote, with no streetlights, so the stars were dazzling. This would be an inspirational place to write.

While Kevin enjoyed growing plants for a mediocre living, he truly wanted to be a successful writer. And he had come so close to breaking through in Los Angeles, he still couldn't believe it hadn't worked out. He had almost sold a "very big!" script to a "very big!" studio. There were many meetings and many promises—an "A" list star had even been attached—but it all fell apart.

Kevin and Faith brought in his couch, flatscreen, bed, and coffee table. Inky ran around wagging her tail the whole time. Kevin could tell that she loved being in the mountains. It was probably the smell of the forest, there were trees everywhere. With all the hiking trails and rabbits, this place was Labrador paradise.

The forest was a lot nicer than the Target parking lot where he had bought her for fifty bucks. A gorgeous black lab puppy. He could not turn that down. She went from a tiny football to a full-size dog in the hellish year he had spent in Merced.

When they barely escaped, he promised himself on the way out of town, Inky would grow up in a nicer place. He was keeping his promise. The mountain was perfect.

Kevin relaxed into the couch, and Faith joined him. They watched a couple of classic episodes of *THE X-FILES* until the sun went down. When it was dark, they sneaked the growing equipment into the house. Though the neighbors weren't on top of them, they could still see what they were doing if they looked out their windows.

They lugged the lights and the bags of food, and then Faith passed out. Kevin was too wired to sleep, so he set up the rooms. It needed to get done, so he did it.

The bedroom was roomy enough that he could run a mother cabinet and a shelf for clones. He had preserved six clones from Merced, and he was going to turn one of them into a big mother plant. A plant that would feed him and pay the rent, the golden goose.

Kevin was the only person who had the strain—

Madman—because Todd had given him a seed he had accidentally created. So, Kevin grew it, and it turned out to be a holy grail plant. A plant that growers were looking for. It had the stink of lemon Pledge, the smell the dispensaries wanted, with the large heavy buds that smokers coveted.

It had yielded half a pound off of one bucket. Just one bucket! Now he would fill the new grow house and pull in ten thousand a month.

With that kind of money, he could buy his own house before he was a toothless old bone.

Okay, you can stop counting your money before it's in your hand, he thought.

Inky wagged her tail and let out a quiet bark.

Kevin interpreted it as, "Hey, stoner, stop daydreaming. I'm about to pee."

He grabbed his new Carhart jacket and a powerful flashlight. Kevin leashed Inky, and they headed out the door. He kissed Faith on the forehead on the way out. Was there a way to make a forehead kiss look manly? Kevin didn't think so.

4

FLAPPING IN THE WIND

oddamn, it's darker than King Kong's butt crack. Kevin laughed to himself. It wasn't funny, but in Kevin's experience, the best way to not act scared was to not act scared.

There was a path that went from behind the house down to a wooded trail that ended in a ravine. It was dark, remote, and surrounded by trees and shadows. Kevin, having grown up in Detroit, had little nature experience. Nothing was scarier to him than going for a walk at night, in the woods all alone. With no weapon, just a flashlight.

He unclicked Inky's leash, and she bounced down the path. She already knew not to run out of his sight.

Just keep your thoughts positive and everything will be cool. Whatever you do, don't think about the barn.

Why would I think about the barn?

I'm not.

Good.

God, that barn was creepy.

Kevin started thinking about last night in the barn. The coyotes were annoying, maybe a little unnerving. But the thing that bothered Kevin all day, the thing that made him dread walking in the woods, was what had been standing in the corner. He had only seen two things before it disappeared.

One, it had red eyes. And two, it had long silver fangs. He could have written it all off as a Stephen King incited imaginary hallucination if he hadn't seen those damned footprints.

Why am I thinking about this right now?

He would not tell Faith about this. She had already been to hell and back in Merced. He did not want to dump more paranormal strangeness in her lap. She was still recuperating.

"Ink stain, let's go." He heard nothing. "Inky."

He looked into the blackness, but he couldn't see her. It didn't help that she was even blacker than the night. He didn't want to go into the shadows to find her. He saw movement. She burst out of the bushes.

Okay, good, he thought. *We can get the hell out of here.*

Kevin wouldn't say he was afraid of the dark. More like afraid of the dark woods in the middle of nowhere. That seemed logical. Inky stopped and growled. Her hair stood up like a mohawk down her whole back. Kevin heard a strange flapping sound. It reminded him of a flag whipping in the wind.

He looked around for the source, seeing nothing. Kevin used the flashlight but only found trees. He pointed the flashlight up. There, floating twenty feet above him, was the red-eyed man. His trench coat flapped in the wind. Kevin noticed his long, clawed fingers, before he bared his fangs and flew straight down at him. Kevin threw himself into the dirt. The thing flew right over him.

The house was one hundred yards down the trail. Kevin sprinted for it.

"Go, Inky!" They ran.

Kevin heard it dive bombing again. He lay down and rolled over on his back. He pulled his legs up and kicked, catching it in the face. He felt his right ankle crunch. The flying man shrieked and pulled up. Kevin rolled over and ran. He almost fell the first time he put weight on the ankle, but he kept his balance and made it home.

Inky was waiting at the door. Hair still standing. Faith woke up when Kevin slammed the door. He was lying on the floor, holding his ankle.

"Sweets, what's wrong? What happened?" she said.

"Twisted my ankle. Stupid tree root." He tried to hide his heavy breathing.

Faith motioned him over. "Get over here, let me look at it."

"Fine."

"You know I'm the boss when it comes to medical stuff," she said.

"Yeah, yeah." He hopped over to the couch on one foot.

She took his size nine foot in her hands. Kevin felt warm electricity go through it. Faith had healing powers.

"Feels like a light sprain. Nothing too serious," she said.

Kevin kept his eyes on the door. "Can you do the thing where you make it heal faster?"

"Sure. And it's called Reki," Faith said.

"Yeah, that thing, rice-a-roni."

"It's energy healing," she said.

Kevin hoped she couldn't feel his racing pulse through his ankle. *What if that thing kicks down the door?* he wondered. Inky wasn't big enough yet to hold anything at bay. Let alone a red-eyed, flying vampire.

Yes, his mind repeated, a real vampire.

What if it kicked the door down? He had no weapons. No gun, no knife, no club, no bat. Not even a goddamn stick. Wait, there was the axe for firewood. It came with the house.

"Hold on." He got up.

He limped to the back closet and came back with an axe.

Faith laughed. "What is that for? Is this where you admit to being an axe murderer? Now that you got me alone in the woods?"

"No, we need to get firewood. If I leave the axe in the corner, I'll remember tomorrow," he lied.

"Now, come over here and put something good on."

Kevin picked up the remote.

"We've got the new episode of *Ancient Aliens* on the DVR," he said.

She clapped her hands. "You know I love that show, babe."

They watched together, sharing their body heat to stay warm. Faith fell asleep first, leaving Kevin to keep staring at the door. Eventually his eyes got heavy, and he fell asleep too.

Kevin's eyes snapped open when the howling started. It sounded like the house was surrounded. Kevin went to the corner. He felt better with the axe in his hands. Faith woke up to the noise.

"What is that?" she asked.

"Coyotes."

"Sounds like an army of them." She rubbed her eyes.

"I wish I had a gun."

"You should have said something sooner." Faith pulled a large silver revolver out of her purse.

"What? How long have you had that?" Kevin asked.

"My daddy gave it to me when I turned eighteen. He said

if a man doesn't take no for an answer, just point it at his crotch. I always have it with me. I thought you knew that."

"I would have remembered that you have a cannon in your purse."

She handed it to him. "Just don't blow your own foot off."

Kevin felt it in his hand. It was heavy. He liked it. He read the stamp on the side of the barrel: 357 magnum.

They listened together. After a few minutes, the howls moved on.

Kevin stood up. "Let's go to sleep in the bedroom. I've had enough of the couch."

"Sounds good to me." They got into bed together.

Faith snuggled up to him. Her warmth was a relief. She was quickly snoring. Normally that would've put Kevin to sleep, immediately. Instead, he stared at the window, waiting to see a pair of red eyes, waiting to unload the magnum in his hand.

5

THE GREENEST LAWN EVER

When Kevin woke up, it was already eleven in the morning, and Inky was giving him that look again. He was going to grumble, but he knew there was no arguing with a full bladder. Besides, better she go outside than inside.

"Let's go, Ink."

The sun was bright, but Kevin didn't feel like going down the back path into the woods. A casual walk with Inky was the perfect excuse to check out the surrounding neighborhood in the daylight.

Pine Mountain Club was basically the exact opposite of where he grew up in Detroit. Here the roads were wide and pristine. There were no traffic lights, just stop signs. No trash or graffiti, just trees and more trees. He could have sat in the road and read a book. Cars drove by maybe once an hour. It was quiet, beautiful, and not nearly as creepy when the sun was out. The houses were all set back from the road by fifty yards. You could usually tell how wealthy a neighborhood was by how close the houses were to the road.

All the houses on the street had giant pine trees on their property. They had massive thick trunks, and were as tall as buildings. They were impressive. The houses blended into the forest. It was like the owners were embarrassed about being human. They didn't want to stick out. So, the houses tended to be log cabins.

But cabin was an understatement. These were more like log mansions. They were big, with multiple floors, oversized windows, and long porches that stretched around the house. The wood was luxurious, colored deep red or dark brown. Each house was its own accomplishment.

Kevin felt very lucky that this was his new neighborhood. He wound his way down the road and found an empty lot. He let Inky off her leash.

"Go make your deposit, girl."

She ran off.

He didn't want to piss anyone off by letting Ink do her business on their lawn. Not that there was anyone around to see it. Most of the houses were empty during the week. These were weekend getaways or summer houses. Occasionally he would pass a little A-frame house. Normal, not rich people lived in them and they were there year-round. The A-frames looked lived in, while the mansions did not.

He thought about Faith sleeping back in the cabin. How much longer could he keep these new attacks from her? Did that put her in danger, or should he keep her in the dark? It was only a year ago that he didn't believe in the paranormal. But that all changed with the knock knock game.

The stupid knock knock game.

$\sim$

evin had recently moved into one of the empty houses on the ranch in Merced. They hired him to grow an outdoor crop behind an old garage that no one used anymore. The plot of land was perfect. It bathed in sun all day and was hidden by a pair of hills.

Kevin was playing with puppy Inky in the house. Actually, it was more of an ambitious shack than anything. He was teasing Ink with a rope toy; he would swing it around just out of her reach and then he would clap his hands. Inky loved it. She would jump up and bark, wagging her tail. Kevin danced around her and switched from clapping to snapping his fingers. Inky loved this too. Kevin switched again. This time he started knocking on the walls. He would knock twice and then say, "Who's that?" and Inky would bark.

He knocked twice and was about to say, "Who's that?" when he heard two loud knocks back. Kevin froze and then realized it was someone at the door. It was probably Faith. She must have gotten off work early and was at the front door. He walked over and opened it.

There was no one there.

Kevin looked around. Faith must be playing a game. He walked to the back of the house. Nothing. He walked back to the front. No one. This was a private ranch; there was no random foot traffic. Kevin slowly closed the door. He looked around, suddenly not very comfortable in the house. Inky watched him. He walked up to the wall. He knocked twice. He waited. Nothing. He looked over at Inky. "See, you're being paranoid for nothing. Silly dog."

The wall knocked twice.

Kevin stepped back quickly. He scooped up football-sized Inky and left the house. He stood outside, wondering where the hell he was going to sleep.

He snapped back, realizing Inky had been off doing her thing for a few minutes. Kevin spotted her farther into the woods than he wanted. He whistled and called to her, "Get over here, Stink. You know you're not supposed to go that far."

Inky looked up and then came running, tail wagging.

"Causing trouble, Missy?" He clicked her leash on. "Let's get out of here."

He walked with her down the steep road. Around the corner and up the street, he would be back home, having made a wide circle around the neighborhood.

But he was in no rush to get back. The air out here was pure, the smell was wood and dirt. It made his heart happy. He could do some real writing here. Maybe he would start today.

And then he saw the house. The shining white house with the greenest lawn ever. It was emerald. It was neon green. It was so green it almost looked fake. In front of the lawn, forming a protective wall, were dozens of swollen, crimson roses. On either side of the lawn were titanic twin pine trees. They looked like the tree that was lit up every year at Rockefeller Plaza for Christmas. They must have been twenty feet wide. And they were a deep green color like none of the other trees in the forest.

The house looked strange too. It just didn't fit in; it looked like it should have been in Washington, D.C. It was stark white and had stately columns. There was a painting of an eagle above the heavy wooden door.

It was almost like someone had flown the house over the forest and dropped it down in the middle of the neighborhood.

Kevin was still staring when the door opened, and a man stepped out. He was holding oversized garden shears. They looked like two machetes. There were black leather gloves on his hands. He wore shiny shoes, grey suit pants, a brilliant white shirt, and a grey vest.

The man's clothes were pristine. He, however, looked like he was a day away from death. His eyes were sunken, his thinning black hair was ragged, and his skin was a dull grey.

This creature created that lawn? Kevin wondered. He realized that Grey Face was watching him stare at his house. Kevin went red, and he waved. He started walking again.

Grey Face just watched him walk by, following with his eyes, not moving his head. Like a crocodile. Kevin kept walking. "Real friendly around here." Inky wagged her tail.

That night Faith made delicious lasagna with both beef and sausage. They watched a couple of episodes of *Game of Thrones*, and they had passionate, primal sex on the couch.

Normally Kevin would be very satisfied with that Friday night. But he kept his eye on the clock the whole time. He couldn't wait to walk Inky and get back to the house with the greenest lawn ever. At night, in the dark, he could watch that house all he wanted, without being spotted by Grey Face. There was something about that lawn. Something about that house that didn't sit right. Kevin felt like it was important to watch it. He got dressed and put Ink on the leash a little early, but he didn't care. Dark was dark. Grey Face wouldn't see him.

This time he took the .357 revolver and stuck it in his pants. It was too big, so he tried his jacket. The front pockets were too small. He tried the inside pocket. It kind of fit, but the grip stuck out at a funny angle. It was obvious what he was carrying.

But Kevin thought about it. There were no cops up there.

Literally. None. The closest police station was about half an hour away, down winding, twisty roads. There was a tiny private security force up there, but all they carried were flashlights. They barely patrolled. So, Kevin could do what the hell he wanted, without worrying about getting caught.

I'm beginning to like mountain living, he thought. He walked out of the house with the magnum sticking out of his jacket.

The moon was brilliant. So bright that he could see the color of his own sneakers. He didn't need the flashlight to see. It was like a darker daytime. With no streetlights, the moon actually made a difference. He would pay attention to the phases of the moon from now on.

Inky did her business on an empty, grassy lot, and they continued walking until they came to the super green lawn house. The tall trees threw long shadows. Kevin found one and stood in it. He was totally cloaked. He was thankful that Inky was blacker than a ninja.

Kevin watched, motionless, for fifteen minutes. He would have felt like a creepy stalker, but he wasn't watching a girl. He was watching a weirdo sickly man puttering around the downstairs. He watched Grey Face go from room to room, cleaning or whatever—Kevin couldn't tell—but what he did know was that this was boring. Nothing of interest to watch. Clearly, he had misread the vibe of the house. Maybe a green lawn was just a green lawn.

Inky was getting impatient just sitting there on the cold road. Kevin was ready to go back when he looked up at the second floor. All the rooms upstairs were dark. The black windows showed nothing. Kevin's heart stopped and then galloped when he saw the pair of glowing red eyes looking out at him.

He took off down the street, Inky running next to him. Kevin was sure the red eyes were following him.

6

TODD THE FAKER

Todd pushed the white Saab convertible to ninety as he crested the hill. There was rarely a cop under the overpass. Todd was happy to gamble. He was usually lucky.

It was another beautiful day in Southern California. Todd wondered why more people didn't have a convertible. *If you're not enjoying life, you are just dying slowly.*

He looked over at the duffel bag in the passenger seat. He made sure it was zippered shut. It was thousands of dollars' worth of product. No way he was going to let that blow away in the wind.

A motorcycle cop shot out from behind a construction sign. Todd looked in the mirror. Now was a good time to exit the freeway. After a bend in the road, he scooted across two lanes and then hid behind a truck. As he exited, he saw the cop motoring past, looking around, trying to find him.

"Suck it, officer." He laughed out loud.

Todd made his way down Foothill Boulevard and pulled into the dispensary parking lot around the back of the building. He got to use the special vendor's entrance. There was extra security here because of all the money that came in and out. He walked through the metal detector; security looked through his bag.

"Go ahead," said a bulky guard with a Glock hanging off his hip.

Todd walked into the dispensary show room. This place did business right on the floor amongst the customers. Todd preferred this to doing business in a back room. In the back, there were no distractions. People paid closer attention to his pitch. He didn't want that. Out here there were enough distractions that they would give it a quick look, giving Todd enough time to tell a story, and then they were putting a fat wad of cash in his hand and he was on to the next dispensary.

"Hey, man, thanks for coming in." The owner was a short fat guy who looked more like a stay-at-home dad than a weed store boss. Todd remembered Fat Dad was named Edmond.

"No problem, Edmond, my man. I only like dealing with good shops because it reflects on my rep, and your spot gets great reviews."

"Thanks, appreciate it." Everyone loved to be flattered. Todd always used this approach. "Now tell me about this batch," said Edmond.

"Well, this was a very special run. These are all F2 seeds, created in the optimum humidity environment to guarantee 95 percent germination rates. I backcrossed the original legendary Krakken mother with a new Super Krakken male to revitalize the genetics of the line. This is by far my best batch of seeds yet. We are talking heavy yielder, short stature, quick flower time."

Todd pulled out a small vile. He dumped two big colorful buds onto the counter. They were gorgeous, magazine centerfold, quality flowers. "Here is an example of what these seeds turn into. This came from these exact seeds. I grow out every run so I can guarantee their quality. And as you know, no one else on the planet has this strain," Todd bragged.

Edmond marveled at the colorful, fat buds. Todd had purchased them from the store next door ten minutes ago. "My patients are going to love these flowers," Edmond said.

Todd knew he almost had the sale. Now for the finishing move. Todd unzipped the bag and pulled out a packet of seeds. The packaging was beautiful, modern and slick. It was a plastic square container, with rounded corners, grey foam inside, and a 3D silver foil design on the front. The logo was a mountain outline with the words "Secret Mountain Genetics" across the image.

When Todd had started out, he sold the seeds in little envelopes. He hardly sold any. When he switched to expensive packaging, he sold every single pack.

Life was about illusion. Make people think they were getting something expensive and they would pay all day. But it had to look good.

Edmond looked over the packaging and whistled. "These seeds look great."

Idiot. You couldn't tell the quality of a seed by looking at it. It was the packaging he was reacting to. Another sale made.

Edmond made up his mind. "I'll take a thousand packs."

Todd charged fifteen dollars per pack. The stores would turn around and sell them for forty.

He put $15,000 into Todd's hand. Todd had long ago learned never to count the money in front of dispensary owners. They liked to feel like they could be trusted. The big boss's word was good.

"My patients love growing special genetics. You make my place look good. Come back anytime." He shook Todd's hand.

Todd walked out with the bag on his shoulder and a roll of cash in his back pocket.

My god, people are stupid, he thought. All that scientific jargon had been straight-up bullshit he had read on the internet. Todd had no idea what an F2 was, and he certainly couldn't backcross anything. He didn't have a clue. He knew it sounded like a lot of work, and he wasn't down with that.

Seeds could be made one of two ways. You could breed male and female plants, grow out their seeds, select for the best traits, combine them, and then grow seeds again. They did this over and over until the genetic line stabilized, and the seeds grew similar plants every time.

This was a slow method, but it ensured that growers got good strong genes that would turn into good yielding, easy-to-grow plants. The other way to do it was the Frankenstein method. You got a female plant and stressed it until it turned into a hermaphrodite and literally laid itself. The result was hundreds of seeds. Todd had jars and jars of them.

The problem was that seeds from hermies tended to turn into hermies themselves. Hermaphrodites were a grow-er's worst nightmare. Instead of flowering big female buds, the hermaphrodites suddenly sprouted male flowers that would pollinate the entire grow room and ruin the crop. Dispensaries wanted female buds, not buds with male hermaphrodite flowers. They had much less THC and were basically a waste of everyone's time. You couldn't give them away.

But Todd wasn't worried; he had a solution. There were many things that could go wrong during a grow, so it wasn't always easy to pinpoint weak seeds as the culprit.

Todd was ordering real seeds on the internet. He would take one of those seeds and put it in every other pack he sold. This way 50 percent of the people that bought his ten-seed pack would get one good seed. Once they grew it out, the results would amaze them. And then they would tell all their friends how great "Secret Mountain Genetics" seeds were. And anyone that complained about his seeds would be written off as a bad grower—simple.

In the meantime, Todd would stack more and more money. He really didn't care that his seeds would ruin hundreds of grow operations. That's what they got for trusting him. And in about six months, he would quit selling seeds and move on to something else. Before some grower or weed store owner came looking for him. But in the meantime, he could probably make $250,000.

The drive home felt way quicker than the drive into the city. The fifteen thousand in his back pocket made Todd so happy he didn't even notice the traffic.

By the time Todd pulled into his garage, the sun was almost gone. When he walked into the house, *Christly Knows Best* was playing on the flat screen. Todd always kept the TV on when he left. He found coming home to a silent house unnerving.

He put two French bread pizzas in the toaster oven and got a beer out of the fridge. But a beer wasn't complete without an oxy. Although he grew plants and made seeds, he never smoked. It made him too paranoid. He didn't need that kind of stress in his life. He'd rather be smiling than frowning. He pulled open a drawer and looked at a pill bottle. It was almost empty.

Shit. Running low.

Todd sat down in front of the TV and ate his dinner. For dessert, he took his pill. He started zoning out but remembered his plants. He should check the water level before he got too stoned.

He went downstairs to the storage room. It was really a half-finished basement, but around here people called it a storage room. There was a grow tent in the middle of the floor. Off in the corner were supplies. A bag of dirt, pots, bottles of food. He tried to keep the place tidy; it made everything easier.

Inside the grow tent, he felt the soil. It was getting dry. Good thing he had checked. Todd mixed liquid food into a bottle with filtered water and fed each of the four big plants. There were seeds all over the floor. He scooped them up and dropped them into a jar.

It would only take four plants to make some real money. An idiot like Kevin had to grow many more plants in order to make a fraction of what Todd was hauling in. And Kevin had to work for two months for his harvest. Todd perpetually had seeds. Yeah, they were imposter garbage seeds, but no one knew that, for now.

Tomorrow he would hit the Hollywood dispensaries. After that, Malibu. He would not let a day go by without making sales. This business had a ticking clock on it. The thing was, he didn't even need the money. His family was very rich. His bank account was always full. He was selling seeds because at the end of the day, it was funny. Like a huge prank he was playing on everyone, and they happily put money in his hand for the privilege.

And, being honest with himself, he liked the semi rock star status that being a seed seller brought him in the dispensary community. The girls all thought he was a badass, and the guys were in awe of his coolness. He would walk in and people would be like: *That dude is a weedepreneur. He must have a huge grow op somewhere in the mountains.*

He zipped up the tent, laughing to himself. Four plants in a basement, that's all. Also, some advertisements in *High Times* and the best packaging he could buy. It was all so easy.

Had Kevin really spent the night in his garbage barn? Jackass. He only offered the barn because he thought it would be hilarious if Kevin did it. That and he thought Faith was hot. Doing them a favor made Todd look good to her. She could see his big house, his big barn. He had so much stuff that he could let her little boyfriend use some. Successful and generous. That had to affect her, even if it was on a subconscious level.

He would be fucking her before Kevin knew what was happening.

Todd put the full jar of seeds on a shelf with a dozen other jars. He would sell all of these seeds. And then a quick retirement. Or maybe he could switch to an internet business model. Then in order to come after him, they would have to find him. Good luck with that. Plenty of other mountains out there. Plenty of other states, even.

Todd froze...

Did he just hear a noise behind him? Coming from the dark, unfinished part of the room? He turned around slowly, trying to act casual, not scared. He looked into the darkness. He couldn't see anything; it was thick blackness.

Relax, no one could get into this room without me seeing them, he thought.

And there was the expensive security system that he had installed. He put one in every house he ever rented. He was just being paranoid, which was probably an excellent trait in someone that was doing what he was doing.

Maybe I should keep the shotgun in the grow room from now on. And then behind him, he heard braying, screaming laughter. Todd jumped straight up, easily the highest he had ever leaped. His whole body was covered in goose pimples, and there was so much adrenaline dumped into his system that he saw stars.

When he landed, he stumbled because his feet were already moving, like a cartoon. He flew up the unpainted stairs two at a time. He remembered to slam the door on the way out. Todd grabbed the dining room table and shoved it in front of the storage room door. He then ran upstairs and got his Winchester shotgun. He racked it.

Todd came back downstairs and rummaged through drawers. He was looking for something he never thought he would need. It might be in one of the kitchen drawers that he didn't use. He was pretty sure he remembered the house coming with one.

He pulled open the drawers. Nothing. He kept looking. There, in the bottom drawer, all by itself, the Holy Bible. Todd spent the night sitting in his recliner, shotgun in his hands, the Bible in his lap. The news was on his TV until the morning, though Todd wasn't really watching. The volume was barely audible. He was listening to the sounds of footsteps on his roof.

He wished he could believe they were restless squirrels, but he knew what they were. The laugh disturbed him deep down. It wasn't really a laugh; it was a cackle. A witch's cackle. He knew it was a witch because some creatures could instantly recognize their arch enemy. Since Todd had been a child and seen *Snow White*, the idea of a murderous old witch scared him more than anything. And it was something he never outgrew and refused to tell anyone. All through college, he had the same recurring nightmare he'd had since childhood. He was being chased by a laughing witch.

When the sun came up, Todd drove to the supermarket. He parked, dropped his seat back, and went to sleep. He felt much better passing out, listening to the sounds of people walking past him.

7

GUN STORE

Kevin pulled into the large parking lot. The big red sign on the gun store said, "2nd Amendment Superstore."

He had done some research. This was the biggest gun store in Bakersfield. It was an hour from the house, but he didn't mind getting away from the mountain. Though it was odd being around this many people after spending so much time in the quiet forest. Cities were loud.

Kevin walked in and was immediately glad he chose the store. It was huge, and there were weapons everywhere. The first counter displayed all kinds of knives. On his left was the archery section. He always wanted to learn how to use a bow. Now, living in the forest, he would be able to.

He was there for two things: ammunition and a holster. Although a few minutes of browsing was understandable. He looked at a row of revolvers. One was so big it looked like something a clown would pull out of his pants.

But Kevin already had a revolver. Maybe a rifle. Something powerful enough to blow a hole through a vampire floating in the sky. He was pretty sure they wouldn't sell him anything if he started talking about the flying undead.

Kevin found a holster that he could slip his belt through. Perfect for walking the dog.

Now all he needed was ammunition. The wall was covered in ammo boxes. He looked over the .357 magnum section. It was hard to read all the details on the boxes. He was leaning over, trying to see. Did anyone make silver bullets?

"Please don't lean on the glass, young man." An older man came over. "What can I help you with today?"

"I'm looking for some .357 magnum ammunition," Kevin said.

"Oh, I see," said the man. "And what do you need it for, if you don't mind me asking?"

"Sure. I'm dealing with some big aggressive animals around my house."

"What kind of animals?" he asked.

"Um, like big birds. Like really big," Kevin said.

"You know it's illegal to shoot condors."

"Of course, sir. These aren't condors. They're bigger. I think they're bats."

"I don't know of anything bigger than a condor. Hmmm. What kind of bats?"

"I think they're,"—Kevin hesitated and lowered his voice —"maybe, vampire bats."

Kevin waited to see the man's reaction.

He looked Kevin over carefully. "Where do you live?"

"Frazier Mountain."

The man looked Kevin in the eye. "Yeah, I've heard of problems like that up there."

Kevin was so relieved he almost hugged the man. Maybe he wasn't insane. "So I'm looking for—"

"Silver bullets," the man finished his sentence.

"Exactly!" Kevin said a little too loudly.

"Nope, sorry. No one manufactures anything like that."

"Oh." Kevin tried to think of a solution. There had to be another way.

The old man pulled out a piece of paper and scribbled on it. He looked around. He put it in Kevin's hand. It was an address. "Now, you didn't get this from me, but he may be able to help you. He makes his own custom bullets. He specializes in rare, aggressive animals." The man looked at him soberly over his glasses.

"Thank you," Kevin said and shook his hand.

Kevin drove through the back streets of Bakersfield, looking for the address. After passing it twice, he found it. The house was actually two houses connected by a small brick covered courtyard. The garage was caving in on itself. It looked like a Fred Sanford paradise. Kevin parked and approached the front. He had a feeling he was being watched. Through a rifle scope. He knocked on the door.

A voice yelled from inside, "Are you good or evil? Evil will be met with great force."

"Definitely good," Kevin said. "No need for great force."

"How d'you find me?" He was at the door.

"Guy at the gun store," Kevin said.

"I told him to stop doing that."

"Please," Kevin mumbled, embarrassed, "I need help."

The door swung open. A big guy with shaggy hair, an Iron Maiden t-shirt, camo pants, and combat boots stuck his hand out.

"I'm Diego, but you can call me Diego. I think I can help you. Follow me." He led Kevin through his house. There were books everywhere. Paintings on the wall of weird creatures. There were multiple suits of armor. Kevin saw a weight bench and dumbbells in the middle of the living room. *Interesting decoration choices.*

They came to a big wooden door. Diego unlocked multiple locks. He had to pull hard to get the heavy door open. "Step into the armory."

Kevin entered. Diego closed the door behind them and locked it. "I don't like to leave this door unlocked. Things in here are too dangerous."

Kevin looked around. There were old school weapons in glass cases along the walls. He saw a large ornate battle axe. Kevin tried to open the case.

"No, don't touch that," said Diego. "Some of these weapons are very haunted."

Kevin stepped back.

"What are you looking for?" asked Diego.

"Silver bullets."

"So, vampire problem or werewolf issues?"

"Vampire."

Diego opened a drawer and pulled out a box of bullets. The tips were very shiny. "I'm assuming you got a .357 magnum?"

"Yeah," said Kevin. "How d'you know?"

"No one tries to kill a vampire with a .22."

"How much?"

Diego held one up to the light. "Five hundred bucks for six of them."

"Ouch, that's a little expensive."

"Hey, you can always try Walmart. See if they have any pure silver bullets there."

"You're right," said Kevin. He pulled five hundreds from his wallet. He handed them to Diego.

"Pleasure. You may want a backup weapon in case you lose the gun, run out of bullets, or can't fire in a crowded situation."

"What kind?" said Kevin.

Diego led him over to a case.

"Maybe a bladed weapon? I have this gorgeous double handed bastard sword. A crusader blade."

He was right; it was gorgeous. It gleamed.

"How much?"

"Five thousand," said Diego.

"It's too big. I can't lug this around my neighborhood when I'm walking the dog. And if I used it in the house, I would destroy all my furniture in one swing. Also, goddamn, that's expensive," said Kevin.

"How about this? Shorter but still lethal." Diego could sense Kevin's interest, so he unlocked the case and put the short sword in his hand.

Kevin unsheathed it. It was heavy. He liked it.

"Spanish dagger, a thousand."

Kevin whistled. "That's not cheap."

"It's authentic. And it was blessed by a pope," said Diego.

It was the most beautiful, ornate piece of metal Kevin had ever seen. It should have been in a museum.

"I'll take it."

"Good choice," said Diego. "Now in order for this to actually injure vampires, it has to be pure silver. But silver is very soft, so you can't get into any long battles with this blade. It will bend and it will break."

"Got it." Kevin counted ten hundreds and handed them over.

Diego looked wistfully at the dagger. "You're obviously serious about this. If you feel you need some help, I offer my services for hire." He gave Kevin a business card.

"Good to know." They shook.

Kevin walked back to his car. His phone buzzed in his back pocket. It was a text from Todd.

NEED HELP ASAP. MEET AT MY HOUSE.

Shit. Todd needed help. Kevin really liked Todd. If he needed something, Kevin would not let him down. He jumped in his car and peeled out.

8

CHEST FULL OF GOLD

Todd looked at his phone. Kevin should be there any minute. He pulled the kitchen table away from the basement door and picked the shotgun back up quickly. He kept it pointed at the door.

Kevin would definitely have questions if the table was blocking the door. The plan was simple: get Kevin to help him move his stuff out of the basement without telling him anything. Use him as a human shield, if necessary, then close the door and never open it again. After nailing it shut.

There was a knock at the door.

"Hey, dude, I came as soon as I got your text," said Kevin. "Woah, what's with the shotgun?"

Todd pulled him inside and closed the door quickly. "That's why I called you over. I've been having some intruder issues."

"Issues?" asked Kevin.

"The past couple of nights I heard people trying to get in through the windows and the back door. And I'm not about to call the police," said Todd. "I figured I'd call you."

"That makes sense. I can help."

"Thanks man, I really appreciate it," said Todd. "I knew I could count on a genuine friend. Let's go downstairs."

He opened the door and held it open so Kevin could go first.

"I've always liked your set-up, man. So clean," said Kevin.

"Thanks."

Todd held back a few steps to let Kevin take the lead. He had the shotgun ready. He was looking everywhere around the room. But he saw nothing.

"Let's get this out of here." Todd grabbed jars of seeds. He took them upstairs. He put them into a black duffel bag on the table.

Todd came back for more. Kevin also took jars and moved them upstairs. He stuck them in the bag.

"You got a lot of seeds, dude. That's pretty awesome. You have really helped the grow community with all these great genetics."

"Thanks," said Todd. "To be totally honest with you, I would do it for free if it didn't pay. It just feels good to help people out." Todd rolled his eyes internally. How much more full of crap could he be? He would have found the whole thing hilarious if he weren't terrified of what might still be down there.

After all the jars were moved, he turned off the lights in the grow tent. *Sorry, ladies, I won't be coming back. You are going to die of thirst.* He sprinted up the stairs and closed the door for the last time.

Kevin was in the living room, rolling a big blunt. "We deserve a little reward." He lit it up and then passed it to Todd.

Todd took it and smoked, pretending to enjoy it. He

wasn't about to tell anyone in the weed business that the great marijuana seed expert hated smoking it.

Kevin walked around the room. He looked out the window, trying to seem casual.

"What, do you see anything?" asked Todd, too anxiously.

"Just looking at the moon. You sound a little paranoid. Everything all right?" asked Kevin.

"Yeah, yeah, I'm fine." Todd sat down in the EZ chair. "It's just, this mountain has a weird vibe, you know?"

"I know what you mean. I think it's the lack of streetlights. It's dead black out there."

"Yeah. It's really quiet too. At night, alone in this big house, I hear things," said Todd.

"Things?"

"Ah, it's probably just the house settling or something. Or kids trying to get in. I am the prefect candidate for a robbery. That's why I don't tell anyone what I do. You haven't been telling people, have you?"

"No. For sure not," said Kevin.

"Good. Thanks. If you want to stick around and watch some *Rick and Morty*, I'll order pizza."

"Yeah, right, no one delivers out here."

"Okay, it's frozen pizza, but it's still good. French bread. With sausage," said Todd—a little pathetically.

"You had me at French bread. I'll roll another fatty."

"Sounds great." Todd wanted another body in the house with him. If smoking was the price he had to pay, so be it.

They watched *Rick and Morty* for a couple of hours. If he could keep Kevin there, maybe he would also hear the cackling. Then Todd could be sure he hadn't gone insane. He tried to entice Kevin into a long Fortnite session, but he finally got up and stretched. It was getting late, Kevin announced, and Faith was waiting for him at home.

Did he mention Faith to rub it in his face, Todd wondered? *No, he's too nice for that. Now I am being paranoid.*

"Hey, man, thanks for coming over. It was a big help," said Todd. "Here, take a bunch of these seeds as a thank you." He poured out a handful and put them in Kevin's hand.

"You don't have to."

"Just take 'em."

"Cool, man, thanks," said Kevin.

Todd walked Kevin to the porch.

They both looked up at the sky, while trying not to look like they were looking up. "Thanks again," said Todd.

"You got it." Kevin waved over his shoulder. He got in his car. "See you soon." Kevin never saw Todd again.

Todd went back inside and locked everything. Door, windows, whatever. He turned on every light in the house. He shoved the kitchen table back in front of the door.

In the garage, Todd found some of his two-by-fours and a can of nails. He put a hammer in his back pocket. He reentered, looking forward to the relief of nailing the door shut. Then he stopped.

It was dark. The lights were out. Every light. By the glow of the TV, he could see the kitchen table was moved—the door was wide open.

Todd dropped everything in his hands. He spun around, trying to see the whole area. He grabbed the shotgun off the table and walked backwards to his room. The long hall was one black shadow.

His bedroom was dark. He felt under his bed for his suitcase; nothing there. He went to the closet and opened it, gun ready. No one in the closet. He kept his eye on the doorway, not that he could really see anything. He found the suitcase —it had all of his packaging inside. No way he was going to leave it. It was practically a chest full of gold. Without the packaging, his seeds were useless.

He stopped. Did he just hear something? Time to get the hell out. He pulled the heavy suitcase down the hall while awkwardly carrying the shotgun under his arm. He stumbled to the kitchen and got the duffel bag around his shoulder. Todd was at the door when he heard it again.

That horrible braying laughter, ending in a cackle.

And it was close. Todd saw something short and dark moving fast at the end of the hall, coming at him. He threw the suitcase down the stairs and ran after it. He made it outside, sprinted to the garage, and shoved his luggage into the car. Todd pulled out just as the door to the house opened.

Something leapt at the car, but he gunned the engine and it missed. Todd raced down the street, the passenger door still open. He drove down the mountain road. He was not stopping for anything, not a coyote, not a bear, nothing. Todd kept his foot on the gas. His high beams stayed on, blinding everyone he passed.

Todd kept looking up at the night sky. The road finally exited the dark forest. A truck stop and a pair of gas stations lit up the road with their harsh multi-colored lighting. Civilization.

Todd's body relaxed so much he partially swerved into the oncoming lane. He was suddenly exhausted. There was a Days Inn by the freeway. A warm bed and a shower sounded like heaven right now. Todd pulled into the parking lot. Tomorrow he would figure out a plan. He could get a house somewhere else. Not on a mountain.

He pulled the suitcase to the front desk. He would not leave it in the car with fifty thousand in cash in the side pocket. Todd paid, got his room key, and dragged the big bag. He threw the suitcase on the fake leather couch and put the duffel bag next to the mini fridge.

Todd took the shotgun out and put it on the bed next to him. He was too tired for a shower. He would come up with his new plan tomorrow. Tomorrow. He passed out.

9

LITTLE MAP

There were hardly any stores in Pine Mountain Club, so Kevin went down to Frazier Park, where there was an actual supermarket. Faith had worked all night at the hospital, so he let her sleep.

In the center of Frazier Park was a four-way stop sign and a gas station. There was a realtor's office and a large park across the road. It had a baseball diamond, a long winding path for walking, and a skateboard park.

Kevin drove farther into town, past the sheriff's station. He made a left and headed towards the supermarket. He passed a cluster of stores in a shopping area that looked like an old German alpine village.

He saw a video rental store. An actual video rental store. Kevin couldn't believe it. He pulled into the supermarket. It was painted avocado green. The town looked like it had been frozen in time. Around 1975.

Kevin had to admit, he loved it. Two of his heroes, John Carpenter and Steven King, were young men in the 70s. He often thought about that analogue world, where typewriters and cigarettes ruled. The last gasp of tactile humanity before the digital revolution took over everything. Bell bottoms, leather jackets, big sunglasses, and obnoxiously huge cars. He would have been comfortable with the 70s lifestyle.

The supermarket was small. Compared to the giant airplane hangars in Los Angeles, it was tiny. The aisles were narrow, and the shopping carts were miniature. *I guess things were smaller in the 70s*, he thought.

He picked up juice, vegetables, and then he made his way over to the meat counter. Kevin had never seen meat so red. It practically sparkled under the lights. He walked out with an armload of steaks and chicken wings. His mouth was already watering.

Kevin was driving to the hardware store when he saw a cool little thrift shop. He pulled over. He was looking for a coffee table. The closest furniture store was in Bakersfield, which was forty-five minutes away. This place could be his only hope in this little town. And they probably had some cool used books.

The shop was a former garage. You could tell by the giant roll-up door and the grease stains on the concrete floor. There was a pink-haired girl at the counter. She was tall and pretty, with a button nose.

"Hey, how's it going," said Kevin. "I'm looking for a coffee table."

"Yeah, we got a couple of those. That way, end of the aisle."

"Thanks. And do you have any used books?" said Kevin.

"Oh, yeah. We have stacks. People bring 'em in, but hardly anyone buys any." She rolled her eyes.

Kevin walked through the aisles. The shelves were covered in random stuff. There was a pair of ice skates next to a toaster, next to a power drill. He saw used dolls, old dishes, a box of candles. He could see the coffee tables towards the end, when something caught his eye. A big wooden crucifix. This one was ornate. Kevin picked it up; it was heavy. He looked over a couple of coffee tables and chose the dark cherry wood one. He put the crucifix on top of it; Kevin was taking it too.

Along the far wall there were piles of used books. They looked like they were six feet high. Kevin started at the end and worked his way methodically through the stacks. There were a lot of paperbacks. A ton of Tom Clancy. Clive Barker, Dean Koontz, and plenty of Stephen King.

I guess a cold black mountain is a good place to get scared, he thought.

He kept looking. He wanted something different. Something special that would only appear in a small place like this. Not something from Barnes and Noble.

He found the first book in the middle of the stacks. It was a big leather-bound book, *Ancient Egyptian Magic, a History*. This was not a bookstore book.

The next book he found a few minutes later was a glossy book, *Secret Aircraft in the Desert*. Edwards Air Force Base wasn't very far away. The jet propulsion lab, skunk works, even Area 51 was just an afternoon drive. Someone probably worked there and donated this book. It would definitely make for some cool reading.

The last book was the most interesting, *Demons from Far Away*. This one was a small paperback. It was the title that caught Kevin's eye. It was so trashy. He was about to put it back when a piece of paper fluttered to the floor. Kevin bent down and picked it up. It was folded many times. Kevin unfolded it.

It was a map. A detailed map of an old mine. Someone had taken a lot of time making it. He stuck it in his pocket.

He would look it over when he got home. Kevin put the books on top of the cherry wood coffee table. He carried the table to the cash register.

"Find everything you need?" asked the girl with pink hair.

"Yeah, found it all; you guys are great. These books look cool."

She looked them over. "Oh, yeah, this one on secret military aircraft is a good one. Lots of people up here see lights in the sky at night."

"Really?" asked Kevin.

"Oh, yeah. Talk to the right people and you will hear a weird story."

"Thanks for the tip," he said.

Kevin opened the trunk to his car, and he lowered the back seats. Good thing it was a hatchback. It made moving things a lot easier. The table just barely fit. He put the crucifix and the books on the front passenger seat.

"You are having trouble with vampires."

Kevin spun around.

"What?"

"I said you are having trouble with vampires. Am I wrong?"

It was a woman standing in front of a small store n with a sign, "Psychic Readings." She had long curly hair, brilliant blue eyes, and a flowing dress covered in roses.

"Um, no, I'm fine. Thanks. No problems here."

"Okay, well, I'm open if you need a reading," she said.

"Thanks."

He got in his car and drove away. Kevin was not about to waste his money. He looked in the rearview mirror. Something about him said vampire problems? She must have seen the big crucifix and made a joke. His mind settled for that answer.

Kevin drove back home up the mountain road. He was happy to get the hell away from this weird part of town. He thought about Todd. The idea of intruders breaking into a local grow operation bothered him.

He decided to swing by Todd's house just to make sure he was okay.

10

A DARK BASEMENT

When Kevin pulled onto Todd's street, he could already see that there was a problem. The front door was wide open. Kevin pulled into the driveway. The garage door was open too, and Todd's car was gone.

The lights in the house were off. But it was still light out, so he could probably see inside. He opened his glove compartment and looked around—no flashlight. *Dammit.* And he realized now the gun was at home sitting on his nightstand. *Double dammit.*

Kevin checked under the passenger seat. The dagger was still there!

He called Todd's phone and heard it ring. The phone was sitting in the grass. Kevin got out and picked it up. This was a bad sign. Todd didn't go anywhere without his phone.

He approached the door with the dagger by his side. He wasn't really worried about neighbors. No one called security about the house being left open, and he guessed there weren't many people on the block right now.

"Um, Todd, you in there?" Kevin called out. "You okay?"

No response. Kevin turned on the flashlight on his phone. He stepped inside. It was darker than he had expected, and his phone flashlight lit up very little. Kevin could quickly tell Todd had left in a hurry. Things were thrown all over the floor, including jars of seeds and some cash.

Kevin listened but heard nothing. He knew that down the hall was Todd's room, but something told him not to go into that dark hallway. Behind him he heard a sound. Like something shuffling. Kevin held up the dagger in front of him. In the low light, it practically glowed.

He didn't see anything or hear anything else. He explored deeper into the house and came to the basement. The door was open. The light to the grow tent was still on, but everything else was off. Kevin started down the stairs. Something caught his eye. In the darkest corner of the room, he saw something crouched down. It was trying to hide, but its breathing gave it away.

He pretended he didn't see it. Kevin backed up casually. The thing stood up. Kevin reached the door. He could hear it running across the room at him. Kevin slammed the door shut and ran out of the house. He made it to his car and took off. The front door to the house was still wide open. Kevin didn't care.

He arrived back at his house. Kevin sat in the driveway for a few minutes, catching his breath. He didn't want Faith to see his panic.

Put on a regular face, he thought.

He unloaded the groceries and brought them in first. Next, he moved the coffee table. He kept looking over his shoulder, hoping nothing followed him. One thing was for sure. He would not tell Faith any of this. She dealt with enough pressure with her job as an ER nurse; no point in making her paranoid on her off hours. They had already survived one paranormal encounter in Merced. If they faced another, she might think he was jinxed.

11

FAITH'S BAD RABBIT

Faith drove south on the 99. It was still dark out. She had just finished her shift at the hospital. She turned up the radio, trying to stay awake. At this hour there were hardly any cars on the freeway, so driving became hypnotic. She rolled down the window, hit the gas, and sped up. Looking out for hiding CHP cops would keep her alert.

She made it to her exit without getting a ticket or falling asleep. Success! She passed through the sleepy town, happy to be close to home. Being an ER nurse afforded her front row seats to a horror show four nights a week. Being that close to death made her appreciate the good things in life. Like being in a cabin with her boyfriend and their dog, in front of a cozy fire.

She hadn't always been so positive as a kid. Getting teased for being tall all the time had made her sour. Developing at twelve and the never-ending looks from all the boys made her anxious. And eventually bitter. But all that changed after nursing school. With nights filled by accident victims, gun-shot wounds, burns, stabbings, and children with cancer, going home healthy and alive put a big smile on her face. Every time.

Tonight was no exception. She made her way past the town and headed up the mountain towards the higher part. The houses were bigger, and it was a lot quieter. That's what Faith had learned while being friendly at the supermarket.

The girl at the cash register told her two things when she found out Faith was living at the top of the mountain: Make sure you have a lot of firewood, and get spikes for your boots. Faith would do both before the real winter started. It was already super cold at night, but the snow wouldn't start for another two months.

She made it to what she called the enchanted forest. Kevin called it the black woods. He was as negative as she was positive, and the balance worked nicely. A few miles up the treelined road and she would be home. She rounded a corner—there was an immense tree trunk across the road. She hit the brakes and stopped with a few feet to spare. Good thing she had been paying attention.

Faith backed up. There was no way to go around. One side of the road was a steep hill that was impossible to drive, and on the other was a guardrail. This was the only road that went up the mountain. Someone had to call the police and let them know that the road was blocked. Might as well be her. She tried to call, but there was no service.

Let's think of another solution, rather than getting mad, she thought.

She calculated the fastest solution would be to turn around and drive back to town to the sheriff's station. *That's a solid plan*, she thought. But first a light nap. That couldn't hurt. The car was locked, and no one was around. She would be fine. She closed her eyes...

Faith woke up and thought she was in the middle of an

earthquake because the car was rocking from side to side. She looked in the rearview mirror and saw a huge hairy arm moving the car. She thought it was a bear, then realized it was standing up on two legs like a man. But it was eight feet tall.

Faith grabbed her phone, but it still had no service. The car stopped rocking. She looked behind; it was gone. She looked up through the sunroof and saw a gigantic face looking back at her. It roared so loud she had to cover her ears.

It scratched the roof like it was trying to peel it open. Faith made a quick decision. It was time to go. She opened her door when she remembered in her purse—the gun. She grabbed it and ran.

She sprinted down the road and heard whatever it was coming after her. It was getting closer, so she veered off and jumped over the guardrail. The first few steps she kept her feet under her, but the hill quickly became too steep, and she tumbled and slid down until she hit the ground.

She was scraped and a little bloody, but she still had the gun. She looked around, pointing it everywhere.

She listened but heard and saw nothing. The moon was bright so she could see pretty well. Faith felt in her pocket for her phone; she would use it as a flashlight. It was still in the car.

Oopsie daisy, she thought.

At least she had the gun. The big .357 magnum revolver. She could see the moonlight shining off the chrome finish. Whatever it was, she would scare it off with the enormous boom that the gun made.

She knew what it was, but she didn't want to think about it. Faith should get back to the road. There was a chance of running into another driver or a cop up there. She would skirt the road from the side and then climb up when it got less steep.

She walked through the woods. She heard the noise behind her. Footsteps running, close. She turned and brought the gun up.

The hairy giant jumped over her head, soaring ten feet in the air. It landed, claws out, ready to charge again. Faith aimed and fired. But it was already jumping away. The loud bang and the fireball from the muzzle sent the creature running into the darkness.

More like hopping into the darkness, she thought.

Faith knew this creature because she had seen it once before. When she was a tiny girl. And it was the scariest moment of her life. She didn't have a gun; she only had a blanket. She was five years old. Her family had just moved into their new house. It was big and creaky. She liked her new room, even if she had to share it with her baby sister.

The entire house had been asleep. Faith heard a noise and woke up. Rain was tapping against her window, which was open. She didn't remember the window being open when she went to sleep. She sat up and rubbed her eyes. Maybe the thunder had woken her up.

She looked over at her baby sister's crib. Standing over her was a huge, giant, hairy monster. It was tall and had long claws. When it realized Faith was awake, it turned around.

It was pink and scarred, like it had been burned. Its eyes were black, and it had fangs. But Faith recognized the face from cartoons she had seen. It was the face of a giant rabbit.

It hissed and stepped towards her bed. Rabbits were cute and cuddly. But this thing was a nightmare beast. She noticed the drool falling to the floor, dripping from its open, sharp mouth. There was no question in her mind that this thing intended to eat her.

She remembered calculating that she had two choices. She could pull the blanket over her head and close her eyes and hope it went away. Or she could scream louder than she had ever screamed. She thought it would be easier to hide. But then she got mad—this thing was in her room, threatening to eat her and her sister. Who the hell did this Rabbit think it was, trespassing through her house? She would not let this stand.

She opened her mouth and screamed like a siren. Faith screamed for what must have been minutes. She heard her parents getting up and running. The creature heard them too because it jumped out of the open window.

When her dad ran into the room, he saw the open window and the footprints leading up to it. He knew something had been there. And so did Faith. At no point did she think she had been dreaming. She knew it had all happened.

And now here she was in the middle of the woods, with the same monster. Two decades later.

She made it back to the road. Although there were no streetlights, the sky was getting lighter. It was almost sunrise. She could go back to the car and wait for the monster rabbit to come back and finish what it started twenty years ago, or she could walk the road until she made it home.

So, she walked. She kept her eyes on the woods bordering the road, the gun in her hand by her side. If something was following her, she wanted it to see the big gun. At one point she thought she heard something large moving next to her, so she turned and aimed at the trees. She heard nothing after that.

When she finally saw the house, the sunrise was orange and pink. The day was starting. She walked to the door and felt in her pockets. The keys were still in the car.

Of course. Perfect way to end the night.

Faith looked through the window and saw Kevin asleep on the couch. He had been waiting for her. Inky was asleep on the floor next to him. She tapped on the glass. Inky heard the noise and started barking. Kevin woke up and unlocked the door. The perfect chain reaction.

He looked her over. She was scratched, cut up, and bloody. She was still holding the gun.

"What happened to you?" Kevin asked. But he already suspected the answer.

Faith needed a shower badly. She tore off her ripped and dirty clothes and threw them in a pile on the bathroom floor. Kevin stood outside the shower so they could talk. Faith told him everything from the downed tree trunk to the jumping rabbit monster. Kevin shared his story about the vampire and the house with the greenest lawn.

They agreed from now on, with monsters, they would tell each other everything immediately. No point in hiding things that could be dangerous.

He told her about Diego, the silver bullets, and the Spanish dagger. Faith informed him they now had just five bullets left.

"Oh, yeah," said Kevin, "something's happened to Todd."

"What?" Faith couldn't stand Todd—he was gross—but she said nothing because Kevin seemed to like him.

"I went by his house and it was wide open. All the doors. And he was gone," said Kevin.

Faith turned off the water and dried off with a big purple towel.

"And when I went inside to check on him, there was

something there. Something bad . In the basement. It chased me out of the house."

"Was it the vampire?" Faith asked.

"No, this was something else."

"Where do you think Todd went?"

"I don't know. But I have a bad feeling about him."

12

THE SMURF

Todd was not thrilled with his room at the Days Inn. It was small, and the bed was uncomfortable. It was time to move on. He did an inventory. He still had fifty thousand in cash, minus a few bills that fell out during his escape from the house. Todd also had jars of seeds and enough packaging to make a small fortune.

He would move to a new house in Santa Clarita, right outside of L.A. His commute would be shorter and there would be no mountains. That sounded about right to him. He would check out early around 9 a.m. and get a good start on the day. If he was lucky, by the evening he would be in a new house, setting up a new tent for his plants. The only thing he was missing was a bottle of pills. There were a couple of oxys in a drawer at his house, but he really didn't want to go back there. Maybe if he bought a really powerful flashlight?

No, no, forget it. I will not get myself killed over some goddamn pills. Though I could really use one right now. Forget it! he thought.

Todd was getting claustrophobic. He felt like stepping

outside for some fresh air. The sun was rising, throwing pink streaks across the sky. It was chilly, but he wanted to wake up, so it was good. Todd was about to go in. When he turned to go, there was a man standing right next to him. Todd hadn't heard him approaching.

"Good morning," said Todd, trying to be polite.

"Sure is." The man was obviously a truck driver. "It's going to be a beautiful day."

"For sure," said Todd, trying to be agreeable.

"I know how to make it better."

"Oh, yeah?"

"Yeah," said the trucker. "There's this little old lady in town. Used to be a pharmacist. She's still being a pharmacist. If you know what I mean."

"Um, why would I need to know this?" asked Todd.

"Oh, no reason. I'm just saying if you got any kind of need. She can fill it."

"Okay. Thanks. I didn't need that information, but have a good one." Todd hesitated and lowered his voice. "Where is she exactly?"

"Oh, she's next to the hardware store. It's a little red house. Red as an apple. You can't miss it. Just tell her Buddy sent you. She'll let you in."

The truck driver waved as Todd went back inside.

I guess I look more desperate for a pill than I realized. Fucking strangers can see it on me. He picked up his bags, closed up the room, and loaded the car. Todd put the shotgun in the back seat and covered it with a sweatshirt. He was taking no chances.

Todd pulled out of the hotel and headed towards the freeway entrance. He slowed down. The pharmacist lady was just five minutes away.

Just get on the freeway and go. Or I can take care of this problem right now and then set up the new house in a much more relaxed state of mind.

Todd turned right and headed back into town. Was there really any doubt? Todd pulled up in front of the house. No point in being subtle. This would be the first and last time he came here. He pulled two hundreds out of his wallet and put them in his back pocket. Why show a stranger how much money he had?

He checked out the block. It was sleepy. A big black bird landed on a fence post and looked right at him. A few cars drove by, but there were no people on the street. He got out and casually walked to the front door. He knocked. He heard noise from behind the door. Shuffling slippers.

"Hold on, dear, I'll be right there."

She sure sounds like a little old lady.

"Who is it?" she asked.

"Um, just a friend. Buddy sent me?"

"Oh, wonderful. I do love making new friends."

She opened the door and invited him in, looking exactly as she sounded. She was a tiny raisin with a little helmet of curly white hair. She led him through the living room to a neat, bright yellow kitchen. There was something familiar about the way she walked. *She looks like Sofia from* The Golden Girls, *he thought. That must be it.* He tried not to laugh.

"Please have a seat. Make yourself comfortable."

Todd sat down at the table.

"So, what are you looking for, young man?" She poured a glass of lemonade from an ornate glass pitcher.

"I could really use some oxys. Maybe like a hundred."

"Oh, you have to be careful with those. They can be very addicting." She smiled.

Todd was ready to get up and leave; he was wasting his

time. She came over with a tall glass full of ice and lemonade.

"Now, now, young man. Be patient. I'm only teasing you. Have some of this lemonade. It's delicious." She put the glass in front of him. "I'm Hilda."

He was going to say "no thank you" to the drink, but it looked really good. It was a light yellow and the condensation on the side showed off how cold it was. A brilliant wedge of lemon floated in the liquid. It was the yellowest lemon he had ever seen. Before he knew it, he was drinking it down. It was delicious. He could use another glass.

She was pouring it before he even asked.

"I can do a hundred," she said.

"That's great." Todd smiled, relieved.

He handed her the money.

"Thank you. I'll go get them. Be right back." She scuttled off. She was faster than she looked.

Todd kept drinking his lemonade.

"I was a pharmacist," she said.

"Like at Walgreens?" he asked.

"No, at a hospital. I had access to everything. It was great. Every day, I took a couple of extra pills home. I thought of it like a retirement account."

Todd noticed an old license plate that hung up on the wall behind him. He hadn't noticed it when he first came in. It said "SMURF." He laughed. A Smurf was someone who stole pills. *This old lady is cool.* She came back and put a vial of pills in front of Todd. It was filled to the top.

He went to grab it, but he couldn't move his arms.

Hilda sat down across from him. "But being a pharmacist can get a little boring. So when it got slow, I would kill people," she said. "It was so easy. How could they expect you not to kill people?"

This old lady is no longer cool, Todd thought.

He tried to get up, but he couldn't move.

This bitch fucking drugged me! his mind screamed.

"Now and then I would slip a little extra surprise in a bottle of pills. Something that would cause a massive heart attack. Something undetectable." She stood up. "I did the world a favor. People are dirty."

Her face transformed into something grey and scaley. Her eyes became black balls. She looked a thousand years old. Hilda jumped up onto the table with the agility of a gymnast. "I just missed you last night, Todd." Her voice became lower, more raspy. It was not the voice of a little old lady. "You made it out of the house, before I could eat you."

Her mouth was full of sharp needle teeth.

Todd tried to scream, but he couldn't make any noise.

She pulled a long butcher knife out of her apron.

"But I still got you. I still got you. Ha ha."

Todd felt an explosion in his chest. Suddenly he couldn't breathe, like he was being squeezed by an invisible python. He realized he was having a heart attack. Everything started going grey. With some relief, he knew it was his final breath.

The last thing he saw was an ancient witch running at him, knife raised.

13

BLACK MAGIC IS REAL

Kevin and Faith slept until sundown. They had both stayed up all night. When Kevin woke up, Inky was sitting next to the bed, staring at him.

"Okay, okay. Give me a minute."

He got out of bed and got dressed. Faith rolled over, awakened by the noise.

"What's happening?" she asked.

"I think you should come with us," said Kevin.

"Really, and here I was comfortable and warm," she said.

"I want to show you something."

"Don't we usually do that here?"

"No, seriously. It's important." Kevin put on his jacket. He attached the dagger to his belt.

"Okay, okay. This better be good and not like 'check out this pretty tree I saw.'"

She put on sweats and Ugg's. Inky sat wagging her tail, waiting to be leashed. The sun was throwing a last gasp of purples and violets. It would be dark soon.

"Where are we going?" asked Faith.

"I want to get your opinion on something. Before it's too

dark to tell. I have a weird feeling about this place," said Kevin.

"What do you mean?"

"We are each being attacked by some sort of childhood monster. Something that tormented us as kids." He kept his voice low. It was quiet enough that his regular voice echoed down the block.

"Yeah," said Faith. "We left a haunted house for a haunted mountain. That's a really bad trade."

"It's too much of a coincidence that this is happening to us at the same time. I want to know what's causing it."

They were at the top of the hill. They rounded the corner.

"There's this place coming up. Don't stop and stare. I have a feeling that this place is involved."

"Involved?" asked Faith.

"Like it's the cause or the center. Something. Maybe I'm being paranoid. This could just be really stupid."

The house was now in sight.

"Don't stare. I don't want to be too obvious that we are spying."

Faith saw the house. The lawn was even more neon brilliant in the fading sunlight. She stopped and stared.

"Yeah. This is the cause. That's for sure. One hundred percent," she said.

"Shhhh! Keep moving. He'll see you," whispered Kevin.

"Who?" She started walking.

"Grey Face. He looks like he's half dead and totally evil. Just keep going."

They walked past the house and down the block. When they turned the corner and their own house was in sight, Kevin relaxed a little. They made it home. Kevin locked the door and looked through the peephole. No one followed them.

He pulled down the shades.

"Why did you say that place was the cause?" Kevin asked.

"Besides the fact that that's the greenest lawn I've ever seen. It was practically glowing. The house looks like it's from another dimension. And those are easily the biggest roses ever. That's some powerful magic."

"Exactly," said Kevin.

"Here's what's really disturbing. That guy is so casual about what he's doing, that he's using magic for landscaping? Does that seem like he's really all that concerned about someone discovering him?" she asked.

"Not at all."

She got up from the couch and starting pacing.

"What do we know about this guy? Other than you said he's frightening, and he has enormous garden shears," said Faith.

"I didn't say I was frightened. I said he looked like death."

"Oh, excuse me," she said.

"I have a plan. Tomorrow we follow him."

"Good. I like it," said Faith. "Let's be proactive and not reactive."

In the morning they took Inky for a hike in the woods, a few miles from the house where hiking trails led to a big, wide-open meadow. Kevin, being from a big city, couldn't believe a place that nice was empty. They saw no one the whole time they were there. He loved not seeing people.

The mountain might be haunted, but it's still beautiful, he thought.

They walked back to the car. Rather than drop Inky off at home, they took her with them.

Kevin drove the car past their house and around the corner. He parked in a shady spot on the street. Luckily, the block was quiet. Most of the houses were empty. Security was not likely to get a call about a car parked suspiciously. Kevin planned on staying until Grey Face drove by. No matter how long it took.

A car drove by.

"That was him," said Faith.

It was a grey nondescript Honda.

"Of course it's grey."

"Go, go," said Faith.

"Just wait a minute. We can't let him see us."

Kevin took his time and then pulled out. He went slowly down the mountain road. From far away, he could see Grey Face's car half a mile ahead of them. There was no way he could tell he was being followed like this. If he got on the freeway, it would be a different story. The freeway had long straightaways where his car could be spotted easily.

"Maybe he has a local job on the mountain," said Faith.

"Unless someone is hiring him to scare local children, I doubt it."

They followed him down, through the center of town, and onto the freeway.

"Figures. Too easy to stay in town," said Kevin.

Kevin let him get far ahead.

"Okay, I'm going to concentrate on staying out of his sight. I need you to stay focused on watching him. Make sure you tell me if he exits. Or we're just going to keep driving like idiots for no reason," said Kevin.

"You got it."

Grey Face traveled on the 5 south for twenty minutes.

Kevin stayed back as best he could. Faith could spot him every time they came to a rise, and she could look down on the freeway.

"He's exiting!" Faith announced. "He's getting on the 138 East."

Inky barked in the back.

"Awesome job. Thank you," said Kevin.

He slowly exited and merged onto the 138. It was a lonely, dusty two-lane freeway. There were huge telephone polls on both sides, so going off-road was not an option.

He hung back as far as he could without totally losing the grey Honda. He kept multiple cars between them. The sky was overcast. For once, the sun was not baking the desert. Kevin was thankful.

"Where do you think he's going?" said Faith.

"Weirdo convention? Worst complexions ever anonymous?"

"Seriously."

"Seriously?" said Kevin. "I have no idea. This guy is creepy, and he seems dangerous. You said there was something weird about that lawn."

"No, I said he was using magic," she said.

"Well, um…"

"You don't believe in magic?"

"I believe in the paranormal. We've seen plenty. Demons, monsters, a portal to hell," said Kevin.

"Yeah, I don't miss Merced either."

"But, like, a dude saying enchanted words out of some old leather-bound book and getting magical powers? That's a wizard. I don't buy it. That's some literary nonsense a guy with a quill pen came up with hundreds of years ago," said Kevin.

"You know I have healing powers."

"That's different. It's explainable. It is a genetic ability to manipulate human energy. Something you were born with. Like ESP. Just because science can't understand it doesn't mean it's not real. I'm talking about magic spells and sorcery. That's *Game of Thrones* stuff. It's cool, but it's made up," he said.

"I've seen magic. Black magic. And I'm telling you, it's real," said Faith.

"Really? Where?"

"The hospital. I am not a liar, and I was not confused. I know what I saw."

"What did you see?" Kevin asked.

"There were two incidents. Both happened before we met. The first one happened five years ago. I was still working in the South. A young man was brought in; he was in his mid-twenties. He had fallen into a coma."

"Okay, I'm sure you guys did tests," said Kevin.

"Yes. We ran every test we had. We came up with nothing. There was no reason that man should have been in a coma. And he wasn't acting. He was breathing through a ventilator. That's literally impossible to fake," said Faith.

"Right. So he was for sure in a coma."

"Yes. And no one could figure out why. No one, nothing. The next day the mother pulls the doctor aside and tells him a story. A new lady had just moved into their neighborhood. She was known for putting roots on people."

"What the hell is a root?" asked Kevin.

"It's Southern for curse."

"Got it. Super crazy."

"So she begged them to bring in a local root doctor to get rid of the curse," said Faith.

"There's no way they let her bring in some witch doctor."

"They did, but it wasn't official. He came in as a family

visitor. And he did his ceremony behind a closed door," she said.

"Did it work?"

"The next day the man was awake and talking. He was totally fine. The whole thing made no sense. Unless you believed in magic. Then it was understandable," said Faith.

"It could have been a coincidence that he woke up after the root doctor came," said Kevin.

"After all that I told you? Okay, technically it could have been a coincidence, but it wasn't."

Understandable. "Um, hmm. You said there were two incidents," said Kevin.

"Yeah, with this one there is no way you can claim coincidence."

"Okay," he said.

"This lady came in with kidney failure. Again, something you can't fake. She was in her mid-forties. One day, when there was no one else around, she grabbed me by the hand, and she confessed."

"What did she say?" asked Kevin.

"She told me someone put a root on her because she cheated with a married man. There was an evil inside of her, and it was going to bite her heart on the way out. It would leave her body in the form of black liquid."

"That's pretty specific," said Kevin.

"A couple of days later she went into cardiac arrest when I was on duty. I ran in there and found her sitting up in bed. She tilted her head back and threw up. Thick black liquid shot out of her and hit the ceiling. She upside down vomited. I never forgot that. It went up and behind her. And it was black, just like she said it would be," said Faith.

"Has that ever happened before? Is that a normal thing with a heart attack?

"No and no," said Faith, "I've never seen that before or since."

"Mental note: don't let anyone put a root on me," said Kevin.

"That's a good policy. Do you believe me?"

"If you say it happened, then I believe you," he said.

"Then you believe in magic?" said Faith.

"Sounds like black magic is real. You haven't given me any proof of good magic yet."

"True, but given the balance of nature, you could always assume if one exists, then the other must too," she said.

"Yeah, but I don't like to assume anything."

They followed the grey Honda when he exited onto the 14. It drove for a couple of miles and got off the exit for Edwards Air Force Base. Kevin exited too. He followed and watched as the Honda turned into the massive entrance gates to the base. Kevin drove straight past. He didn't turn to look, not wanting to be obvious.

He got back on the freeway, lost in his own calculations.

"Edwards? I don't get it," asked Faith.

"Well, Edwards is the center of a lot of conspiracy theories. A bunch of them."

"Like what?"

"I'm not an expert, but I've heard things about exotic technology, alien bodies, dimensional portals. All kinds of weirdo rumors," said Kevin.

"What does that have to do with black magic, vampires, and giant rage bunnies?"

"Good question," said Kevin. "We're going to find out."

14

DRONE NINJA

L ater that night, Kevin pulled a box out from under the couch. He opened it and put a tiny drone on the coffee table.

"Check this out," he said. "I used to play with this a lot before we met. I got really good with it. Watch this."

Kevin steered the tiny drone around the room. Faith sat on the couch, watching.

"It's so small," she said.

"And now for the landing."

He brought the drone to a gentle landing right on Faith's knee. She gave him tiny applause.

"Coolness aside, why are you showing me this?"

"There's a miniature camera on the bottom. So, I was thinking tonight, when we take Inky for her walk, I'll fly this drone onto a branch right outside one of the second-floor windows of the super green lawn house. We'll be able to watch what Grey Face is doing and he will have no idea."

"What if he sees it?" she asked.

"I'll maneuver it next to some leaves. It will be camouflaged."

"You think you can pull it off?" asked Faith.

"For sure. I'm a ninja with this thing."

They waited until after midnight and then they stepped onto the porch with heavy jackets—it was cold now. Faith had the revolver in her pocket. Kevin wore the dagger on his belt, but it would not be easy to get to under his Carhart jacket. They walked up the street. They could see their own breath. It was cold, but the stars were bright and twinkling.

Wow, stars actually twinkle, thought Kevin.

There were no streetlights, so the stars were unbelievable. People in cities had no idea. When they looked up at the sky, they saw a few dozen stars. Out here, it was millions.

"Let's keep quiet and stick to the shadows. We don' t want him to see us. He'll probably come running out of the house with a rifle," said Kevin.

"Or a decapitated head."

"You are very dark," he said.

"You love it." And she kissed him.

They approached the house. The trees threw jagged shadows all the way across the road. They made a pattern that looked like the street was candy striped. They stopped and lurked. Kevin took out the drone and started it up. He launched it. It did an awkward dip and then it was on the way, rocketing to the house.

He was suddenly aware of the strong wind. That would change everything. He had only used the drone inside, and the idea of gusts of wind never even occurred to him. Kevin did not want to fail in front of Faith. He would keep the drone moving fast, giving the wind less time to push it around.

He steered it around the house to the back where there was a big tree by an upstairs window. A powerful gust shoved it sideways, and it skipped off the side of the house, making a slight knocking noise. The wind was loud enough that it was barely audible.

"Oh, no," said Faith.

Kevin got control of it and kept flying.

"Nice!" she said.

Kevin steered the drone closer to the ground where the gusts would be weaker. He slowed it down at the base of the tree, and then he ascended straight up to the big branch. He landed it perfectly. Right on a flat, broad tip of a branch. Kevin switched to his cell phone, started up an app, and the camera went live. He could see perfectly through the window. He showed it to Faith.

"Wow, it totally worked. You are awesome," she whispered.

A powerful gust of wind blew through the forest. The drone was knocked off the branch and became tangled in some leaves. It dangled, hanging over a walkway. It could not have been more obvious. He worked the controls, but the rotors were just getting more stuck.

"Oh, no," said Kevin.

"If he sees that thing, he's going to know someone is spying on him."

"You're right. And he's going to suspect us," he said. "I'm going to have to get it."

Kevin walked away.

"No!" Faith whispered. She tried to grab his sleeve, but he was already too far. Inky whimpered. She did not like this situation either.

Kevin kept low and stuck to the side of the house. He ducked down under the window. He heard a noise and froze. Someone was inside the house, moving around.

Kevin kept on moving. He crawled under the window and made it to the back. The drone was dangling. He jumped up to grab it, but it was just out of his reach. Kevin tried again. He couldn't get to it.

Of course I'm too short. Of course. I'm always too fucking short. Couldn't have fallen on the ground, oh, no. Always just out of reach. To humiliate me, with Faith watching.

Now Kevin was really mad. He decided that he would get that drone back, no matter what. Even if he had to pound Grey Face with his bare hands. Height would not stop him this time.

There was nothing to stand on. So he climbed the tree. He crawled up and got his hands on a branch. Then he pulled himself up from branch to branch. The drone was right in front of him; all he had to do was crawl onto the end of the branch and grab it.

It was silent. Nothing was moving. Kevin made his way towards the end of the branch, like a snake, sticking to it. He was reaching for the drone when the back door to the house opened.

Grey Face stepped outside. Kevin stopped moving. He held his breath. If he didn't move, the man wouldn't see him.

Grey Face looked up at him and stared straight into his eyes. Kevin was busted. He thought about jumping down and running when Grey Face's hands started moving. He motioned at Kevin, and he was instantly pulled out of the tree and held in midair.

Grey Face was holding out his hands. He screamed at Kevin, "How dare you spy on me. You will regret your insolence. Before I end you, I will rip your limbs off and make you watch."

He jerked his hands and smashed Kevin into the ground. He raised his hands and Kevin was suspended back into the air.

Kevin wanted to say something cool or witty. Something

dangerous. But the wind had been knocked out of him. He couldn't say anything. Kevin couldn't breathe.

"And that's what you get for spying," Grey Face barked. He threw his hands forward and launched Kevin across the lawn and into the street. He landed hard but got to his feet immediately.

"Go!" Kevin yelled. He and Faith ran down the street with Inky in the lead. The only sound they heard was Grey Face's laughter echoing behind them.

15

UNLOCK THE DOOR

William was getting sicker.

He was pretty sure he could fix it, but it was definitely getting worse. The constant blood loss was making him woozy.

A giant truck blew past him the other way. The wind from the truck rocked his grey Honda. He grabbed the steering wheel with both hands. This was not the place to go off the road. The huge telephone poles would demolish his compact car.

They promised to fix him as long as he did what they said, but William was having his doubts. But what choice did he have? It's not like he could walk into an ER and tell them he was suffering from molecular degradation because he was opening portals to other dimensions.

No, if they wanted something, he would give it to them. They were simply too powerful, too advanced, to trick into anything. William had never believed in karma, but that was, unfortunately, starting to change.

A clump of his own hair fell into his lap. *Jesus*, he

thought, *I can't really spend a lot of time at the office like this. Someone will definitely see.*

They were already starting to suspect that something was wrong with him. He looked like he needed a transfusion, badly. If only it were that simple. William suddenly felt a tickle in the back of his neck. And just like that, he knew he was being followed. His body was falling apart, but the powers he was gaining were impressive.

WIlliam looked in his mirror. He knew it was the car all the way back at the top of the rise. He slowed down and looked closer. *Sonofabitch. It's that idiot from the neighborhood. That nosy, stupid jerk with the dog and the girlfriend. The girlfriend they keep asking about.*

His exit was right there. He could swerve suddenly and lose them, but then they would know they had been spotted. No, better to take it slow. Like he had no idea. He would draw them in and then spring a trap.

All of this because of a stupid book. A stupid, stupid book.

William was a scientist, so he was a kind of detective. He worked on facts and clues, while trying to solve a scientific mystery. So, tracking down a rare book was a problem he could solve. He hadn't expected it to be so difficult. William was also a sociopath. He was well aware of it and had learned to work within the constraints of his special wiring. He saw it as an advantage. Everyone around him was a sheep, while William was a man-eating shark. He just had to hide it.

He had heard about the history of the lab and the book at the end of his first week at the Jet Propulsion laboratory. Someone casually mentioned the founder of JPL and the rumors about him. All it took was ten minutes with his phone and he was up to date on the story of Jack Parsons.

Jack was a genius and a rebel. His propensity for blowing things up was the very beginning of the laboratory. Jack would invent solid state rocket fuel and become a rich man and a legend in aerospace history.

But Jack liked to play at the edges of science and life. In the late forties, Jack began experimenting with black magic. To learn the secrets of the universe, Jack started unlocking doors that he never should have had access to. With too much money and time on his hands, Jack and his new roommate, a charismatic and soon to be famous science fiction author, started performing long and intricate spells given to them directly by Aleister Crowley. They were all members of the Ordo Templi Orientis cult.

While the accepted story claimed Aleister was not happy that Jack and Ron were doing his spells without his permission, William's research told him differently. Aleister had been impressed with their success, so he encouraged them. He gave them a special book. His most powerful book.

Aleister was a devotee of chaos. And by his calculation, giving the two maniacs the book was like handing a baby a loaded gun—something bad was going to happen. The rumor was that the end result was the first wave of modern UFO sightings, starting with the Roswell incident in '47. They had unlocked the door and let them in.

The book that Aleister had given them, the key to opening the door, was what everyone was hunting. And no one could find it. But William had a clue few people knew about. A clue he painfully extracted from an old family member with a blowtorch. Jack had kept a very detailed diary. That diary would lead William to exactly where that book was. Now all he had to do was find the diary.

While they were hunting for the book, William would go

around them and find the diary, and then he would be the first to the book. Secrets were easier to keep before the internet, William thought.

After enough online lurking, he picked up the name of the bar where members of the current Pasadena OTO hung out.

16

HOMICIDAL GHOST

I f there's one thing a cult likes, it's an idiot with a lot of money. William figured he would become a regular at the bar, throw around a lot of cash, and act like a dumb ass. In two months, they invited him to come to a meeting. He was too tempting of a target for them to pass him up.

William had to make two calculations for his plan to work. One: that a cult would appreciate an expensive bottle of red wine at their next meeting, and two: if they had Jack Parson's diary, it would be a treasured thing they brought out to impress prospective members. He was right on both counts.

The location was exactly what William expected. It was an old abandoned church. Dramatic, predictable, cheesy. It disappointed William to be right. They weren't creative, and they did not know what they were doing. But this would make his mission easier. They would never see it coming. Then again, most people were idiots.

He parked his car in the crumbling parking lot. Of course they sent the blonde girl with green eyes, Holly, out to escort him. They were hoping to dazzle him or distract him with her obvious beauty.

"Mister Baxter, please come this way." She held her hand out for him to take.

He took her hand, and she led him through the debris.

"Please watch your step," she said.

Yeah, yeah, I get it. The parking lot is full of rubble. Ohh, spooky. William laughed to himself.

The inside was exactly what he thought it would be. Candles everywhere and a banquet table set up where the lectern used to be. There were half a dozen people standing around, waiting for him. Introductions were made, but William didn't remember anyone's name. It didn't matter.

They sat down. In the center of a table were plates of cheeses, ham, and salami. Next to it were little mini pieces of toast. They were too sophisticated for crackers. So, William began his trap. First, he complimented their choice of venues; he talked about their history to show he had done his homework. And then he started waving money in front of them. He had all this cash burning a hole in his pocket from his nightclub(a lie) and he wanted to support their cause.

When he said a hundred thousand, he could feel the entire room get excited. They must have been hard up for cash because the smiles all around looked like something out of a cartoon. Hoping to seal the deal, they placed an ancient, heavy wooden box on the table.

And there it is, thought William.

They opened the box and held up the actual eighty-year-old diary. They knew enough to be proud, but they didn't know he had left clues to where the actual spell book was hidden.

William acted impressed (he was), touched it with fake

reverence, and then declared he would double his donation. The room practically cheered. When he uncorked his expensive bottle of wine, they were so giddy they had no suspicion. He poured everyone a healthy glass and poured himself one. He was not about to trigger a subconscious warning on anyone's radar when he was this close.

He raised a glass, and everyone drank happily. They didn't notice that William only pretended to drink. They all died quickly. William had injected the poison through the cork. There was enough cyanide to kill a herd of buffalo.

William watched as the light went out of their eyes. It was the highlight of his week. When his fun was over, he scooped up the diary and waltzed out, light on his feet. They had no video surveillance, and there would be no witnesses. He was in and out like a homicidal ghost.

He read the entire diary that night. There was no way he could sleep when he was this close to the treasure. According to his understanding of the diary, Jack spent his last days on the base in old Building 21. Which was long since abandoned. He had hinted that there was something of immense value in the wall behind his desk.

So, there was William, walking around the base with a sledgehammer hidden inside his coat. Luckily, the old part of the base had been largely forgotten. There was a guard, but he walked around the entire area. It was easy to get past him.

He slipped into the building, turned on his flashlight, and went down to the basement where Jack had done a lot of his work. The building was big enough and deep enough that no one could hear William smashing the wall open. And no one heard his cheers either. He raced home that night, the old leather-bound book in his briefcase.

Had Parsons figured out how to contact beings from

another world? Was it all just a part of his legendary myth? Something engineers gossiped about when they got bored? If Jack had figured it out, William could as well. Jack might have been a genius, but William was a predator. He was relentless. He would make contact, figure out their weakness, and then force them to give him formulas and secrets. They would make him powerful, famous, and then legendary.

If it actually worked.

That was a big "if." But the book had been hidden in the wall. Would Jack have hidden a book behind a wall if it didn't work? William doubted it. But it would be quite a practical joke if it didn't work at all. Maybe the whole thing was a story Jack told to make himself sound cool. William was not very patient.

He read the book the minute he got home. It was thick and heavy, bound in old beaten-up leather that might have been snake skin. It was so old it was hard to tell, but it was definitely animal skin. And there was something else. There were spots on it that William was sure were blood stains.

He was halfway through when he realized his shoes were still on. When William finished the book, he went to sleep. He would need all his energy for tomorrow. The spell required a lot, so he would get some rest.

When he woke up in the morning, William called in sick to work. This was far more important. Intergalactic travel was now his top priority.

He prepared the spare upstairs bedroom and moved out all the furniture until the room was completely empty. He brought in a bowl, a brush, a chair, then screwed a large hook meant for storing bicycles and tied a noose to it. Now the room was ready.

He ate an enormous meal. He drank as much water as

he could. And then he entered the room. According to the book, he could not leave the room until the spell was complete. If he did, it would not work. And it was going to take hours.

The spell was simple but intricate. There were two steps. The first consisted of the spell caster writing out the entire spell word for word on the floor. In their own blood. In the middle of the floor, they drew a symbol that looked like a crop circle. When completed, they put the noose around their neck and jumped into the symbol on the floor. If the spell worked, the rope would break and it would transport them. If it didn't work, then the house would smell terrible after a week.

William was willing to take the risk. The reward was too great. He wasn't afraid of much—death, sure, but not like a typical person. Death was something that he was friendly with, so he wasn't scared of it. He knew it was inevitable and when his mission was over, he could lie down and rest forever. But not before it was done.

The only thing that scared William was being crippled. He could handle monsters, heights, bugs, even physical pain. But losing his body parts was a fear he could never shake.

William got down on the floor and cut his left hand open. He held it over the bowl and made a fist. Blood poured into the bowl. He would have to be careful. There were a lot of words to write. He needed to use a lot of blood. But not so much that it actually killed him.

William started writing. Soon he was boiling. He was not allowed to open a window. The entire room had to stay sealed. He took his shirt off and continued. He wrote as small as he could in order to use less blood. In a couple of hours, he was almost done. He started getting dizzy. The room started to smell like ozone. Maybe he was just imagining it.

By the time he finished, William was streaked with sweat. The room seemed to have grown bigger. It was probably a hallucination from the loss of blood. William stood up on the chair. He stopped himself from toppling over. He straightened up.

Now was the moment of truth. Would he really put the noose around his own neck? He had come this far; he wasn't going to stop now.

17

MASSIVE SHARK

William put the rope around his neck and jumped off the chair, aiming for the symbol in the middle of the room. The air crackled with green energy. The rope snapped, and William fell through the floor. He kept falling. And falling.

It was minutes that he was in the air. Finally, he hit water. He tried to swim, but he was pulled down under water. It was freezing and dark. He glimpsed a shadow underneath him. It was gigantic. William felt tiny. It swam right past him. It was a shark. A massive super shark. Much bigger than any whale. It was a thousand feet long. William was a flea next to it. It smacked him with its enormous tail, and William was thrown right in front of it. The shark opened its jaws. William's hand instinctively went to his belt —there was a knife there! He grabbed it and propelled himself towards the shark...

Now William was running down the halls of an asylum. He was being chased. He looked behind him. Of course there were zombies. They stumbled after him, faces rotting, limbs falling beside them. They kept coming; there must have been a hundred of them. Some of them were holding long knives. Others were holding hammers and cleavers.

He laughed. "Really?" he said. He had always hated zombies. He thought they were the least scary, stupidest horror invention ever.

William turned, grabbed a zombie by the arm, and then kicked as hard as he could. He tore the arm off and took the hammer that was in its hand. He attacked the zombie horde. He smashed their heads in one by one. Spinning, dodging, and swinging. Geysers of zombie blood erupted all around him. William laughed maniacally.

William was now in a dark forest, surrounded by trees and blackness. What would they throw at him next? They were obviously trying to work on his fear. He suspected that they had never run into a sociopath before. If they wanted to find what scared him, they would have to dig deep. There would not be much there.

William spotted a large man in the distance. He was wearing a hockey mask. Suddenly there was a loud mechanical noise. The large man started up a chainsaw.

"Is this some sort of golden oldie from the eighties or something? You idiots do not know what you are doing," William said.

He ran at the masked man, full speed, and picked up a log as he ran; he leapt high in the air and crushed the man's head with the log. William picked up the chainsaw off the ground and cut the man into pieces.

William woke up in the driver's seat of a speeding Camaro. The speedometer said 120. He looked around the car; there was no way out. He held the wheel and tried to keep the car steady. It was still going faster. William knew what this meant. There would be an accident and he would be crippled. His heart was racing.

He tried hitting the brakes, but that only made the car speed up. Now there were two trucks coming his way. There was no going off-road because cement walls bordered the road. The trucks were bearing down on him.

William closed his eyes and held his breath, and *boom*. There was an explosion of glass and metal. He was pinned behind the crumpled dash; he couldn't move his legs. The car was now on fire and he was trapped.

He tried to get out, but he was stuck. William used his shoulder and back muscles to wiggle out. He pushed himself away from the dash and shoved himself out of the seat. He sprawled across the asphalt and dragged himself away from the wreck. It was going to explode soon.

Using just his arm strength, he pulled himself farther away. He looked down at his legs. They were mangled. His arms were shredded from the road's surface. He was bleeding everywhere.

So, this is how it ends, thought William, *crippled in the middle of a road*.

He heard a noise and looked up, just as a truck ran over him. William opened his eyes. He was in a room—actually, it was more like a space. It stretched out in all directions as far as he could see. The colors of the room were shifting, moving, like an aurora borealis.

He was kneeling. He tried to stand up, but he was stuck. William pulled his arms up, but he couldn't. It was like he was chained to the floor with invisible shackles. This was not good.

"Perhaps it would be easier for you if we made your mind visualize actual chains."

William saw he was not alone. There were three beings with him. They were short and grey. They had bulbous heads, slits for eyes and mouths, and almost non-existent noses. The chains were in his head. William could feel it. They were in his head and they had him immobilized. It was going to be difficult to bully these creatures. That didn't mean William wouldn't try.

"Do not plot your attack. You won't be able to affect us. We can freeze you with our minds; you can't fight that."

William wasn't going to stop looking for an opportunity.

"I am called Lam. I am from a far planet much more advanced than yours. You opened a doorway and invited us in. What is it you want from us?" he asked.

"Answers," said William. "Formulas, elements, advanced science."

"Ah, a seeker of knowledge. Knowledge from outside of your galaxy. We can help you with that. But first, you will help us."

"What if I say no?" said William.

"You can't say no. It is not an option. We admire your bravery, William, but we will have no mercy on you. Mercy is not built into our system."

"It is not in my system either."

"Then you understand us. There is no escape. We are relentless. You know it in your mind. In the next couple of days, you will notice parts of your body breaking down on a molecular level. It is this bridge."

William gritted his teeth. *So, it's a trap*, he thought, *of course.*

"It is not a trap; it is an agreement. You help us and we will cure you. That is a fair transaction."

"Yes, very fair." He doubted they could understand sarcasm. "How do you want me to help?"

"You have opened a doorway. We need it to be larger. This must be done from your side. You will do this for us, and we will cure you."

"What do you need me to do?" asked William.

"This doorway is powered by entropic energy. The most chaotic energy a human being can create is fear. We need more fear."

"How the hell am I supposed to do that?"

"We will give you tools. You will turn the mountain into a fear generating engine, and we will all come through the door," said Lam.

"That's good for you, but what about my questions? I want knowledge."

"Yes. We will give you special knowledge. You will become rich and famous. We will cure you. Here is your tool."

Lam tossed him a shiny metal machine that was shaped like a scarab beetle.

William reached forward, still kneeling. He picked it up; it was iridescent. The surface had tiny lines that formed a pattern. It seemed to glow blue.

There was technology in this thing. It was not some decorative souvenir, thought William.

"You are correct. It will let you know how to use it."

"What does that mean?" asked William.

"Now go."

"Wait—"

William woke up on the floor of his spell casting room. The smell of blood was making him nauseous. He ran out and puked in the upstairs bathroom.

Did that really happen or was that a horrible vivid nightmare, wondered William. He looked down. The alien beetle was still in his hand.

18

WINTER WONDERLAND

The next couple of weeks were uneventful. That did not make Kevin feel any better. He was constantly waiting for the hammer to fall. He knew something bad was coming, he just didn't know when. And it was driving him crazy.

He slept with the dagger under his pillow. The revolver was on the nightstand. But he didn't really sleep. He lay there listening to Faith's snoring, trying to hear any other sound that was out of the ordinary. Sometimes he would catch an hour of sleep at sunrise.

But rent was still due, regardless of Kevin dreading a monster attack. So, he concentrated his efforts into his plants. They had just taken off. They were getting taller and growing more branches, while the stalks were getting thicker. Soon he would switch the light cycle so they would grow large, heavy buds. But right now, it was all about vegetative growth. He would guide them from little baby clones to wide bushes in weeks.

The secret to their turbo charged growth was the hydroponics system he was using. Bubble ponics, the advertising screamed. *This high-tech bucket system will bring you the yields of your dreams!*

Kevin saved up his money and was all set to order it online. But first he made a trip to the local hydro store for grow supplies. Maybe they would have the bubble ponics system and then he wouldn't have to wait for delivery.

The hydro store was small and crammed full of supplies. Kevin suspected the store was making a small fortune despite the size, probably because of it. Kevin found the clerk in the back. His name was Peter, but everyone called him Big Pete. He was six foot four, with a burst of red hair and blue eyes. He made everything in the tiny store seem even tinier.

Kevin explained the hydro system he was looking for.

Big Pete laughed. "Listen man, if you believe all the advertisements you see, you are going to go broke really quick."

"What do you mean?" asked Kevin.

"That system costs what? Hundreds of dollars?"

"Eleven hundred, actually."

"Hilarious," said Pete. "Listen, man, I got nothing to do right now, so I'm going to show you how you can make your own system, the exact thing they are selling you. For under a hundred bucks."

"Yeah, right."

"No, really, we have all the stuff here to make it—it's easy. Go get a five-gallon bucket, a water pump, an air stone, plastic tubing, and a net pot. Oh, and get a lid."

Kevin walked through the mini aisles and picked up each item. He brought the armful of equipment back to the counter.

"Okay, so pay attention. I will not be repeating myself. You take the lid, cut a hole in the top so the net pot can drop down into the bucket." Pete could see that Kevin was confused.

"Like this." He sighed. Using a Sharpie, he traced a circle around the bottom of the net pot. He pulled out a box cutter and traced the circle. He punched it through, and there was a perfect hole in the lid.

"The net pot goes in here." He placed the pot in the lid. The lip of the pot was bigger than the hole, so it suspended the net pot perfectly.

"Got it," said Kevin.

"Now attach the tubing to the air pump. The other end goes into the air stone. Like this. Now the air stone goes into the bucket. And that's pretty much it."

"What? I was going to pay a thousand bucks for that? I mean, it came with six buckets and had a cool logo, but that's, what, like two hundred dollars? The ad made it sound really complicated and high tech."

"They use big words to make you feel like it should be expensive. This system is as simple as it gets. The air stone creates bubbles in the water, which pop right under the net pot. The water and nutrients splash the roots of the suspended plant. When the plant realizes where it's food is coming from, it sends all its roots down into the bucket. The five-gallon bucket can hold a giant root ball. The bigger the roots, the bigger your flowers. Very simple," said Pete.

"You make it sound easy."

"It is. Just make sure the water stays fresh and cool and the rest will work out. Plants are a lot smarter than we are."

"How?" asked Kevin.

"Listen, most people gravitate towards crap. They get a crap husband or a crap job, maybe a crap house or car. It makes them feel like crap. But that's what they're used to, so that's what they go to. Plants always grow towards the light and the food. They are smart enough to reach for the good things in life. They're not dumb. Don't forget that."

He didn't. Kevin treated them well, figuring they would treat him well in return. He got the best food he could buy; he changed their water often, and he watched them grow fast. Kevin was using big 1,000-watt lights meant to mimic the sun, so they got all the energy they needed.

"How are they looking in there?" asked Faith.

"Super healthy, switching to flower soon." Kevin sat down on the couch next to her.

"Oh, goody, I love that part. They get so beautiful."

"And valuable. Let's go outside. How about a walk in the woods? We live here, we might as well take advantage. How about that?" said Kevin.

"Don't you think it's dangerous?"

"It's daytime. We should be fine. We can't be stuck inside like prisoners all the time. Otherwise, we should just get the hell out of here and never come back."

"I'm tired of running from the paranormal," said Faith.

"I agree. We gotta make a stand someplace. Let's do it here."

He took her hand and kissed it. Then he bit it.

"Beast!" Faith laughed. "Let's go walking. Inky, you ready for an adventure?"

She jumped up, tail wagging.

There were hiking trails that led to the meadow, but farther past there was a trail that wound up the side of a steep mountain. It was a tough hike, but Inky loved it. There were woods on both sides of the trail, and she ran in and out, crossing over the path to jump into the forest.

It was a beautiful sunny day that looked more like spring than the end of fall. Kevin was wearing shorts and a t-shirt, and Faith was wearing jeans.

They walked up and up, past a shooting range, around corners and past caves and meadows. The only animals they saw were rabbits and squirrels. Kevin kept an eye out for bears, but he wasn't too worried; he left the gun at home. It was too sunny out to be worried about vampires or mutant bunny men.

It took them about an hour to hike to the top. The view was massive. They could see for miles in all directions. Kevin was trying to catch his breath. The smell of the flowers and pine trees was strong, like a perfume.

"This is why we live up here. This is incredible," he said.

"We are so high up, the clouds look like the ocean."

Inky's tail stopped wagging. She whined.

"What is it, girl?"

"What is that?" Kevin pointed in the opposite direction.

They both looked—there was a black wall of clouds moving fast. Faster than they had ever seen clouds move.

"Seriously, what is that? It's moving too fast. Is that a tornado?" asked Faith.

"No, we're too high up. It looks like a quick-moving storm."

Inky started barking. The clouds blotted out the sun, and the temperature plummeted. The first snowflakes fell as wind swirled.

"Are you serious?" Kevin asked. He started shivering.

"Let's get out of here." Faith was shouting to be heard above the wind.

"Yeah, back to the car," yelled Kevin.

The snow was already sticking to the ground. Kevin's arms and legs stung from the cold. Faith pulled her hoodie on and tied it tight. She thanked god that she had taken a sweatshirt.

It took them a minute to find the trail. By the time they

walked down, there were a couple of inches of snow on the ground. And it was getting deeper, quickly. The wind was screaming; they were in the middle of a raging blizzard.

They walked down the trail maybe a hundred yards, but the snow was already at their knees. There was no way they would make it to the car without freezing to death.

They held on to each other and stumbled through the snow. Kevin kept Inky's leash wrapped around his hand. If she slipped away, he might never find her again.

They kept walking. Faith pulled Kevin close.

"What are we going to do?" she yelled.

Kevin wasn't sure. They didn't have too much longer in the freezing weather with nothing but summer clothes. His mind was panicking. Where could they possibly go?

The caves!

He screamed the words to Faith, who understood. A little farther down the trail they had seen caves—it was their only chance. They walked through the belligerent wind and thick flakes, looking at the side of the trail for the caves. They kept looking. Is it possible they passed them already? It was easy to misjudge things in the storm.

Faith squeezed Kevin's arm. She pointed. They could see a dark shape in the side of the white hill—a cave opening.

They ran through the woods to get there, tripping over bushes and branches that were now hidden under the snow. A frozen sticker bush raked Kevin's legs, but he didn't care; his legs were numb. He guided Faith around the obstacles, and they made it to the cave.

Kevin hesitated for a second. There might be something else in this cave taking shelter. But the choice was freeze to death or brave the unknown. It really wasn't a choice. The cave opening was small, but they squeezed through. Once inside, the cave got bigger, taller, and wider.

"Tttthhheerrreee cccccoouuuuulld bbebbbebeeee annnimallllllsssss." Kevin tried to speak, but he was shivering too hard. Faith took his clothes off, down to his boxer shorts.

"We have to get you out of these wet clothes before you get hypothermia," Faith said. Faith took her clothes off too, and they held each other until they stopped shivering so badly.

"We need to start a fire."

"With what?" asked Faith.

"Maybe there are some sticks or bushes in here. Let's look."

He took his phone out. 95 percent charged. He had learned from the barn—charge your phone. Faith was still shivering. Boy shorts and a soaked bra were not keeping her warm. They used their phone lights to search for anything they could burn. They found a couple of sticks, some branches, a few scraggly bushes. They made a pile. It was not very impressive.

"This really isn't enough," said Kevin.

"I'm not being dramatic here, but as a nurse, I can tell you if we don't get a fire going soon, we're going to die in here."

19

SAVED BY A JAY

Kevin stood up. "Okay, we need a fire. Come on." He led her to the small mouth of the cave. The storm still raged outside. If they were cold before, it was much colder by the entrance. Kevin stuck his head out. He looked around. Under a group of large rocks next to the cave was a dry patch where a bunch of dead branches lay on the ground. They were barely wet with snow. Kevin pulled back inside. He got his wet shoes on. No socks.

"What are you doing?"

"I saw some wood. It looks pretty dry. I'm going to get it."

"I would say don't go, but we need a fire."

"I'll take care of it."

He paused in the entrance to the cave, trying to look heroic. Faith thought he just looked cold. "I'll be back."

Inky whined. He stepped out. The wind immediately slapped him, and he went sprawling into the snow. Kevin picked himself up and kept walking. He leaned against the hill so that he wouldn't get lost in the blizzard.

He made it to the wood and scooped it up in his arms.

The branches dug into his skin and started cutting him, but he couldn't feel it; his body was going numb. He looked around the forest. The snow was now at least three feet deep. Kevin was amazed.

He stuck to the hill and stomped his way through the deep snow. It got so deep that he was hardly able to lift his legs. He fell down and walked on his knees the rest of the way. He crawled through the cave entrance and threw the wood on the floor.

"This should be enough to get us warm," he said. Kevin would have shivered, but he was losing all sensations in his body. He lay down and closed his eyes.

"Get up!" yelled Faith. "You can't go to sleep now. You won't wake up."

"I'll be like Sleeping Beauty." He started passing out.

Faith grabbed him by the wet feet and dragged him away from the howling cave entrance. She made a pile of sticks in the middle of the cave. She pulled Kevin into a seated position. And then she slapped him hard. Kevin blinked awake.

"Owww. What the hell?"

"How am I supposed to start the fire? I don't know how to hit rocks together like a cave woman."

Kevin laughed. It was a weak sound. "We have been saved by a joint."

"What do you mean?" asked Faith.

"It's in my shorts. I rolled a fat joint for the top of the hill. I forgot all about it because of the snow."

"So what? The joint will be wet and useless."

"Yes, but there's a lighter in there too." Kevin smiled.

Faith ran to his shorts and went through the pockets. She stuck her hands in the pocket and pulled out a neon green lighter. She held it up.

"Yessss!"

She kissed Kevin all over his face. "Your love of joints saved our lives."

She struck the lighter and it lit. She held it to the pile of kindling she had placed under the bigger branches. It took a second, but the little sticks caught fire. More lit until there was a mini blaze under the branches. The wood smoked from the moisture on the surface, but eventually the white smoke died down and the branches caught fire. A good size, healthy fire. Faith almost cried, it felt so good.

Kevin's eyes opened. "You saved us."

"You did too, by getting the wood," she said.

They both stood over the fire, warming themselves. Inky lay down close to the growing blaze.

"I don't think anything has ever been so wonderful," said Faith.

"I have to agree." His muscles relaxed; he was no longer shivering. The smell of the burning wood was as delicious as dinner.

"We should dry our clothes."

"Good idea," said Kevin.

They laid their clothes next to the fire. The storm outside was still going. It hadn't slowed down at all. The screaming wind echoed off the cave walls.

"Not to sound paranoid, but—" Kevin started.

"This storm seems mighty suspicious," finished Faith.

"Exactly. I have never seen a storm form so fast in my life. Not even close."

"Totally agree." She sighed.

"It was kind of the perfect trap. We go out like it's summer and we get hit with a blizzard. Insane. I'm glad we ate before we left."

"Me too."

They finally sat down, both raising their feet to the fire.

"Ahhhh, this may be better than any jacuzzi, ever," said Faith.

"Yeah, we'll rent this cave out as a VRBO." Kevin laughed.

Faith threw a pine cone at him.

"Hey, don't waste that. We're going to be out of wood soon."

"Are you going to go get more?" she asked.

"I don't think so. There wasn't much else, and the snow is even deeper now."

"Then we'll have to find some more in here," she said.

"I was thinking the same thing, but let's enjoy this fire a little longer. And how about sharing a little body heat?"

Faith came over and sat next to Kevin. They wrapped their arms around each other, enjoying the heat from their skin contact. They sat for a long time. The fire was dying down.

"It's almost out," said Faith.

That got them moving. They put their mostly dry clothes on. They turned on their phone lights and walked farther into the cave. The tunnel sloped to the left so that they could no longer see the entrance. If not for their lights, the cave would be pitch black.

They went deeper. The tunnel opened until they were in an enormous cavern. The ceiling was high and there was no hint of outside light. They searched along the ground for more branches and sticks. They picked up whatever they found.

"Let's make a pile and then we can figure out how to transport it," said Kevin. He dropped an armload of sticks on the cave floor.

"Good idea." Faith added to the pile.

"I think we can keep the fire going for a few more hours."

"And then what?" she asked.

"And then we get the hell out of here. Whether it's still snowing. When night comes, the temperature will drop and we will die when our fire goes out," said Kevin.

"But we'll freeze before we get to the car."

"Maybe not. It's downhill, so it makes running easier. And we can heat some rocks and stick them in our pockets. Like hand warmers. That will help."

"Maybe it will stop snowing before that," she said.

"Somehow I doubt it. Let's get some more wood. You cover that side, and I'll look over there."

They split up. Inky followed Faith, tail wagging. Kevin went farther into the darkness. His light found more wood. He bent down to pick it up when his light went out.

He was immersed in blackness. He hit the phone and the light came back on.

Standing in front of him was the red-eyed vampire.

It lunged at Kevin, fangs and claws flashing. Kevin threw himself backwards and yelled, "Run! He's here!"

Instantly the vampire was on top of him. Kevin used his arms and legs to keep him back and avoid his bite. But he kept driving forward like some sort of crazed animal. His teeth were getting closer.

Inky snarled and launched herself at him. She bit into his thigh. Mr. Red Eyes turned and raised a claw to slash Inky. Kevin's hand went to his belt and found the silver dagger. He thrust up as hard as he could.

The dagger punctured the vampire through the chest. He screamed silently and turned into a puff of black smoke. It stank of rotten eggs.

"I got him! I got him! Faith, did you see that?"

He heard a noise and swung his light up. Another vampire hung from the ceiling. It jumped down right on top of him. Kevin kicked and ran. In front of him was another vampire.

"There's more of them! Get to the entrance!"

Faith ran, three vampires chasing after her. Inky barked and bit them. Kevin sprinted behind them—he was also being chased. The vampires were close; he could smell them. They turned the corner, and the entrance was ahead.

The fire was still burning. The vampires realized they were about to escape, so they ran harder. Kevin jumped over the fire, turned, and kicked. He showered them with sparks and orange embers. It gave them enough time to make it through the narrow crack in the wall.

Kevin fell into the deep snow. Faith and Inky were running down the hill. He picked himself up and followed them. He saw claws reaching out after him. Black smoke came off their arms as they hit the daylight. The snow was still blowing hard, but Kevin's adrenaline gave him the strength he needed to run through the snow. He caught up to Faith, grabbed her arm, and pulled her faster.

By the time they got to the car, they looked like snowmen, but they didn't care. They were relieved—they had made it. The car started and Kevin cranked up the heat.

"Now let's get the hell out of here."

"You don't have to ask me twice." Kevin gunned it. They skidded through the snow, but they found the road and never stopped.

20

A KIDNAPPING KIT

Villiam was thinking of poisoning the town's water supply.

But then he figured that mass murder wasn't the best way to generate fear, just death. There would be no one left alive to be afraid. So, he started planning a serial killing spree. If he killed maybe three of his neighbors in some sort of ritualistic way, the entire town would be paralyzed with fear and he could satisfy his new masters.

Maybe he could order a scary mask off of Amazon. He could also order a chainsaw. He wondered how many murderers ordered their equipment from Amazon. The one-stop killer shop.

Just then, the electronic beetle they had given him started buzzing. At first William couldn't understand what the buzzing from his pocket was. Then the beetle crawled out of his pocket and opened up its wings. It flew up and behind William. He turned around, trying to watch it, but it kept flying behind him. It landed on the back of his neck and sank titanium fangs into his flesh.

William screamed and fell to his knees. He closed his

eyes and got nauseous. He was flooded with images of being mangled in a car wreck. Genuine fear took hold in his stomach. That was the energy needed to open the doorway. When he opened his eyes, he was back on the alien bridge. Rainbow colors faded in and out of his vision.

"We have become aware of a human we would like to study," said Lam.

William tried to stand up, but their mental shackles were keeping him on his knees. "There has to be an easier way for us to communicate!" William shouted.

"We are talking over a bridge through spacetime. Do you have any better suggestions?"

"How about a phone call?"

"Perhaps we should gag you as well. Would you like us to cure you?"

"I'd like to see you—"

William could no longer talk.

"There is a girl. She has significant powers compared to everyone else around her. She could be useful to us. Find her, capture her, and then bring her to us."

Lam shot a bright white beam out of his eyes and into William's eyes. "We have given you the ability to see her. She will glow to you. Find her, get her, bring her. Or else."

William tried to scream one last profanity, but he still couldn't speak. Everything went black. He woke up on the floor of his kitchen. His neck was killing him, like something had bitten him. He remembered something had.

He stood up and looked around. William lost his balance and fell down. He needed to find this girl and help these parasites open their doorway. Then maybe he could escape, and they wouldn't come after him. Maybe.

William made it to his car, taking shaky steps. He got behind the wheel and took a deep breath. William started up the car and drove down the street. He circled the neighborhood a few times but didn't see anyone. No one was walking around. No one was even walking a dog. It was a quiet day at the top of the mountain.

He drove down the road to the "blue collar" town. The one with the old timey video store. He could get some supplies and he could keep a lookout for the girl. Whoever she was. And by supplies, he meant a kidnapping kit.

He drove through the forest. Anyone who watched *Dateline* with any sort of seriousness knew: you never buy all the tools of your murder kit at the same store. Far too many idiots had been caught like that. William refused to be that stupid.

First stop was Ace Hardware. This was one of the few actual stores in town. It was the closest thing they had to a Walmart. *Small town charm*, he thought.

He wandered through the aisles and found some sturdy rope and a rubber mallet. A rubber mallet would be less likely to crack a skull when he whacked her over the head. She needed to be taken to the bridge alive. Preferably conscious.

"You find everything you need?" asked the woman behind the counter. She wasn't a teenager, but she was still good looking. William tried to turn on the charm.

"Not everything. I'm looking for a beautiful woman. What aisle would she be on—oh, wait, here you are behind the counter," said William.

She gave him a fake smile and said nothing else. She handed him back his change silently.

William walked out of the store, slightly embarrassed. He used to have a certain way with the ladies; some would have even called it charisma. But now with his new grey complexion, falling-out hair, and haggard face, those powers of persuasion were gone. In fact, most people shrank away from him now, or they pretended not to see him. Was this what homeless people dealt with? People in wheelchairs? If William had been wired for empathy, he might have felt bad; instead, he was furious that he was now at society's bottom rung.

Besides, hobos don't communicate with aliens across space-time bridges. He knew he was still special.

He thought he could bully them, trick them, or if he had to, hurt them. William couldn't have been more wrong. He was powerless. They controlled him easily. He was their prisoner thanks to the tiny beetle/torture device they had stuck him with.

His complexion had gone grey because of that damn machine. Every time it needed to create a new biological creature, it took a literal chunk out of William. It sank its teeth into his skin and removed a piece out of him, the size of a bullet. That slice of his flesh was used to grow a new entity. They came directly from William's body. Losing blood kept him weak and near collapse. If not for bandages, William would have bled to death by now.

The snowstorm and the gang of vampires had been very painful. The beetle took successive chunks out of his left arm. William had thankfully passed out in the middle of it. He bandaged his arm, and eventually the bleeding stopped.

William looked up and realized he was in the parking lot of the Dollar General. His second stop. He wandered the aisles until he found zip ties and rubber gloves. He didn't bother to try chatting up the girl at the counter.

He stopped at the gun store for an important piece of the puzzle. The man who ran the store wouldn't shut up. He had an opinion about absolutely everything. William wished his assignment had been to kidnap this idiot. But he kept his mouth shut and could finally walk out with what he came for: a stun gun.

His last stop was the supermarket. William found some bleach and duct tape. He picked up a carton of juice so it would look less obvious. The dude at the register didn't even look up at him.

On his way to the car, William saw a glowing light. He followed it across the street into the parking lot of Mike's Pizza. It was a tall girl getting into a small red car. She was radiating light like a small sun; it was almost blinding. William had to squint. It was her! And she was with the idiot from his neighborhood. The one that had followed him. It was his girlfriend. Suddenly the new assignment became a lot more enjoyable.

William walked back to his car, humming.

21

TOYS

By the time Diego pulled up to the house, it was already dark out. He hauled two duffel bags out of the back of his pickup, walked into the house, and plopped them down in the middle of the living room. "I brought some toys."

"What kind of toys?" asked Kevin.

"The kind that are sharp, dangerous, and a little explosive."

"That's the best kind," said Faith.

"Normally I would wait to unzip these just to build up suspense, but judging from the vibe in the room, you guys are in no mood to fuck around."

"I wouldn't have called you if it wasn't important."

Diego unzipped the bags and started pulling out weapons.

"Now you mentioned vampires, but you weren't very specific, so I've brought a variety of arms," said Diego. He laid a couple of shotguns on the table. "Classic and simple. The scattergun. You can just throw silver scraps down the barrel and now you have a silver shrapnel launcher. You can take out multiple blood suckers with these."

"Nice," said Faith.

Diego removed what looked like a wooden bear trap. "This may look old-fashioned, but it's not. These teeth are made of wood because they are wooden stakes."

"Yeah, but we can't leave bear traps around the house. Some kid could wander into one," said Kevin.

"That's where the new tech comes into play. These traps are only armed when you press this button,"—Diego pointed to a remote control—"and unless the trap is armed, it won't go off. Even if you dance on it. We will set up a perimeter with these."

Diego took large industrial-looking lights and put them on the floor. "Now these motion sensing lights are killer. They run on bulbs that are on the same frequency as daylight. You want to make a vampire explode, let them walk into this light. I'll install these on every corner of the roof. If they get past the traps, they run into our lights. Good luck getting through these defenses."

"But what if they do?" asked Kevin. "Not trying to be a dick. I'm just saying."

"That's a fair question," said Diego. "That's why I brought these." He put a sword on the table, followed by an axe. "Both silver blades. For the up close and personal part of the program."

"Yeah, but when we get to these, we are in trouble," said Faith.

"Well, that's why I brought the coup de grâce." Diego took metal pieces out of the bag and started screwing them together with tools. When he finished, he stepped back and bowed. It looked like a Gatling gun. It was basically six crossbows, combined into one cannon.

"You crank this handle, the barrels spin and fire these silver tipped arrows fed through this here belt. Just keep turning the handle and you have two hundred arrows to fire. Any vampire that gets through that is not a vampire."

"Yeah, about that," said Faith. "It's not just vampires. I was attacked the other night by something else."

"Werewolf? Zombie? Witch? What? Go ahead, tell me. Nothing fazes me at this point."

"A huge, monster, mutant rabbit," blurted out Faith.

"What?"

"A giant weirdo killer rabbit."

"Like a gigantic fluffy bunny?"

"Don't be ridiculous. It had the body of an immense man, like a bodybuilder, but with the head of a pink insane rabbit. With murderous eyes and big fangs."

"I wasn't there when she was attacked," said Kevin. "I mean, if I was there, it would have been a different story."

"Bodybuilder rabbit, that's really specific." Diego whipped out his phone and started looking something up. "I have an extensive database of witness accounts of monsters and cryptids."

He got one hit on giant killer rabbits. He read through the file. "Talk to me about its abilities."

"I was running for my life; I was preoccupied. It was really fast. It could jump over my head without a problem, and I got the distinct impression that if I didn't have my gun, it would have tried to eat me," said Faith.

"According to this file, one other person has ever seen this thing. And he came away from it missing a hand. Anything else you can tell me?"

"Yes, I saw it once before," said Faith.

"When?"

"Twenty years ago, when I was a kid. It came into my

room and I screamed. It jumped out the window before my dad ran into the room. It has been my recurring nightmare ever since."

"That's not good. I'm afraid I already know the answer to this question, but Kevin, were vampires your childhood nightmare?" asked Diego.

"Yeah, my stinkin' older brother showed me the original *Nosferatu* movie, and it scared me silly. It stuck with me for years. I mean, I don't have those nightmares anymore or anything."

"Right. I'm going to have to drive home and get some more damn traps and weapons," said Diego.

"Anti-bunny man equipment?" asked Faith.

"No, it's more than that. Seriously, I would almost keep all of this to myself, but I have a feeling that being honest might save our lives," said Diego.

"What do you mean?" asked Kevin.

"It's pretty obvious that whoever is doing this is using our deepest childhood fears to create these creatures. Fear is a big part of this equation. I could easily just be like, yeah, nothing scared me as a kid, I'm good. But there was this one time."

"Doesn't sound good," said Kevin.

"I had a fairly normal childhood for a while, considering my parents were monster hunters. Until this one day when I used a shortcut through the oil field."

22

DEATH WORM

A twelve-year-old Diego walked down the street on his way home from school. He came to a corner.

If he turned right, it would be a twenty-minute walk through a rough neighborhood. If he turned left, he could cut through the old, abandoned oil field.

In 2020, those oil fields would be humming with working oil rigs and dozens of men. But in 2008, the economy was dead. Diego had heard his parents talking about it, many nights.

The big oil machines stood silent, unmoving. They were dusty from years of standing still. No one came to this field. Like there was some sort of invisible putrid smell. People just knew to stay away. There was no graffiti, no broken beer bottles. No signs of lurking teenagers. Nothing.

Diego's mother had taken him by the hand and made him promise repeatedly to stay away from the field. He had promised without a problem, silently vowing to do whatever the hell he wanted.

His dad had been less adamant. He thought Diego could stand to be a man once in a while, but his mother was having none of it. The field was empty and dangerous. He was forbidden from walking through it.

But for Diego, it cut a twenty-minute walk to a five-minute walk. It was hard to turn that down. And besides, he always did whatever the hell he wanted. And what he wanted was to cut through the damn oil field.

The field was surrounded by chain-link fence topped with razor wire. But Diego knew where the holes were. He slipped through and trotted down the embankment to the flat, dusty field. What Diego didn't understand was that when your parents were monster hunters, their children became very appealing targets. Many monsters wanted to get their hands on him, either for blackmail, leverage, or just good old revenge. Diego knew his parents were monster hunters. He even admired their rare occupation. He just didn't realize there was a neon glowing target on his back.

The weather had gotten unusually cold for Bakersfield, so Diego didn't have to worry about rattlesnakes or scorpions. He walked between old, frozen machines, enjoying the solitude. This was one place he didn't have to worry about running into anyone.

And then she stepped out from behind one of the oil drills. A beautiful woman in a breezy white dress. Diego stopped walking. He was not expecting to see anyone. There was something weird about the woman. She was beautiful, but there was something unnerving about her. Diego couldn't figure out what it was.

She waved to him. She wanted him to come closer.

He automatically took a couple of steps forward before he knew what he was doing. And then Diego realized why she looked strange. She had black eyes. All black, no white. Diego stopped walking. He backpedaled. She waved to him, more frantically this time. He turned and ran. He looked back, but she was gone.

He slowed down. Maybe he should take the long way home. He kept looking over his shoulder, but she wasn't there anymore. He relaxed a bit. A long walk seemed like a vacation compared to looking into her eyes.

The ground started shaking. Like an earthquake. He heard a sound behind him, like the earth cracking open. Diego turned around slowly. He knew there would be a monster there.

A giant worm rose out of the split in the ground. Normally a worm, no matter what size, would not inspire Diego to run so fast that he almost jumped out of his shoes. This worm had a giant gaping mouth, filled with long shiny teeth. They looked like icicles.

Diego didn't stop to wonder how it could live in an empty oil field in Bakersfield. He didn't wonder if it was seeking revenge on his parents. The only thing he cared about was running even faster.

The worm's side started swelling and a long tentacle burst out.

A slim, cold tentacle caught up to him and wrapped around Diego's ankle. It clamped down and dragged him backwards. He could feel the suckers digging into his skin and sucking his blood.

He pulled at it and beat it, but it was too strong. He was getting pulled closer to the massive mouth of icicle teeth. Diego grabbed on to a metal leg of one of the big oil drills. He would not let go.

The death worm pulled harder. The tentacle slipped down to Diego's sock. That was all he needed. He let the tentacle yank his sock and shoe off. And then Diego was free. He was up and running instantly, not caring about his missing shoe or his bloody footprint.

He could hear other tentacles behind him, but Diego beat them to the fence. He made it through the hole without slowing down. The last sounds he heard were the tentacles sliding backwards. He ran down the street with just one shoe.

For most, that would be the end of the story. They would never ever go back to that oil field under any circumstances.

Diego went back the next day.

He had new shoes on. He unzipped a duffel bag and took out a hatchet, a slingshot, and a super soaker. Diego put a football helmet on and slung the super soaker around his back. He stuck the hatchet in his belt, and he held the slingshot in his hand.

Diego was his parents' son, Monster hunting was in his blood, and he was not about to be bullied by one. So he walked across the field, proudly...

The woman in white stepped out from behind a rig. She waved to Diego again. He paused and pretended to be interested. Then he gave her the finger and fired his slingshot.

The metal ball hit her dead in the face. She flopped backwards, shrieking. The ground rumbled, and the worm came up. It wasted no time shooting tentacles at Diego.

This time Diego did not turn and run. He pulled out the hatchet. He chopped and severed the first half dozen tentacles that reached him.

But there were more. And they wrapped around his legs. Diego slipped out of them easily. He had covered his pants in a thick layer of Vaseline. The monster could not hold on to him.

Diego pulled the super soaker off his back and ran at the monster. He dodged more tentacles and ran harder. He pumped up the water gun, slid under a hungry tentacle, and jumped up. Diego was so close to it he could smell it. It had the same stench of seaweed that washed up on the beach. It smelled rotten.

Diego hit the trigger and unleashed a stream of gasoline. He soaked the worm's body and made sure to get it all over the nasty, gaping face. He flicked his lighter and tossed it as he ran past. The monster exploded into flames. It crackled and shook. It wailed and shriveled, falling back into the crack in the ground. Diego hacked a tentacle off and put it in his duffel bag. He wanted to show his parents.

That was the first day of Diego's monster hunting career.

23

JOEY OR KRAMER

Faith listened to it all with her mouth open. She couldn't believe Diego's bravery.

To Kevin, it sounded more like insanity. And he didn't like the way Faith was now hanging on Diego's every word.

"So now you have nightmares about giant worms?" said Kevin.

"No, that was a story about how I conquered my fear. I don't have nightmares."

"But we were telling nightmare stories. So basically, that was a humble brag about how you are fearless," said Kevin.

"I guess you could look at it that way," said Diego.

"You said you were going home to get more equipment?" prompted Kevin.

"Yeah, I think I got something for that bunny man."

"So, you're going to come right back?" asked Faith.

"Yeah, I'll be quick."

"What do we do in the meantime?" asked Faith.

Diego set the crossbow cannon up in front of the window. He secured the tripod. He shook it; it was sturdy.

"If trouble comes knocking, just open the window and start turning the crank. You have two hundred silver tipped arrows. I think you'll be okay," said Diego.

"We'll be fine," said Kevin.

Diego stepped outside.

"Take your time," said Kevin.

They watched Diego's pickup truck rumble away.

"I've got the first watch," said Kevin. He stood next to the cannon.

Faith found John Carpenter's *The Thing* on Netflix. She thought it would be funny to have a scary horror movie in the background while they kept watch for actual monsters.

The porch light only illuminated a couple of feet from the house. After that it was all trees and thick black shadows. It was impossible to see anything. But that didn't stop Kevin from trying. He spent hours in front of the window, looking out. Eventually, Faith fell asleep on the couch. He found *Big Trouble in Little China* and streamed it. Kevin thought a comedy would help lighten the mood.

Faith woke up just as Jack Burton was battling David Lopan over Samantha from *Sex and the City*. She stood by the cannon the rest of the night. Which wasn't that long. Sunrise started soon after she got up. Judging from the vampires in the cave, sunlight was not something they could withstand. Crazy muscle-bound rabbits, on the other hand, were an unknown.

There was a moment when she got ready to start the cannon. A deep rumbling startled her from a standing slumber, but it was just Diego pulling his truck into the driveway.

Faith liked Diego; he was cute and exciting. He was obviously brave, if not a little crazy. But he wasn't for her. She and Kevin were a good team. She didn't want to trade that.

She did, however, like the way Diego made Kevin jealous. She thought it was funny. Kevin made her laugh, more than he knew.

Diego brought duffel bags inside. Faith led him up the stairs to the loft. It was mostly empty except for a couple of boxes and a few stacks of buckets and trays. There was a single bed in the corner.

"You can sleep here. Make yourself comfortable. We will have dinner breakfast when we wake up in the afternoon."

"Sounds good to me. Thanks for the hospitality."

"Do you think the equipment is going to make a difference?" asked Faith.

"Definitely. But at some point, we're going to have to stop playing defense and switch to offense. We'll run out of ammo, eventually. We need to find the source and stop it."

"We can take you to the source, but he's dangerous and insane. Also, he has telekinetic abilities. He threw Kevin across a lawn with just his mind."

"Wow."

"Yeah. We'll talk about it in the afternoon-slash-morning. Get some sleep," said Faith.

Faith and Kevin woke up to the sound of a hammer. They went outside and found Diego on the roof installing floodlights.

"What are you doing up there?" asked Kevin.

"Floodlights. But I've installed something a little extra. If anything lands on the roof, like a giant mutant rabbit, a spring-loaded spike trap will go off. And go right through its feet."

"Sounds painful. I like it," said Faith.

Diego got down and wiped off his hands. "One more thing to take care of."

Diego took a spool of fishing wire out of his cargo pants. "I'll be right back."

He walked down to the woods bordering the house. He unspooled the fishing line and started weaving it between the trees a foot off the ground. He made a maze of trip wires.

When he was done, he stopped and took a deep breath. The air was fresh and piney. It was much nicer than Bakersfield, which smelled like a tire fire. Maybe he should move soon. He heard a noise for a second and froze. Did he hear something? It sounded like a crunch on the forest floor. Twigs and leaves.

Diego took the silver sword off of his back. The forest was still. No sounds. Even the birds held their breath, like they sensed the tension. He waited patiently. If there was something out there, he would wait for it to move first.

Minutes went by. Diego's shoulder was hurting from holding up the sword. Still no movement. Finally, he sheathed the sword and walked back to the house. By sundown, everyone was tense. They were ready. They could barely eat dinner; they knew a battle was coming.

But by midnight, nothing had happened. They took Inky out for her late-night walk. They avoided the house with the super green lawn. By two in the morning, they were all asleep in the living room. The same thing happened the next night and then the next and the next. After a week, Diego went home. There was no point in living in their house, if there was no monster battle. He wasn't Joey or Kramer.

Diego packed up his car and said his goodbyes. "Just call me if anything goes down. I will race up here any hour."

Kevin and Faith were both sad to see him go. He had been a fun distraction, and it had been comforting having a third soldier in their army.

24

WHIPPING THE KNIFE

William was trying to get used to his new powers.

He was practicing knife throwing against a dart board he had nailed to the wall. Only he wasn't using his hands. He was using his telekinetic abilities. The knife was in its sheath. But using his mind, he pulled it out and whipped it across the room. It landed solidly in the dart board, just to the left of the bullseye.

No one would expect that. He had the element of surprise on his side. The guy with the girlfriend would not see it coming. Using his mind, William pulled the knife out of the dart board. He floated it back to his belt and into the sheath.

He had been practicing for days. His condition made it so that leaving the house wasn't a very appealing option. His hair kept falling out in clumps, and sometimes he got a headache so bad he would fall down and cry tears of blood. Not very cool in public.

And then it happened again. A bloom of pain behind William's ears. Like he was hit with a baseball bat. He fell down, silently screaming. He lay there for a few minutes before he woke up, face hot and sweaty. Another wonderful side effect of his visit to the spacetime bridge. He needed to hurry up and kidnap the girl. The sooner he gave her to them, the sooner they would cure his unstable condition.

When he was able to stand, William angrily walked around the house, putting together his kidnapping kit. He shoved his tools into a backpack. He walked out of the house and enjoyed the cool air on his skin. The molecular instability kept him feeling hot all the time.

The black night was perfect cover. With no streetlights, it was easy not to be seen. He didn't want some nosy neighbor taking his picture and putting it online for the local Facebook community to remember. His plan was simple: he was going to sit and wait outside their house. When they came outside to walk their dog, he would strike. He was going to bury the knife in the guy's chest, strangle the dog, and then take the girl. The stun gun guaranteed that any struggle would be minimal.

William heard a noise up ahead. The jingle of a dog collar. He saw a golden shimmer in the dark. It was them! He dove into the bushes and crouched down. Did they see him? Should he attack now? Was this the best chance? He held his breath and didn't move. He had lurked many times before. Not moving was like being invisible. The blackness was his friend, his comfort blanket. It would keep him safe.

He relaxed. No, he would wait. It was not a good idea to attack them out in the open. Why risk it, when he could wait and dictate the ambush on his own terms. They passed him ten feet away. The dog perked up and growled, but they ignored it and kept walking.

Next time, listen to your dog, dummies, he thought.

They walked down the block. William waited until the

sound of the dog collar was far away. He slunk out and made his way to their house. He stood outside, observing. Maybe they left the door unlocked. He could be inside when they got back. They would never expect that. He would kill the man and the dog quick.

He took two steps, and a pair of brilliant spotlights came on. He shielded his eyes and stepped back and then fell over a trip wire.

"Goddammit," he muttered. William got up. They had booby trapped the area. He was going to have to be more careful. He took a step back and stopped suddenly.

Is that a bear trap? William thought. *They trying to cut my fucking leg off?*

Now William was angry. They wanted to play rough, then he would oblige them. No mercy. He had been considering letting the dog go in the woods. Now he would definitely kill it in front of them. And it would be their fault. He leaned up against a tree. William would wait here.

He looked up at the sky. The stars were brilliant against the jet-black night. Somewhere out there was Lam. On a planet, in a ship, William wasn't sure. He was sure of one thing, though; he would have his revenge. First, he would let them cure him, and then he was going to slaughter them and dance in their blood. No matter what it took.

Perhaps he could explode Lam's heart with his new telekinetic powers. Sure, he was some sort of alien creature, but he had to have a heart, right? Maybe two of them? William would explode them both if he had to.

He was fairly sure that Lam could read his mind. He would have to think about something else. He had always loved the roadrunner and coyote as a kid. Maybe he could play it as a loop in his head to trick them. He would have to practice. William was picturing the coyote on an Acme rocket when he heard them coming back. Suddenly he was gripped by the beginnings of a laughing attack. He started giggling.

He was about to start howling, so William punched himself in the gut. That stopped him. They were closer now. How should he attack? The trip wires and the bear traps made it a lot harder to run and jump out of the darkness.

The floating knife. He wouldn't even have to move. He would guide it through the dark and then whip it at the man. Nice and simple. No booby traps could stop his knife. He waited for them to come closer. They walked in front of the porch, and the security lights came on. William stepped farther back into the shadows. Now was the time. Now!

He floated the knife out of his sheath. He drove it through the trees. He took a deep breath. There was a vibration in his pocket. *Oh, no. Not now!* The beetle flew out of his pocket and landed on his neck. *No!*

The beetle bit into his neck, paralyzing William with pain. The knife fell down and landed harmlessly in the dirt. Blade down. He sank to his knees as the beetle started taking chunks of flesh out of his back. He wanted to scream, but he jammed his fist in his mouth. The metal teeth dug into his trapezium muscle and worked its way across in a line, taking chunks out every few inches.

William had been through this already. In a second a monster would grow from his chunk of flesh. It hurt, but it would be over quickly. Only the beetle wasn't stopping. It got to the end of his back and started over again, in a new row. The last thought William had before he passed out from the blood loss was, *How many monsters is this thing making?*

25

BRILLIANT STARS

I t was a quiet night. Quieter than usual. But Kevin didn't mind. A quiet night meant no vampires. He was fine with that. They ate a dinner of Faith's amazing fried chicken and then settled onto the couch for an episode of *Oak Island*. The episode lulled them both into a nap. Kevin fell asleep sitting up, while Faith snuggled onto his shoulder and started snoring. Kevin was awakened by Inky bumping him with her head.

"Really, Ink? It's barely nine o'clock," said Kevin.

She looked at him.

"All right. When you gotta go, you gotta go."

He tried to get up without waking Faith, but it didn't work.

"What's happening?" she asked.

"Ink stain apparently needs to go outside and do her business. I can go without you. You can stay here, all warm and comfortable."

"I'm awake now. I don't mind taking a walk. Some fresh air might be good," she said.

Kevin put his sneakers on and slipped on his heavy

Carhart jacket. Inky was wagging her tail and doing 360-degree spins in place. Kevin opened the door. Ink would have taken off if not for the leash. They turned the corner from their woodsy niche and started up the block.

"Yet another pitch-black night," said Kevin.

"Yeah, but it makes the stars stand out. Look how beautiful."

Inky was pulling harder now. She had zero interest in the stars.

"Okay, okay, we're going. Clearly she needs to make a deposit at the doody bank."

Faith laughed. "Does she use an ATM or a teller?"

"For sure a teller," said Kevin.

They were silent for a minute. Inky kept pulling.

"What if the attack never comes? It's been a couple of weeks," said Faith.

"Then we go about our lives, happy that we never had to battle the forces of evil."

"But I feel bad," she said.

"About what?"

"Diego. I feel like we wasted his time."

"Of course, Diego." Kevin rolled his eyes. "I wouldn't worry about it. I'm guessing he didn't have a lot to do anyway."

"What does that mean, 'of course, Diego'?" asked Faith.

Inky started growling. They told her to be quiet.

"You know what it means. You seemed awfully interested in what mister tall dark and Latin had to say."

"You're just imagining things. I thought he was helpful. He brought a lot of cool equipment," said Faith.

"Yeah, I'm sure."

"Stop being so jealous. It's really not attractive."

"You got it," said Kevin angrily.

They walked down the rest of the block in a furious silence. When they got to the empty lot, Kevin checked with his flashlight for coyotes, and then he let Ink off the leash.

"Come back quick, no messing around," he said.

Inky took off into the shadows.

"It's cold tonight," said Faith.

"Yeah, you can feel winter is coming."

They listened to Inky sniffing around the bushes.

"She loves to sniff," said Faith.

"It's her favorite thing in the world. Well, that and food."

Kevin whistled softly. Inky came trotting back out of the darkness, wagging her tail.

"Let's go home, girl. There's a soft warm bed waiting for you." He clicked the leash onto her collar, and they walked back down the street. When they got to the house, they walked up the porch, triggering the security lights.

Kevin hesitated for a second on the steps. Did he just hear something? No, he was just being paranoid. Maybe Faith was right; there would be no attack. The whole thing was over. He would grow his plants in peace while Faith continued to be a badass ER nurse.

When the latest episode of *Yellowstone* was over, they decided to sleep in their bed instead of being scrunched up on the couch. Kevin had insisted that they sleep in the living room for the past few weeks, and then they would be ready for any attack. But that seemed overly cautious now, so they stumbled to the bedroom.

Kevin was the first to wake up to Inky's barking. It wasn't her usual a-squirrel-is-taunting-me bark. This one was her some-serious-shit-is-going-down bark. The same one she used when she smelled a bear outside. It meant, "come here, right now." Kevin jumped up and ran into the living room.

The floodlights were on, and he heard a bear trap go off. Two vampires ran into the light and burst into flames...

"Oh, no. Faith, it's started. The monsters are attacking!"

She came running out of the bedroom. "What do we do?" she asked.

"Get ready. Grab a weapon. So far the defenses are holding."

Faith picked up a silver sword.

They heard something land on the roof. And then the spike trap activated. Something howled in pain.

"Wait, vampires have to be let in. They can't enter without our permission," said Faith.

"That could just be a myth. Besides, they don't need our permission." He pointed.

Hopping into the light were two huge mutant rabbit men.

"Oh, no. Multiples," she said.

"Dammit, they have no problem with the lights." Kevin picked up the shotgun. "But I bet they aren't bulletproof."

The rabbits jumped twenty feet and landed on the front porch.

"Babe, can you open the window?"

Faith slid the window to the side.

"And do me a favor, cover your ears. Inky, get out of here. Go to your bed." She took off, Kevin racked the gun and fired. The buckshot blast blew the rabbit men backwards off the porch. If they weren't dead, they would be soon.

"That worked," said Kevin. He looked into the darkness. Dozens of red eyes looked back out at him.

"There are lots of monsters in the woods. We're going to have to get Diego." Kevin picked up his phone and hit Diego's number.

It rang and rang, but no no one answered.

"He's not picking up."

"Maybe he's asleep."

"And maybe he's supposed to be on call in case we need him. Like we do now!" said Kevin.

Another rabbit man hopped out of the woods. Kevin fired. The bunny mutant was thrown back into the darkness.

"Text him!" said Faith.

A large pack of vampires stepped out. They hung back from the spotlights, looking for a way around. A rabbit mutant landed on the porch and attacked one of the spotlights before Kevin could get a shot off. Now they were down one light.

"Where the hell is Diego?" yelled Kevin.

26

POPCORN AND A MOVIE

Diego was bored. He was all keyed up for a battle that never happened. It was a big letdown. What do you do for fun instead of fighting an army of unholy nightmares?

Sure, he would probably get a call or two in the next few days to document a ghost or investigate a chupacabra sighting or something, but even that wouldn't compare to the war he had been looking forward to. Maybe a walk through the armory would cheer him up. It always did. He turned on the lights. The weapons gleamed. He smiled; it was working.

He passed by the knives. They brought good memories. He looked at the gorgeous dagger he had bought in Tibet. He hadn't used it yet, but he was looking forward to it. Then his eye landed on the Philippine haunted sword he had used to kill an actual Aswang. That had been an amazing night. He still couldn't believe he survived. But he did, thanks to that sword.

He stopped and lifted the bow his father had given him. His father had put a hole through a real skin-walker with it. He considered it his luckiest weapon. He brought it upstairs with him. Holding it always made him feel better. Diego sat down on his recliner. He surfed the satellite until he found something watchable. Syfy was showing *Escape From New York*. That was a movie he could always watch.

Diego laid the bow down on the couch and went into the kitchen. A movie like this definitely required popcorn. He grabbed a bag and stuck it in the microwave. He set the time and waited.

And that's when the sneezing started. Diego had an attack that lasted more than a minute because when he was finally done and gasping for air, the popcorn was ready.

Diego steadied himself and got a carton of juice out of the fridge. He gulped it down without a glass. Bakersfield was always dry and dusty; it clogged his sinuses and gave him sudden, intense allergy attacks.

Maybe it was time to move to the mountains. The air was clean. There were hardly any people there. Traffic was a myth. Sure, there were vampires and giant mutant bunny men, but at least no allergies.

And then it came again, another wave of sneezes. He held on to the counter but almost fell over anyway. When it finally stopped, he could barely breathe. He opened a drawer and dug out an inhaler. He took two quick puffs.

That was an improvement. He could breathe better. But his nose was now sealed shut. He tried to blow it, but it was closed up. He was going to have to resort to Benadryl. He didn't want to, but he enjoyed having the use of his nose. He knew he was on call, but he also needed to breathe.

Two Benadryls would unlock his nose and he would be back to normal in a few hours. It would also knock him out and make him dead to the world. But it always solved his allergy issues. He swallowed the pills, poured the popcorn bag in a big ceramic bowl, and settled into his chair.

He happily watched Snake Plissken kill punks with his Mac10 submachine gun. *Now that was a gun*, he thought. *I need to get my hands on one of those.*

He started to pass out. His last thought was, *They'll be fine for the few hours I'll be sleeping. No big deal. They won't even notice.*

27

ASSAULT ON PRECINCT 13

They were down to one spotlight. They had to protect it no matter what.

Kevin used the shotgun to keep the murder bunnies back while Faith used the .45 Diego left for them. It was a big, heavy, stainless steel pistol, with a 10 round mag. It made an enormous boom and had a real kick, but she could handle it if she used both hands.

"We have to keep them back. If we lose the second spotlight, we're screwed," yelled Kevin over the gunfire.

Faith fired at the tree line, where she saw the glowing red eyes lurking. Her shots and the spotlight kept the vampires pinned down. She ejected the magazine and slapped another one in. They were loaded with the special custom-made bullets Diego brought them. They were silver tipped.

Another gang of psycho rabbits landed on the porch. They went for the spotlight. Kevin fired, racked the shotgun, and fired again. The bunnies were hit and stumbled back.

"Get some of that, you stupid freak rabbits! Get some of that!"

The door was suddenly ripped off its hinges. A large muscly brown and white rabbit man bounced into the room. Kevin turned and fired. He was out of ammo; the gun was empty. The mutant rabbit man grabbed Kevin by the throat.

Kevin pulled the silver dagger off his belt and stabbed. The bunny barely noticed. Kevin remembered—silver didn't mean squat to a killer rabbit monster. Kevin was passing out. He was brought back to reality by the boom of the .45 behind him.

Faith emptied the mag into the rabbit's chest. He let go of Kevin's throat as he crumpled into a ball of fur and blood.

"We need backup. Where the hell is Diego?" asked Kevin. He pulled out his phone and dialed again. Still no answer.

"Someone must have heard the shots," said Faith. "They'll call the police."

"The wind."

Kevin was immediately reminded of the first movie that he had ever watched with Faith: *Assault On Precinct 13*. It was set in Los Angeles in the 1970s. In it, a police station gets attacked by a gang. No one can hear the gunshots because the station is so far away from everything. It was a badass movie, and Faith loved it. It had been a great first date.

"What?"

"The damn wind," said Kevin. "It's blowing too hard. The gunshots will be muffled. There's hardly anyone up here. These are mostly vacation houses. And the closest police station is forty minutes away! By the time they get here, we'll be stiff and dead."

Faith listened. He was right. The wind was roaring. It was like a jet engine. This could not be a coincidence. Someone or something was manipulating the weather.

Their enemy was powerful. She found this unsettling. She might be able to heal, but she certainly couldn't control the elements. That was way out of her league.

"Back to the window," yelled Kevin. He had seen movement by the trees.

The vampires threw one of their own at the spotlight. As he burst into black smoke, another vampire came up behind him and landed on the ledge. They had used the first vampire as a shield. He ripped the spotlight off the roof and smashed it into the ground. The outside went black...

"No, no, no! Keep firing!" yelled Kevin.

Faith shot at every pair of red eyes that she could see. She shot until her hands ached.

Kevin fired the shotgun until he was out of ammo. There were a dozen dead vampires lying on the ground. But the gang of living vampires was growing. And growing. A huge wave of them poured out of the tree line.

"The cannon!" Kevin pointed. He grabbed it and started cranking the handle. Faith fed the belt of silver tipped arrows into the large gun. Kevin aimed it at the tree line.

Puffs of black smoke went up all over like fireworks.

"Keep going!" said Faith.

Kevin cranked harder. Arrows rained down on the darkness, and vampires exploded.

"It's working!" shouted Kevin.

Wave after wave of vampires was smashed as they died over and over. The sound of the cannon spinning went *wump wump*, punctuated by the hissing of dying vampires.

But they kept coming.

"How many of them are there? They won't stop!" said Faith. And then the cannon ran out of arrows. For a second, everything was quiet. And then the vampires realized they were out of ammo, and they swarmed. Kevin pulled out his silver dagger. Faith grabbed the silver sword.

"Fight until we die," said Kevin.

"That was my plan too," said Faith.

The vampires poured into the house. They scrambled through the window; they crawled through the doorless doorway. Like insects in a feeding frenzy. Kevin and Faith stood back-to-back, weapons ready. They were surrounded by fangs and nails. Backed up against the wall. Kevin could sense their attack; they would pounce all at once.

And then he remembered something—the light schedule in the grow room. The lights were on right now. The 1,000-watt lights that used the same frequency... as the sun.

Kevin kicked as hard as he could behind him. The doors smashed in and sunlight came pouring out of the grow room. The living room was immersed in brilliant golden light. And the vampires exploded all at once.

They were now alone. The vampires were all gone. Disintegrated.

"Wow, I can't believe that worked," said Kevin. He picked up the door and tried to put it back on its hinges. It immediately fell again. Kevin kept an eye out the window while they cleaned up the room. "It will be easier for us to maneuver without all the crap on the floor."

"I agree," said Faith.

Kevin walked to the bedroom and opened the door. Inky came racing out, fur standing up.

"It's okay, girl. They're gone," said Kevin.

"The vampires, at least; we still have the bunnies to deal with."

"I think they're regrouping or taking a carrot break or something. I don't see them out there."

"Maybe they got scared off by our amazing monster killing abilities?" said Faith.

"Somehow, I doubt it. They'll be back. Let's be ready."

Kevin laid out their remaining weapons on the floor. A sword, a dagger, a revolver, and a baseball bat.

"It's not much," he said.

"But it's better than nothing."

"I'll stand watch while you take a nap on the couch."

"I doubt I can fall asleep after this much adrenaline," said Faith.

"Give it a try. If worse comes to worse, your feet will get a little rest."

Faith gave him a skeptical look. "I'm not even tired." She was snoring in less than five minutes.

Kevin stayed up for hours. Eyes on the shadows and nothing else. When Faith woke up, Kevin was still standing in front of the window. His neck and back were aching from concentrating for so long.

"Anything happening?" asked Faith.

"Eh, nothing. I mean, I don't think it's over, but I haven't heard a thing. It's dead still out there."

"Good, maybe you can get some sleep and I'll stand guard."

"No, don't worry about it," said Kevin. "I don't need to sleep."

"Really?"

"I'm not a rich man, I'm not a tall man, but one thing I can do is protect you."

"Aw, babe, I appreciate you no matter what," said Faith.

"I'm serious."

Inky started growling.

"You disagree, Ink stain?" he asked.

Her hair stood up.

'She's sensing something," said Kevin.

And then they both heard it, rustling leaves and crunching branches. Kevin picked up the revolver. "Go up to the loft, make sure that window is shut tight. We don't want them coming up behind us."

Faith took the sword and a flashlight and walked up the stairs. "Fine, but I'm coming back. You don't get to kill all the bunnies yourself."

Kevin was glad she didn't argue. There were a lot of mutant bunnies left, and he only had a few more bullets. Maybe he could hold them off long enough for Faith to escape through the back window. "Hey, if things get really hairy down here, I want you to disappear out that window."

"You really think I would desert you?" Faith called down.

"I'm just saying, if it looks too bad—"

"We go out together," she said.

Inky started barking. Kevin saw a monster bunny about to jump. He fired. "Here they come! Secure that window!"

He fired two more shots. Two more went down. But a large group of them was gathering. The revolver was almost out. Kevin counted at least twenty weirdo mutant killer bunny men. He would fight them as long as he could, and maybe Faith would escape after all. Death was coming—no, death was already here.

The bunny monsters got ready to leap.

And then Kevin heard the best sound ever. A deep base that sent vibrations all the way through his body. A helicopter? No, it was the sweet *chop chop* of an AK-47.

Diego was back.

"Yes!" said Kevin. "Babe, Diego is here!"

Boom boom.

The sound of the heavy ammunition coming out of the AK made it impossible to talk. Kevin clapped with joy as a dozen bunnies went down, blood and brains spraying everywhere. Diego made it up the stairs and into the house, firing as he ran backwards.

"Thank god you came back." Kevin clapped Diego on the back. "We were dead without you. What happened?"

A pair of furry arms came through the window. Claws scratched at them. Diego fired through the wall. No more bunny. "I had an allergy attack and had to take Benadryl. It always knocks me out. I missed all of your calls and texts." He slapped in a new magazine.

"So, what woke you up?"

"I had this big ceramic bowl of popcorn. I passed out, dropped it, shattered it, and scared the hell out of myself," said Diego.

"Good thing you like popcorn."

Diego handed Kevin a box of ammo. "Load up. Here they come."

Kevin jammed the bullets into the revolver. The rabbits made a group charge at the front door. Diego and Kevin opened fire. They cut them down before they made it into the house.

"I'm really glad we didn't have to go hand to hand with those things. They were huge," said Kevin.

"I know what you mean."

"Hey, Faith, you can come down now. We took care of them. They're all dead."

"You got that right," said Diego.

They kept watch out the window. There was still no more movement. They kept waiting.

There was just silence.

"Hey? Babe?" said Kevin.

Kevin and Diego looked at each other.

They loaded their guns and slowly walked up the stairs

to the loft. Kevin led the way, his revolver held out with one hand and a flashlight in the other. Upstairs was empty. Kevin shined his light everywhere. There was nothing but the sword Faith had been holding. It was lying on the floor. And there was nowhere to hide. It was just empty.

"What the fuck," said Kevin.

"What was she doing up here?" asked Diego.

"I tried to keep her out of the way. I sent her to check the window."

They both went over to the window. It was unlocked and cracked open. Kevin opened it all the way and looked down. There was a ladder there.

"Oh, god."

"That your ladder?" asked Diego.

"No."

"Then she's been kidnapped."

28

FLOATING

F aith made her way up the narrow steps to the loft. When she got to the top, she realized she had forgotten a flashlight.

For this, William was thankful. He lurked in a dark corner. With no flashlight, he was invisible. He was lightheaded, and blood ran down his legs. That damn beetle. It had taken many chunks out of his back. He was still bleeding. If he didn't stop it soon, he would pass out. He heard Faith go over to the window...

She saw it was slightly open. As he had planned. She hesitated and stepped back. Was there someone in the house already? Faith reached out to close the window, and a hand grabbed her wrist. Before she could scream, there was a blue flash and then blackness.

William shocked her just once with the stun gun and she was out. He grabbed her limp body before she fell over and made noise. He shoved the window open and pushed Faith's limp body out.

As she fell to the ground, William grabbed her with his mind and slowed her fall. He stopped her and floated her two feet off the ground. He had been practicing floating objects, so he knew he could do it.

William slid down the ladder and was moving quickly through the woods. He floated Faith's body in front of him. Up ahead, beyond the pine trees, was a red Nissan SUV that was already running. He pressed a button on the key fob, and the trunk door swung up. William floated her body inside and closed the door. He was inside and driving in a blink. The whole kidnapping had taken less than five minutes.

He steered the SUV up the road. He drove slowly because he had seen too many cop shows where the bad guys were spotted because they were driving like bad guys. No, he would be subtle and careful. Gentle, even. It would be very easy for one of these old crones to be sipping their coffee in front of a window and take note of his speeding vehicle. They might even take a picture with their phone and put it on Facebook. Everyone was now a snitch with a camera.

Thanks for that one, Steve Jobs, he thought, *making my life harder*.

He drove higher until there was snow on the sides of the road. He found the house he had been looking for. It was more of a mansion than a house, actually. Though it was made of logs, it was ten steps up from just a cabin.

This was the house that William researched. He checked online and made sure it wasn't a VRBO. No sudden surprises from a car of tourists. He checked to make sure it wasn't for sale. No nosy realtors coming around, giving tours.

No, someone lived here. And they were about to have a very bad day.

29

IVAN'S GOT AN EAGLE

Ivan was exhausted. He hadn't slept in days. This also made him furious. He was exhausted and furious, and that was tiring. He walked from window to window, careful not to stand in front of the glass. He carefully peeked out and then quickly pulled his head back.

He did this repeatedly. There were a lot of windows. He angrily cursed the world because he didn't get a house with fewer windows. He looked at his $22,000, blah blah Rolex. It said five o'clock. Was that five in the morning or evening? He wasn't sure.

He sat down on the couch. His gigantic back muscles were cramping. He stretched out but could not afford to fall asleep. He turned on the TV. It was the morning news crew. That answered his question. He had made it through another night. Not that daylight meant he was safe. But at least another day had passed.

The more days that went by, the safer he would be. Maybe. Although the organization he worked for would never forgive him for stealing three million dollars from them.

They should learn to let things go, thought Ivan.

He closed his eyes and thought about the worst day of his life. The big game, the biggest poker game in L.A., the game he was in charge of, got robbed. Somehow two idiots had managed to smuggle a pair of .32 caliber Seecamp pistols past security. They waited a couple of hours for big money to be on the tables, and then they were up and firing. First thing they did was shoot the security.

And then they had everyone against the wall, and they were filling bags. Ivan came out of his office, pointing his massive .44 caliber gold plated Desert Eagle, given to him by the big boss on his last birthday. It was an honor and a useful tool. Ivan loved the gun. He slept with it under his pillow ever since. The fireball and boom from the .44 caliber Magnum was scary enough to turn almost anyone into a track star. And it was gorgeous.

Ivan blew the shorter one's face off. Literally. His face disappeared in a red mist. The taller one made it through the door. Ivan followed him with the Desert Eagle and squeezed the trigger. He would not get away. *Click*. Nothing happened. It was jammed.

He cursed in Russian. He ran after him, but he was too slow. He was big and powerful, but he was not fast. By the time he got to the staircase, the skinny guy had jumped to the first floor and escaped.

Ivan knew he was dead. Literally. If he didn't disappear immediately. His boss had given him one command: No robberies. Ever. He didn't have to say "or I'll fucking kill you." That punishment was obvious. Ivan dismissed all the players, promising to get them all their money back by sunup. And once they were gone, Ivan robbed the place himself.

The idiot thieves stole maybe $200,000. They didn't get to the safe. The safe was the house. And the house had to cover all chips. Ivan stuffed the three million dollars into a big suitcase and ran out the door. If the big boss was going to kill him over two hundred thousand, he might as well take all the money and start a new life.

Ivan woke up. He got up quickly. How long had he napped? Shit, he could not afford to slip up like that. He picked up the gold Desert Eagle. He appreciated the heaviness. It was solid, like a brick. Ivan had always loved the strength of metal. As a boy he had adored his heavy metal trucks, and he quietly hated the plastic toys his mother came home with.

The Desert Eagle was all he had now. Back in his L.A. condo, he had a very respectable arsenal. AKs, an MP5, a P90, even a Tommy Gun. And so many pistols he couldn't even count them all without forgetting a couple. But they might as well have never even existed. There was no way Ivan could get to them. The house would be watched, covered by snipers and wired to explode in case they missed their shot.

Ivan would have paid $20,000 for his P90. A 50 round mag filled with mini rifle bullets would have been very comforting right now. More than a blanket and a pillow. All he had was the Eagle. It was pretty, and it was intimidating, but it was impossible to conceal. That made it hard to carry when he was in town picking up supplies. Ivan grumbled. And then there was the nasty little habit the Eagle had of jamming. In fact, if it hadn't jammed, he wouldn't be here right now.

Ivan needed a walk to clear his head. But he was not that stupid. So he settled for a shower. Should he take the Eagle with him? The steam could rust the mechanics of the gun over time. He could leave it out in the living room on the couch. No rust.

Fuck it, he didn't like being unarmed. He left the gun by the sink. He turned on the water and made it scalding hot.

30

ICICLES ARE SHARP

William watched and waited. When he saw the bathroom light go on, he knew the moment was right.

As he approached the house, he feared motion lights, but nothing turned on. He made it to the back door easily. He was about to unlock the door with his TK powers when he spotted some huge icicles hanging from the door frame. They looked really dangerous. William smiled.

He entered the house. It was big. The walls were white, and the ceiling must have been forty feet high. There was a gentle fire burning in the rock fireplace. This was an expensive house. William heard someone singing in the shower. A man.

That gave him time to get the girl. He didn't want to leave her alone for long. His life depended on delivering her. He could not let her get away. He walked back to the SUV and pulled her out of the trunk. The sky was getting light, so he had to hurry. He floated her up the walkway and into the house before any neighbors saw.

William laid her down in the living room on the hardwood floor. He heard the water shut off in the shower. A huge man came out of the bathroom in a tiny towel. It was so small William almost burst out laughing.

He raised a big gold handgun. "You think I shower with no weapon? Ha. Joke on you." He had a thick Russian accent. He pulled the trigger. *Click*. The gun jammed. "Goddammit."

"No, my friend, the joke is on you," said William. He lifted the large pointy icicle into the air, and then he whipped it at the Russian's chest. It actually went through him and hit the wall and shattered. Ivan didn't understand what happened, but he was only confused for one more second before he was dead on the floor.

William had always wondered about killing someone with an icicle. Turns out it worked.

31

THANKS, STAIRCASE

Kevin jumped out the window and somehow ran down the ladder. He landed on the ground and was instantly sprinting down the street. He had a revolver in one hand, a brilliant silver dagger in the other. He didn't care who saw what. He had one goal: get to the house with the greenest lawn ever.

He was going to kill William any way he could. Kevin turned the corner and raced downhill. And then the house came into view. No lights were on. Kevin ran at the door and slammed into it, shoulder first. The door exploded inwards. He heard running footsteps; it was Diego. He came up behind Kevin with the .45 by his side.

They both entered the house. It was dark and quiet. Kevin strained to see, but he had taken off without a flashlight. Then he remembered his phone. He turned on the light function.

"At least we've got that," said Diego. "Sure, we can only see one foot ahead, but it's the best foot."

Kevin was not in the mood to laugh. He had lost the most important person in his world. He had to get her back.

Now. They went down the hall into the living room. Kevin led the way because he had the light. The kitchen was empty. So was the bathroom.

The floor creaked a lot, but it was spotless. Like a museum. The person who lived here was clearly insane. And they loved Lysol, because the place stank of it. Kevin had always hated that smell. It was cheap and suffocating.

"This floor is clear," said Kevin.

"Agreed."

"Let's go up."

Kevin carefully made his way up the staircase, which was even creakier than the floor.

"We've kind of blown the element of surprise. Thanks, staircase," said Diego.

They made it to the top floor. It was a long hallway with rooms off to the sides. All the doors were closed.

"We're going to have to go through each room," said Kevin.

"Of course."

Kevin kicked open the door, gun sweeping the room.

"We don't have time to be careful. Faith is gone," he said. He quickly moved to the next room, and the next. There was one door left. Kevin's patience was gone. He threw open the door and walked into the room. He moved the flashlight around. It was empty. Kevin lowered his gun and took a step.

"This one's empty too," he said. He heard a sound above and looked up.

There was a vampire clinging to the ceiling.

Kevin tried to bring the revolver up, but the vampire was already on top of him. Long claws wrapped around his neck, and large fangs snapped inches from his face.

Kevin raised the gun, but the vampire swatted it away. Its fangs were so close that it drooled on Kevin's face. He could smell its breath. It smelled like a corpse. Kevin pushed back with all the rage he had, but it was like trying to push a car. The vampire was much stronger. It was a wall.

"Hey, ass face. Have some silver." Diego blasted him in the side of the head with the .45.

The vampire flew backward and exploded into black smoke.

"Thanks for that," said Kevin. He jumped up and ran down the stairs. "This stupid house is empty. Let's go."

Diego followed. Kevin walked outside and couldn't have cared less about the brilliant orange sunrise. He spotted the grey Honda. He ran over and pulled open the door. The car was spotless. It was completely empty. If he was hoping for a clue, there was nothing to look at. Kevin slammed the door and kicked it. He was breathing heavily. "It's empty. The car is empty, the house is empty. There's nothing," said Kevin. "How the fuck are we supposed to find them!" he screamed.

"I know, man. But freaking out won't solve a thing."

"I don't even know which direction to run after them."

"Let's go back to the house. We can think of a new plan. Come on."

He led Kevin away from the empty house and up the street.

32

BROWNIES AND MILK

Kevin was sitting on the couch with his head in his hands.

"I should have realized sooner. I hadn't heard from her in like fifteen minutes."

"You were in the middle of a battle with giant mutant killer bunnies. Being distracted is understandable."

"My job was to protect her," said Kevin.

"You will get her back."

Kevin looked up. "How?"

Diego was cleaning the room. He was gathering rubble and debris and dumping it in a big trash bag. "First, we clear our heads, calm down, and get organized."

"What does that mean?" asked Kevin.

"I'm guessing you don't drink or anything."

"No, not really."

"Okay, then you probably have some powerful edibles?" said Diego.

"That's some sort of grower stereotype. And yes, I do. My special atomic knockout triple chocolate brownie bombs."

"Great. Let's have a couple. We can relax and see the situation from a new perspective."

"Okay, that's not a bad idea." Kevin got up, went to the kitchen, and pulled a pan out of the fridge. He took two large brownies and put them in the toaster oven. "We might as well be civilized about this," said Kevin. He poured two tall glasses of milk. "Okay, let's start at square one. Literally, where can we start? What are our options? Do we even have any clues?" said Kevin.

"Right. I think there are three areas we might find clues. First is the actual physical scene. We haven't looked at it yet; we just ran past it. Two is the digital realm. Maybe we can find some information on this guy somewhere. And three, if we think all of this out, maybe we can figure his motive and location."

Kevin put the brownie pan on the coffee table that had somehow managed to not get destroyed in the battle.

"Okay, that's something we can work with. Three avenues. I can get my head around that. We will examine the scene for physical clues. What about online? I'm not clueless, but I'm not a hacker or anything," said Kevin.

"I got someone. A cousin. She's a digital freak. She can find things online like some sort of Mexican bloodhound. She's pretty awesome."

"Sweet. All right, I'm starting to see a teeny tiny glimmer of hope."

Kevin took a big bite out of his brownie. Diego didn't touch his. He wanted to be clear headed. He hoped Kevin would pass out soon. Kevin would need his strength, both physical and mental, if they were going to have any chance at finding Faith. So he decided on a brownie-induced nap.

It would be a lot easier to go over the physical scene without Kevin's manic energy yelling in his ear.

Kevin took another big bite of his brownie. Diego nibbled a tiny corner of his.

"Avenue three, the thought experiment," said Kevin. "What did you mean?"

"Let's see if we can get into this guy's head. What are his motivations, his methods, his tools? Then maybe we can get an idea of his location? Or at least his intention."

Kevin took another big bite of the brownie. It was gone.

Diego took another nibble and then moved it around on his plate.

"What do you know about him so far?"

"Not much. We first noticed his house because the lawn was supernaturally green. He drives a shitty Honda, or he used to. Oh, and last time I ran into him he lifted me up using telekinetic powers from his mind," said Kevin.

"Well, that's something. The TK stuff is good to know. That way we've taken the element of surprise away from him next time we see him."

"Right. Next time we see him, I'm killing him."

"I hear you. Have you ever seen him anywhere in town? Does he have a hangout? Friends?" asked Diego.

"Friends? That guy? Other than vampires, I doubt it. And if he hung out anywhere, they would call the police on him. This guy is the creepiest."

"Okay, good, that's something. No friends. You're not about to run into him at the local bar. So he's living a lonely existence up here," said Diego.

"I know he works at Edwards Air Force Base."

"How the hell did you figure that out?" asked Diego.

"Faith and I followed him."

"So, he's a soldier."

"Nah, I don't think so. He wasn't wearing a uniform," said Kevin.

"Hmm, that gives us a couple of possibilities. Intelligence? Civilian contractor? Scientist?"

"He could be any of those," said Kevin.

"This is good, though. We're narrowing it down."

"Yeah, narrowing." Kevin's eyes started drooping.

Diego stopped talking and waited quietly. Soon Kevin was snoring deeply, stretched out on the couch. Growing up as a kid, Diego had been obsessed with Sherlock Holmes. While other kids had loved the Power Rangers, Diego would get lost in the Sherlock stories that were in his big red book. He loved the idea of noticing things that other people didn't. So he trained himself to be super observant, and it helped him many times.

He started upstairs in the loft. Sunshine poured through the window now; it was very easy to see. The first thing that caught Diego's eye was the pool of dried blood in the corner.

That must have been where he stood waiting, thought Diego. *So, he's injured. That changes everything.*

He went over to the window. The walls and the floor showed no sign of a struggle.

So, he snuck up on her. If Kevin didn't hear a fight, he must have used a stun gun. How did he get her unconscious body down the ladder, being so injured?

Diego tried to picture it in his head. There were no drag marks or scuffs.

Right, his telekinetic abilities. Shit, this guy just went from dangerous to insane super villain.

Diego paused and listened. Kevin was still snoring. He went out the window and down the ladder. He stepped down, imagining Grey Face and what his next move must have been. Diego spotted footprints and a puddle of blood on the wet ground. Still no drag marks.

So, he floated her.

He followed the blood trail to the end of the dirt where there were tire tracks. Diego pulled out his cell phone and took a couple of pictures of them. He smiled to himself. *Imagine what Holmes could have done with a supercomputer in his pocket.*

All the clues pointed to one thing: Grey Face was still on the mountain.

33

A CRYSTAL BALL

When Kevin woke up, he was calmer. He no longer acted like he had an electrical charge running through his body, but there was still a cloud of doom and rage that hung over him.

"Can't believe I fell asleep. Did you find anything?"

"Yeah. I went over the scene. The clues tell me that Grey is still on this mountain," said Diego.

Kevin stood up, ran his hand through his hair, and picked up the revolver. "Then let's go find him. Right now."

"Whoa, hold on, slow down. This is a big mountain; he could be anywhere. We can't just go door to door looking for a Grey lunatic hiding in the house. We're not psychic," said Diego.

"Hold on, I think I know where we can find one."

They drove down the mountain. Diego drove his pickup. It was roomier than Kevin's car.

"I forgot about this because a bunch of other stuff happened. But I came to town looking for a thrift shop. That's where I got the coffee table. And as I was leaving, there was this pretty lady standing in front of one of those psychic places. I never believe in that crap, so I ignored it."

"Yeah, me neither."

"But as I was walking past her, she asked me if I was having any vampire problems," said Kevin.

"What? No way."

"Yeah. Seriously. I was like, do I have a sign on my back? Was that a lucky guess? Is she spying on me? What the hell? I just give off an 'I'm being harassed by vampires' vibe?"

"That can't be a coincidence," said Diego. He pulled into a spot in the parking lot right in front of the Psychic Readings storefront.

The pretty woman came out and stood in front of the door. She was dark-haired with green eyes. She wore a long flowing dress covered in flowers. She was in her forties. Anyone that ever doubted an older woman could be beautiful had never met her.

"I see you decided to return," she said in some sort of exotic accent. "I am Serena. Please, come inside."

She opened the door for them...

The inside was small but decorated for maximum effect. The walls were covered in tapestries, incense assaulted Kevin's nose, and there were candles everywhere. An actual crystal ball sat on the round table. That was too much, and Kevin almost turned around and left right there, but he remembered they had no real clues, and she had been right about the vampires.

Diego looked at the mirror on the wall. He guessed it was a two-way mirror. His radar was up.

"Please sit. I am called Serena," she said with a vocal flourish that bordered on singing. "Sit, sit. I can sense that you are both very skeptical." She paused, closing her eyes.

"But I can also tell that you are in trouble and are looking for help. Yes?"

Kevin and Diego looked at each other and sat down.

"I am—"

"Kevin," she said. "And you are Diego. You're looking for proof before you open up to me. Yes?"

They didn't say anything.

"You both have secrets. You grow magical plants, and you hunt monsters."

Kevin jumped up. "Okay, lady, how the hell could you know that? You've been spying on us? That's information you can't get just by running our plates. Are you working with Grey Face?" He shoved his hand in his pocket and wrapped it around—

"You can take your hand off the revolver, Kevin. I'm not here to hurt you," she said.

"How could you—"

"Did you not see the sign outside? I'm psychic."

Diego said nothing but was paying attention to the two-way mirror.

Serena turned to him. "You fight monsters and mutant rabbits, but you find psychic powers hard to believe? Please sit down."

Kevin sat back down.

"Why are you here?" she asked.

"You tell us," said Diego.

She closed her eyes and put her hands on the crystal ball.

"You've lost something, and you need me to help you find it."

"Not something. Someone," said Kevin. "Can you see where she is?"

Serena paused.

"No. I can't see her."

"Of course not. The one thing we need to know, and you can't see it," said Diego.

"Let me guess, for a few more bucks you might see her. WHERE'S MY GIRLFRIEND?" Kevin slammed his hand down on the table.

The crystal ball tipped off its stand and rolled to the edge of the table. Serena instinctively reached for it and grabbed it before it fell off. As she did, something fell out of her ear and onto the table. It was an earpiece.

Kevin pulled out his gun and leveled it at Serena. "I knew this was a scam," he said.

"How many are in the back room? How long have you been surveilling us?" demanded Diego.

"Who are you working for?" Kevin yelled. "Get up!"

She got up.

"Open that back room!" yelled Diego.

He pulled out the .45 and aimed it at the door.

"No, don't shoot!" She stepped in front of the door, and her accent was completely gone.

Kevin grabbed her and pulled her away.

"Come out of the room with your hands up or I will shoot all of you through the wall," ordered Diego.

They waited. Nothing happened.

"I'm going to count to three and then I start shooting," he said. "One—"

The door swung open. Kevin and Diego stood, guns ready, while Serena begged them not to.

Out stepped a beautiful teenage blonde girl, with her hands over her head. She must have been only seventeen.

"Don't shoot, we are not a threat to you. I know you are both confused and paranoid right now, but we can actually help you."

"Who else is back there?"

"It's just me."

Diego stepped past her and entered the small room, gun up and ready. It was empty.

Diego and Kevin both put their guns away.

"Someone explain what the hell is going on. How do you know so much about us?" asked Kevin.

"I told you before," said Serena in a completely American accent. "Psychic."

"You're still peddling that bullshit. You should know when it's time to drop the con," said Kevin.

"Not me. Her. My daughter, Madison."

"Yeah, right," said Kevin.

Sit down and shut up, stop waving your stupid guns around, and maybe we can start helping you! Madison shouted into their minds.

Kevin and Diego looked at each other and sat down.

"If you have actual psychic abilities, what's with the earpiece scam? Like seriously, what the hell?" said Kevin.

"Yeah. What he said," said Diego.

"Most people will not take a reading seriously that's coming from a teenage girl. But they are much more likely to believe if it's coming from my mom. I do the reading in here and I whisper it to her in her earpiece. It's not a scam; they are getting an actual reading."

"Then we came to the right place. We need your help. Read us, and you'll see we're telling the truth," said Kevin.

"We're serious," said Diego.

She sat down and closed her eyes.

"How long does this usually—"

"Your girlfriend was kidnapped by an evil lunatic, and you are hunting monsters," said Madison.

"Well, he hired me, actually. It's not like I'm just

wandering around looking for monsters. But yeah, that's the gist of it," said Diego.

"What do you want from us?" asked Serena.

"We need your help to find my girlfriend."

"And taking down an evil man and his army of monsters," said Diego.

"Great, you've had your reading. You scared the crap out of us as a nice bonus. Let's just say this has been free of charge, and we hope to never see you again," said Serena.

Madison stood up. "Wait, Mom. This is like the first interesting job to come through that door. How many more 'will I find love' or 'will I strike it rich' readings can we sit through before we go insane?"

"It pays the rent."

"I want to be a part of something important. I can feel this."

Serena studied Madison. She was not going to give in. She turned to Kevin. "We're not working for free."

"I can pay. No problem," said Kevin.

"It's not going to be dangerous, right?" asked Serena.

"No, we will protect you with our lives," said Diego.

"I hope that's not what you said to Faith." Madison walked out the door.

34

NOT SERENA

Diego drove his white pickup back up the mountain while Serena followed in a red VW bug. They all parked in front of Kevin's house.

"Now keep in mind that we just had a monster attack, so my place is a wreck," said Kevin.

The door fell off its hinges.

Madison hesitated. "There was a lot of evil here."

"The key word being *was*. We took care of it," said Diego.

"But not before we lost Faith. Can you look at the scene? Maybe you can pick up something," said Kevin.

"She's not a bloodhound."

"Right, right. Sorry, Serena, I just meant this is the scene we want her to study," said Kevin.

"Yeah, I get it. I just want you guys to be honest with us. I can't stand liars. And it's not Serena. It's actually Susan," said Susan.

"Why would you—"

"Who wants a reading from Susan when they can get one from the exotic Serena? It's all about showmanship." She bowed with a flourish. Kevin rolled his eyes.

Diego led Madison up the stairs to the loft. He pointed to the corner that was muted in dull grey shadow.

"Here is where he was hiding. You can see the pool of blood he left behind."

"Gross."

Madison walked around the room, slowly, carefully. She closed her eyes and inhaled. She watched as a ghost image of Grey Face snuck up on Faith. She let out a little yell when he shocked her. She watched as he floated her down the ladder. She saw him take the girl in an SUV and drive away. The image faded.

Diego and Madison came back to the living room. Inky sat up and wagged her tail, happy to see them return, despite the tense atmosphere.

"Did you get anything?" asked Kevin.

"You don't have to answer that, sweetie. We don't know if these two can be trusted."

"Mom, knock it off. I read their minds; they can be trusted. And yes, I saw everything. It happened exactly as they said."

"Exactly?" asked Kevin.

"Yes. Grey Face used a taser on Faith. He floated her down the ladder and then took her away in a red SUV," said Madison.

"So, you saw them? Which way did they go? Did you see where they went?" said Kevin.

"No, I only saw the SUV color."

"Dammit!" yelled Kevin. He kicked a chair over.

"Hey, man, calm down. It's a start. Now we know to look for a red vehicle. That's a solid clue," said Diego.

"I'll calm down when Faith is back here, safe."

"We're going to find her."

"Yes, but will we find her alive?" yelled Kevin.

35

NOWHERE GOOD

They stood in front of Grey Face's house. The sun was going down in a blaze of purple and pinks. *It is beautiful*, thought Diego, *but that's not going to help us see in here*. Diego took a backpack off his shoulder. He took out flashlights and a battery-powered lantern. He was not going to be in the dark.

"Flashlights for everyone." He handed out lights.

"It's going to be fine. It's empty. We just need Madison to see if she can sense something," said Kevin.

"Okay, but I'm going to stay out here. That place is creepy. No, thank you," said Susan.

Kevin, Diego, and Madison filed into the house.

Susan watched their flashlight beams through window. She was happy that she chose not to go in. She looked around. It was dark. The only light was the sunset, and that was fading fast.

An owl hooted. The bushes rustled. Were those footsteps behind her? Susan quickly changed her mind. She ran in the house.

"I thought you were staying outside," said Diego.

"I figured you would probably need my help."

"Of course," said Diego. "Thank you for coming."

Madison vaguely heard other people talking, but she wasn't paying attention to them. The house had set all her senses on fire. Like an electric charge was running through her on a loop.

The house was freezing. But it must have been just her because no one else in the group was acting like they were cold. Madison would not act scared. She refused to give her mother any reason to exclude her from this adventure. Nothing cool ever happened in her town, and besides, Diego was super cute.

They went through the downstairs, carefully. Kevin was in front and Diego brought up the rear. They kept the women between them.

Madison saw a ghostly image of Grey Face. He looked sick and desperate.

"His name is William."

"That's a start," said Kevin.

She had a feeling that the real jackpot was on the second floor. "Let's go upstairs."

The stairs creaked under the weight of the four of them. The stink hit her like a smack. She smelled something foul; she felt something wrong. It wasn't alive. But it wasn't dead either. She saw a flash of red eyes and fangs. Snow white skin. Vampires had been there.

"Vampires were here."

"Yeah, we know," said Diego.

"Seriously?" said Susan. She turned to leave but realized again she would be all alone. So she turned back.

"Maybe we should get out of here. Like the hell now," said Susan.

"Mom. Hold on, I'm seeing something else. I think this is more important."

They all stood quietly. Diego realized he was holding his breath.

"Oh, crap."

"What is it?" asked Kevin.

"It's a gateway. A door."

"To where?" asked Diego.

Madison tried to see inside. All she got was a sliver of a peek. Tears immediately streamed down her face.

"Nowhere good," she whispered. "Let's get out of here." She walked out quickly and headed for the stairs. If Diego hadn't followed her so closely, he wouldn't have been there to catch her as she fainted at the top of the stairs.

36

AN OLD ANTENNA

adison woke up on the couch in Kevin's house. Everyone was standing over her with concerned expressions.

"It's a good thing it's dark out there. Someone looking out their window would have seen a young girl being carried down the street," said Diego.

"Sometimes the blackness of the mountain can be helpful," said Kevin.

"I know what you mean. Once the sun goes down, I don't have to worry about my hair or what I'm wearing. No one can see anything out there," said Susan.

"What made you react like that? Was it the house? Or what you saw?" asked Diego.

Madison sat up. "What I saw."

"Can you describe it?" said Kevin.

"Hold on. You don't have to, sweetie. If it's too hard, we can just go home."

"Mom. I can do this."

"I'm not trying to push you, but Faith has been gone for

twelve hours now. Every minute counts," said Kevin. "What did you see?"

"It's hard to explain, but I'll try. It was cold and black. Whatever could survive in there, I don't want to meet. It was so different from here."

"Different from where, the mountain?" asked Kevin.

"Different from California?" asked Diego.

"Different from Earth," said Madison. "It wasn't anywhere on this planet."

"Wait, what?" said Susan.

"How do you know?" said Kevin.

"Because I know," said Madison firmly.

"So you're saying Grey Face opened a door to another planet?" said Diego.

"Another planet, another dimension, I'm not sure. All I know is it wasn't anywhere that we should be."

"We?"

"Humans," said Madison. "It was like the bottom of the ocean. Nothing lives down there but monsters that can stand the cold and pressure."

"Hold on, is that where he took Faith?" asked Kevin.

"No, it was just him."

Kevin was pacing. "So you both think he's still here on the mountain."

"With the amount of blood he was losing, he didn't have time to drive far. No, he's still here," said Diego.

"I agree, I can sense a faint trace of him. He's not right next door, but he's still on the mountain," said Madison.

"Is there any way you can just see him?"

"I've tried before and what I've learned is in order for me to locate someone, I need to see the area they are hiding in."

"Okay, good, we can work with that," said Kevin. "There's

a spot I heard about that's at the top of the mountain. It's an old ranger station that overlooks everything."

"That might work," said Madison.

"Well then, let's go," said Kevin.

"What, right now? But it's dark out," said Susan.

"Yes, right now. What are we waiting for? Faith is missing. We have got to get her before he does something horrible to her. That means we leave right now."

"But what about bears and mountain lions? Not to mention vampires and rabbit monsters," asked Susan.

"That's why we have powerful flashlights and guns. We'll take care of your safety," said Diego.

"I'm terrible at playing the damsel in distress. That's why I have my own guns," said Susan.

Diego's truck was big enough that they could all pile in. It was a twisty-turny road that shoved them around from side to side. Madison did not mind. She was crammed next to Diego. His leather jacket had a warm and exciting smell to it.

This part of the mountain was even darker. There were no houses here. Without high beams, they were almost blind. Regular headlights were not strong enough to cut through the blackness. The higher up they went, the more snow appeared on the side of the road. It had snowed up there while the rest of the mountain had gone about its business, unaware.

The parking lot was old and cracked. It had been a long time since people had been up there. All the snow was piled up on the side. Parked by the snow piles were two titanic snowplows.

Diego pulled the truck to a stop. The ranger station was large and imposing. But as they got closer, they could see how rickety it was. A twenty-foot radio antenna stuck out from the crumbling roof.

"Let's get up to the observation deck. You can see everything from there," said Kevin.

They looked at the stairs skeptically.

"All right, I'll go first," said Kevin. "Follow me."

He took his first step and heard the creak of the old boards. He decided a quick run up the stairs was the best strategy.

"See, no problem," he called down from the top of the stairs.

One by one they ran up to the top.

"Hold on to the handrail here. I don't know how much I trust this wood."

Everyone grabbed on to the metal handrail. They made their way to the middle of the deck. They looked down, and spread out in front of them was the entire mountain.

"Now that's an amazing view," said Diego.

"What do you think, Madison? Do you think it will work?" asked Kevin.

"Let's find out," she said. She relaxed her body. Madison had discovered that concentrating and tensing up made sensing things much harder. She slowed her breathing, and a tingle started forming in the back of her neck. The left side of the mountain slightly glowed. She waited to see if the area got smaller. It didn't.

"I can see that he's on that side of the mountain." She pointed.

"So he's still here," said Diego.

"Yeah, but that's still a huge area. How are we supposed to find him? We're running out of time," said Kevin.

"We're really far from everything. It's hard for me to see this far."

Kevin looked around. He spotted the antenna on the roof. "Some people think ESP is electrically based."

"Why are you saying this?" asked Diego. He followed Kevin's gaze and saw the antenna.

Madison looked up and saw it too.

"We can try," she said.

Susan looked up and immediately started shaking her head. "Hell no. Absolutely not. That is way too dangerous," she said.

"Mom, we came all the way up here. We have to try something."

"I'll lead, you follow," said Kevin.

He started up the metal ladder sticking out of the wall. He pulled himself up to the roof. Madison did the same.

Susan put her hands on her hips. "So, no one's going to listen to me. That's the new plan."

"If it makes you feel any better, I'm listening to you," said Diego.

"It doesn't." For the first time, she noticed Diego was cute, in a young and wild kind of way.

Madison got to the top of the ladder; Kevin pulled her the rest of the way. The roof was rickety. The wood had long since disintegrated, leaving a skeleton of metal in its place. They both balanced on the same rusty beam.

Kevin led her to the antenna.

"What should I do?" asked Madison.

"I guess grab a hold of it."

"Okay."

She stepped around Kevin.

She looked up at the antenna. It was a lot taller than her and was made of thick, smooth metal.

She took a deep breath and grabbed it.

"Aahhhhhh!" she screamed. Then she laughed. "Just kidding."

"Not funny," said Kevin.

"So not funny," yelled Diego from the deck below.

"I have to agree," said Susan.

"What did you expect to happen?" said Madison.

"I don't know. I thought maybe it would amplify your powers." Kevin was frustrated. They were running out of time.

Madison looked around. She really could see the entire mountain.

"What now?"

"Maybe try concentrating instead of making a joke?" said Kevin.

Madison sighed. "Since we came all the way up here."

She grabbed it again. This time she actually tried. She reached out with her mind, and a wave of energy suddenly jolted her body.

Madison lifted off her feet and floated to the top of the antenna.

Kevin watched with his mouth wide open.

Madison was weightless, but she hardly noticed because all of her vision had turned bright white. Everywhere she looked she saw white. Except for an area in the far corner of the mountain. That bloomed purple. She looked closer, and her vision zoomed into a street. It went up the street and stopped in front of a tall house with a red door. Madison let go of the pole and dropped straight down.

Kevin dove under her and managed to grab her before she fell past the beam.

Madison looked up at him. "I know where he is."

37

TALKING COYOTES

Madison was easing her way down the ladder when the howling started. She jumped the rest of the way to the deck. The howling got louder.

"Are those wolves?" asked Susan.

"No. Not to worry. Just coyotes," said Diego.

"It sounds like there's a lot of them."

Kevin was still on the roof. He pulled out his high-powered flashlight and shined it around the parking lot. At the edges, he saw dozens and dozens of eyes. They were getting closer. "There are a lot of them."

"Let's just get to the car," said Susan.

"They've cut us off from the car," said Kevin.

"What?" said Madison.

"Yeah, and they're bigger than normal coyotes. Something is wrong here," said Kevin.

"Shit." Diego racked his gun.

Kevin slid down the ladder. "I'm estimating around a hundred of them."

"What?" said Susan.

"Normally, a pack of coyotes can't really hurt a person. But this many? They could tear us to pieces," said Diego. "We gotta go."

"This way." Kevin pointed. "Let's put some distance between us and them."

They jumped from the deck and hurried down the hill into the woods. Kevin led the way, and Diego brought up the rear. The woods were covered in deep snow. It made going quickly a difficult task.

"Let's pick up the pace," said Kevin.

"Easier said than done," said Madison.

They sped up and were soon out of breath. From the top of the hill, they could hear the coyotes coming down.

"Stay close. We are stronger together," said Diego.

The branches were thick, and the snow was deep, but they kept going. They shined their flashlight all around, cutting through the deep blackness. They could hear the coyotes getting closer. For the first time in years, Madison grabbed her mother's hand.

Kevin was almost running. "Let's go faster."

They jumped over branches and slid down the hill. Diego fired a warning shot behind them, trying to keep them back.

"They've got a gun!"

"Hang back."

Kevin sped up. He yelled back to Diego, "Did you hear that?"

"Were they talking?" asked Diego.

"That's what I heard," said Susan. "How is that possible?"

"It's not," said Kevin. "You were hearing things."

"All of us?" said Susan.

"They're werecoyotes," said Madison.

"How do you know?" asked Kevin.

"Because I've seen them in my nightmares a hundred times."

"Dammit," said Kevin. "Keep going. We bought ourselves a little distance."

The hill was getting steeper.

"Watch your steps. You can't fall here," said Diego.

The branches got smaller, and ahead of them was shallow, white, untouched snow.

"Now we run," ordered Kevin. They took off sprinting; they were sliding and running over the slick surface. They were almost skiing on their shoes. Ahead was a black ribbon snaking below them. A road.

"Let's get to that road!" yelled Kevin.

The werecoyotes' footsteps were now coming from the sides. And they were getting closer.

Diego fired again. This time they did not back off. They had the numbers, and they knew it. A thicket of trees rose in front of them. Madison stumbled for a second, but she caught herself and kept going. She veered right to go around the trees. The rest of the group went left.

The pack saw they split up, and they all closed in on her. Madison ran faster. She could hear their heavy breathing now. They were getting closer. She dared a quick look back over her shoulder. She saw the pack was almost on top of her. And they were all running on two legs.

The hill got steeper. Now gravity worked against her, she ran faster than her legs could move, and she tripped. Madison tumbled end over end through the snow until she came to rest on a wall of bushes. She shook her head. No bones were broken. She looked up, and the pack was on top of her.

All she saw were fangs and claws everywhere, desperately trying to tear into her. She heard their snarls and felt their furious breath. They stank of pee and old meat.

This is the end. At least it will be quick, she thought.

And with a second left to live, she closed her eyes and tried a trick she had only done once before. It was something she had mistakenly discovered at the carnival last summer.

38

A GRENADE

The carnival came to their small town once a year, and Madison would not miss it, regardless of what her mom said. When she told her mom she was staying at Katie's house, she forgot to mention that they were going to the carnival.

It was a hot evening, but it was the mountain, so the air had a touch of coolness to it. Like an implied threat about the coming winter.

Madison and Katie had been friends for years. Katie had red hair and freckles. She was taller than Madison and far more athletic. Madison was wearing jeans, a white t-shirt, and a black leather jacket. She wasn't trying to stand out, but with her long blonde hair and brilliant green eyes, she was hard not to notice.

Billy Hooten noticed. The minute she arrived, he spotted her. He followed her all night.

Although Madison's psychic powers were increasing, she wasn't able to read minds constantly like listening to a radio in the other room. Her power was more like a focused beam. In order to read, she had to focus on that person. If she had focused on Billy, she would have grabbed the nearest sheriff hanging around the food stands.

Billy was following Madison when she went on the whip. He was standing in the crowd when she rode the mini roller coaster. He actually took a couple of pictures of her while she and her red-headed companion were riding the Ferris wheel.

Madison's face hurt from laughing so much. She didn't think the carnival would be this fun. She was really glad she had gone with Katie. In two years, they would be in college, so she knew now was the time to make memories with her childhood friend.

They walked towards the food. "I'm thinking funnel cake and corn dogs. What do you say?" said Katie.

"Making my mouth water." Madison checked her back pocket, and then the other. "I think I left my phone in the car. My mom has probably texted me like a hundred times by now. Give me the keys; I'll go get it."

"I'll go with you."

"No, don't worry about it, the car is right there." Madison pointed to it. It was just halfway up the block, within sight of everyone. "Order the food. By the time I get back, it will be time to stuff our faces."

"All right, but be back in five minutes or I'm getting one of those cops."

"You got it. Starting now!" Madison pretended to run.

She walked through the crowds and made it to the path through the trees. By the time she got to the sidewalk, there was hardly anyone around. She waved to a couple on the other side of the street. They waved back. When they were gone, she was all alone. From the carnival, the street looked fine. But now there were shadows everywhere and it was empty.

Up ahead, maybe forty feet, she saw the car. Madison walked fast. She took out her keys—she would grab her phone and turn around super quick. The street was creeping her out—

Then Billy stepped out from behind a tree. And he maced her.

Madison was coughing and gagging. She fell to her knees, blinded, unable to breathe. In one second, she had been completely incapacitated. But her mind was still working.

Billy could hardly believe his luck. His plan had totally worked. Now all he had to do was drag her into his van, and she was his. All for him, forever!

After years of fantasizing, it was finally happening. He reached out to grab her, but his hands were trembling with excitement. She was still conscious, so he looked around and picked up a big rock.

"This is going to hurt," he said with glee.

Madison had always walked carefully when she was inside someone's mind. She had respect for the space because she could feel how delicate the inside really was. It was like trespassing in a house made of thin glass. If she moved too hard or fast, she could do real damage to a person that could last for their entire life.

When she read Billy's intentions, she decided it was time to stop being delicate. That she was blind and couldn't breathe only made her angrier. In one second, she took Billy's fears and secret desires, pointed them at each other, and super-charged them with her fury.

The result was a psychic explosion. He dropped the rock, his head snapped back, and a massive aneurism stopped his brain and then his heart. Forever.

She called it a psychic grenade...

The werecoyotes were piled on top of Madison. They were going to devour her. And she became furious. She took a deep breath and attacked. She dropped a psychic grenade and because they were so close, all bunched together, Madison was able to generate a chain reaction.

In half of a blink, she set one grenade to feed another and another until it became a giant bomb.

One second the pack was on top of her, ready to eat, and then they were all lying dead in the snow, scattered by an invisible explosion. Their faces frozen in horrified expressions, lips pulled back, terror in their eyes. They were literally scared to death by their own fears.

Diego was the first to reach Madison. He was sure she was dead. He was amazed she was the only one alive in a pile of corpses. He pulled her out of the snow and checked her out. She was intact.

"Thank god," he said. "How did you do that?"

"I hit them with a psychic grenade."

"Wow, that's amazing."

"But it's made me reallllllly tirrrrrred." Her words slurred. She passed out in Diego's arms.

39

GIVING BLOOD

William had almost bled to death. But luckily for him, Faith was a nurse. So he took his Browning Hi-Power 9 millimeter, put it to her head, and forced her to take care of his wounds.

Unfortunately, his wounds were all on his back, which made holding her at gunpoint a lot harder. So he floated the pistol with his mind and held it in midair. If she messed with him, he would ventilate her. Very simple.

Faith kept her eyes open for any chance of escape, but she didn't hate William. She realized right from the start that William was mentally ill. Some would have just said crazy, but Faith thought more scientifically than that. He was schizophrenic or sociopathic. Either way, this was not a choice he made himself but something he was born with.

Most people would have said the best cure for a sociopath was a bullet in the head. But if all of god's creatures were special and served a purpose, and Faith believed that down to her core, then William had to have some value. At the very least, she could heal him without murdering him when he let his guard down. But he made it difficult because he was such a dick.

Luckily the house was huge, and it came with an extravagantly large bathroom, which Faith could turn into a semifunctional hospital room. Her patient had two big problems. First, he had lost a lot of blood. It had almost killed him. And he had a lot of wounds that looked close to infection. So, Faith used her healing powers on his wounds to keep them from getting worse.

She hovered her hands over his injuries and they glowed. To William it felt like a warm tickle. When she was done, she tried to convince him to go to a hospital.

William didn't like that suggestion. He told her if she brought it up again, he would shoot her in the foot. So she scrapped that idea. That left only one other option. She would have to give him some of her own blood.

If they had been different blood types, it wouldn't have worked. But of course, they were a match. Faith had no needles for a clean IV transfusion. Before she resorted to a straw and a basting needle, she would at least go through the house just in case someone had a real syringe.

"I'm going to check the house and see what kind of medical equipment I can put together."

"Yeah, right. You go off and climb out a window and run off while I die here? I don't think so."

"I need to find something to work with. Right now, I've got nothing," said Faith.

"Then I'm going with you. Come on."

William shakily stood up. He would have liked a cane, but they were stuck with what was in the house. The big ass dead Russian probably had no cane. He shuffled behind Faith as she went through the house. He was too weak to hold the Browning, so he floated it behind her head. If she tried to attack him, he would put a hole in her skull, and he made sure she knew it.

There was something about this girl that really pissed William off. She was too kind. Like it was some sort of stupid ass performance where she hoped to impress the audience. Why was she so eager to help him when he had knocked her out with a taser? She must be planning to stab him in the back the first chance she got. He was not about to fall for that crap.

So, he was as mean to her as possible. At some point, he would force her real personality to come out.

Most of the house was empty, including the fridge, which sucked because Faith was starving. But in the big Russian's bedroom, she hit the jackpot. Thankfully, his immense bulk wasn't a hundred percent natural. She found a gym bag with steroids and multiple fresh syringes. That would work.

Unless you are a routine IV drug user, it is very hard to inject yourself. Even if you are an experienced ER nurse. This posed a problem for Faith.

The bathroom was clean and ready. William was lying on a table that they had turned into a makeshift cot. Towels, alcohol, and the syringes were all laid out. "I'm going to need your help for part of this," she said.

"Like what?" William demanded.

"I can't draw my own blood."

"Goddammit. What are you, some sort of pussy?" he yelled.

"I've put needles in babies, I've saved people from all kinds of physical disasters, and I've even seen toes fall out of a boot. I am not a pussy. I just can't inject myself. I'll need you to do it."

William sighed.

"Do you want to die from blood loss?" she said.

"Fine. I'll do it. Show me where."

Faith pointed to a blue vein in her arm, and then she looked away.

William moved the needle through the air and plunged it into the vein on the first try. He filled the syringe with crimson liquid and then pulled it out. Faith picked it out of the air and stuck it into William's arm. Not gently.

William thought about slapping her with the pistol, but he wanted to see how far he could push her before she pushed back. So here was her angry side. As far as anger went, it wasn't much. She was, after all, giving him her own blood. He didn't even ask her for it; she just volunteered it. Damn goody-goody. Tonight, he would make her sleep in the vampire room.

40

USE BOTH HANDS

Madison let the hot water run over her. It might have been the best sensation she ever felt. She was amazed to discover how many muscles of hers were sore. The bottom of her feet hurt. That had never happened to her before. Any movement caused about fifteen distinct shocks of pain from various areas of her body.

She stayed that way until the hot water ran out and quickly became cold. She stood there with a towel around her shoulders, going over everything that happened. She nodded off for a second but woke up before she tripped over the tub.

Madison knew if she lay down, she would sleep for a couple of days. They did not have the time. One thing the werecoyote attack had done—it made her mad. She was determined to find Faith and destroy Grey Face. No matter what her mom said, she was going to see this through.

She put on black pants, a dark grey sweatshirt, and a pair of combat boots. She was dressing for fighting, not fashion. Madison found her mother standing in the living room, almost wearing the same thing.

"What are you doing, Mom?"

"I'm just going to avoid a big fight and skip to the part where we make up and agree. I know I'm not going to change your mind. But you will not be able to change mine. If you're going, I'm going. Period," said Susan.

"Fine."

Susan pulled out twin .45 caliber handguns. They were big, heavy, and shiny.

"What are those for?" asked Madison.

"In case anyone gets too close to you, I'll put big holes in them. I'm not a helpless woman; I carry two .45s."

Susan grew up in New York City, on the lower east side. It was during the 80s, so it had been a crime-filled nightmare. Through all the robberies, burglaries, and assaults Susan endured, she always vowed revenge. Someday she would be too strong to mess with. In the concrete asylum, as she liked to call it, no one was allowed to have a gun, so when she moved to California, she changed that immediately.

About five miles down the road from her little house was a secluded area that all the locals used as a gun range. Susan started with one .45. At first it was hard; the kick was heavy, and the boom was very loud. But eventually she got used to it. She even started to like it.

Susan bought old plates and cups at the thrift store. She exploded these from ten yards and then she walked back to about twenty-five. She went a couple of times a week for an hour at a time. After a few of months, she was good. She could explode multiple targets in a row with no problems. It became so easy that she got a second pistol so she could shoot two at the same time. It was a challenge, but she got even better.

If this were the Old West, she would have had a badass nickname. So, she gave herself one: the two gun chick.

41

THE VAMPIRE ROOM

Nails and glass made great shrapnel, so William put bowls of it behind the house's doors. If someone came through the door, William would launch the bowls with his mind, punching dozens of holes into the intruder. No one could survive that.

Come and knock on our dooooor. We've been waiting for youuuuuuuu. William sang to himself over and over with a smile. The house was secured, he had new blood pumping through him, and his wounds were being kept clean by Faith's powers. Only one last thing to take care of.

"Come here," said William, gruffly. He took Faith by the wrist. "Now kneel and get ready. There is someone who really wants to meet you."

He pulled her down next to him. The mechanical beetle knew he needed it. It buzzed in his pocket and flew out. It landed on the back of his neck. When William opened his eyes, he and Faith were kneeling in front of Lam at the gateway.

Every time William had interacted with Lam, he seemed detached and emotionless. Robotlike. Now, however, there was something else in his eyes: anticipation. There was even a hint of a smile. It made William feel nauseous.

"Where are we?" asked Faith.

"Don't speak. Just let that thing do the talking," said William.

William felt no empathy for anyone, ever. It wasn't in his mental vocabulary. But in here, in the weird gateway, he felt something like kinship. They were two humans, dealing with something completely alien. He couldn't help feeling that he and Faith were on the same team, and Lam was not.

"You are a very rare creature. Your genetic mutation is one in a billion. We need to study the bio electric energy you can generate. You will come with me now. There is no negotiating."

Lam took her by the hand. A white doorway opened up behind him and he pulled her through. William could do nothing to stop him. He was still frozen in place, stuck to the ground by invisible chains. Technically, there were not actual chains; they were put in William's mind by Lam. But the effect was the same. He was afraid he would be stuck like that for hours, while they did whatever they were doing to Faith. It was cold, and it was dark. He could see some basic framework of the bridge he was on, but most of it was hidden by shadow.

He was relieved when the door appeared and Faith stumbled out ten minutes later. She looked like she had lost twenty pounds. Her expression was the most disturbing— she was blank. Before William could say anything, they both disappeared.

They reappeared in the living room of the big dead Russian's house. They were both lying on the floor. Faith began dry heaving. She wasn't the experienced interdimensional traveler that William had become. He gave her a minute to recover and then he lifted her to her feet, roughly. She was barely conscious.

"What did they do to you in there?"

She didn't respond. William didn't like that. He shook her.

"What happened to you?"

She looked up at him. "They took my powers."

"What? But I need them to help me get better," he said.

"Well, I don't know what to tell you. They stuck me in the middle of some big machine. There was a bright light and then my power was just gone. I could feel it."

"Those motherfuckers. Did they tell you what they needed it for?"

"No. But it seemed really important to them," she said.

"They can't disrespect me like this. I brought you to them as a gift and this is what they do to me? Not acceptable."

"I'm sorry they upset you so much," Faith said sarcastically.

"Listen, if you let someone bully you, they will always bully you. Until you kill them. That's how life works. Everyone knows that."

"While I feel really bad for you that your alien interaction wasn't fulfilling, I am ridiculously hungry right now. You can try to stop me, but I'm going through the kitchen and finding something to eat. Shoot me if you object."

Faith rummaged through the kitchen and figured out that the Russian must have been buying food from the local restaurants because he certainly wasn't a cook. The cupboards were almost cartoonishly bare. The fridge was spotless except for a couple of bottles of coconut water and a chicken nugget ten piece. She opened one last cabinet and found a package of pasta and a jar of red sauce. That would have to do.

She discovered a pot and a wooden spoon. They must have come with the house; she could not see the Russian shopping for pots when he couldn't cook at all. The pasta and red sauce must have been left by a fairy or something.

In a couple of minutes, the pasta was ready. She heated up the red sauce in the microwave. And then the nuggets. It was the nuggets that got William's attention. Suddenly he was in the doorway, sniffing at the air. "What are you making?"

"It's spaghetti and chicken nuggets," she said.

"I must be really hungry because that actually sounds delicious."

She fixed their dinners on paper plates she found next to the fridge. Faith must have been hungry too, because she inhaled the concoction and loved it. She ate it so fast the last bite was still steaming.

William watched her carefully, not allowing himself to be charmed by her. When he was done, he leaned back in his chair. "I would murder someone for a beer right now."

"I believe you."

"Once the sun goes down here, everything closes. Like everyone's going to melt or something. Not that there's a lot up here."

"Tell me about it. I've had to cook just about every night for months," said Faith.

"Yeah, one pizza place, a bar, and a corner store."

"You forgot the terrible Mexican food," she said.

"I was trying to forget it."

Faith laughed. For one second, she forgot about the fact that he had kidnapped her.

"Why did you move up here? In the middle of nowhere?' she asked.

"I figured at the top of a mountain in a huge forest, I would have the space and privacy to open the door to contact Lam. The real question is, why did you move up here?"

"My boyfriend wanted to move to a place outside of L.A. that was quiet and away from society. He's a medical grower. The farther away from prying eyes and burglars the better," said Faith.

"And how'd that work out for you?"

"Well, there aren't many people, but there are a lot of monsters. So it's kind of a tradeoff. Though I think I prefer the monsters."

"Yeah, me too," said William.

They sat in silence. Faith's eyes started drooping. William watched. She had been through a lot and she was obviously exhausted. She donated blood and lost her powers, all in the same day. Never mind being kidnapped and tased. She could probably use a good night's sleep in a proper bed. There were a couple in the house. And that's when William caught himself almost feeling a sliver of empathy for Faith.

He slammed his hand on the table, waking her with a start. She had almost tricked him. He was furious.

"I told you that you would be sleeping in the vampire room tonight. I was serious."

He took her by the hand and pulled her up the stairs, roughly. The 9 millimeter floated behind her. He was done with trust. He pulled open a door. "You sleep on the floor." He shoved her inside.

She fell and looked up. All along the wall were standing,

sleeping vampires. The light from the hallway was disturbing them—they were waking up.

"When they wake up, they are always the hungriest. And the only thing they will see for breakfast is you. So stay quiet and don't move too much, or they will attack you. Night night." He closed the door and locked it.

42

ASSAULT TEAM

They took Diego's truck and drove up the mountain road. Madison closed her eyes. "Right up here." Madison senses could now direct her. "Left here, and then it's all the way down at the end of the block," said Madison. "The house has a red door."

Diego drove down to the end. There was the house with the red door. He drove around the cul de sac and drove away.

"Where are you going?" asked Susan.

"We shouldn't park right across the street. It's a little obvious." He pulled over and parked halfway down the block.

"Let's go," said Kevin. "We lead."

He carried a silver sword in one hand and the revolver in the other. Diego held the AK in a low ready position. Anyone looking out their window would have been surprised to see a four-person assault team walking down the street. Luckily for them, this was a block made up of large vacation homes. It was deserted. Except for the lights coming from the house with the red door.

They stood together, across the street. The night was black. The wind made itself heard.

"Quiet voices from now on," said Diego.

"How are we going to do this? We can't just walk in the front door," said Kevin.

"Look for a better entry," said Diego. "Stick to the shadows."

They walked around the house, looking for a way in. They found a back door.

"Madison, can you scan the house and tell us what's going on inside?" asked Diego.

"I've never really tried to read an inanimate object, but I can read whoever is inside, and I can get the layout of the house through them," she said.

Madison closed her eyes. The group circled around her because she was so vulnerable when she used her powers.

"Is Faith there? Is she okay?" asked Kevin.

"She's okay. She's upstairs. It's filled with vampires."

"Of course it is," said Susan.

"The downstairs. In front of the doors. Booby traps."

"Dammit. What are they?" asked Kevin.

"They look like shrapnel bombs."

"Okay, so doors are out," said Kevin.

Susan moved away from the group, looking closer at the house.

"Hey," she whispered. "I think I found something. Over here. It looks like a small bathroom window. And it looks like it's not closed all the way."

"Very nice. Good job, Susan," said Diego. He signaled them to follow him. He slid the window all the way open.

It was dark, but they did not turn on the lights. Kevin put his hand over a flashlight and shined it around the room. The light was weak, but they could all see—the room was covered in blood.

"Vampires upstairs, blood all over down here. This is not cool!" whispered Susan.

Diego eased open the door. The hallway was dark too. It seemed like the whole house was dark. They crept forward, carefully. Their flashlights showed a large living room with a high ceiling.

Suddenly Madison yelled, "Everyone get down now!"

Shrapnel exploded over their heads.

43

LIGHT SHOW

William heard the window in the bathroom sliding open, quietly. Someone was trying not to make noise. He immediately turned off the lights and hid behind a big chair.

He watched as flashlights stabbed their way into the room. There were four of them. Something was raising a red flag in William's mind. How did they know to avoid the doors? Maybe they just got lucky. There would be time later to find answers. Right now, four people had to die.

He waited until they got closer, and then he launched the shrapnel. Somehow a girl had shouted a warning just before impact. Did she hear him? He was being silent. Another red flag.

A flashlight beam found him in the corner, and then they opened fire. William was caught with no place to go. Although he had never done it before, he used his telekinetic power to deflect the AK-47's bullets to the side. He imagined a heavy wave of water in front of him, and the bullets deflected into the wall. William smiled; the gunfire was going to bring a wave of vampires down the stairs. Four intruders would make great vampire food.

He had a fleeting thought about Faith, but there was nothing he could do now. She would be collateral damage.

Faith was awakened by gunfire coming from downstairs. She had just enough time to wonder if the sound would disturb the vampires, and then they all woke up and attacked her.

She kicked and punched, trying to keep them off of her, but there were so many of them. She felt fangs plunge into her neck. It was like a fire inside of her skin. In the next second she would be ravaged like a drowning calf in a piranha feeding frenzy. It would be quick.

And then they stopped. They looked around and cocked their heads. They ran for the door. They all sensed the same thing: William was in trouble and he needed them.

They left Faith lying in the middle of the floor in a growing puddle of blood.

Madison instinctively stayed out of the way when the bullets started to fly. She ducked behind a large table, and then she made her way closer to William. While everyone was distracted with the gunfire, she crept closer.

When she was five feet away from him, she hit him with a psy grenade. Or at least she tried to. It didn't work. William's mind was unlike anything she had slipped into. His fears were minuscule. There was nothing for her to grab on to and take advantage of.

He turned to her and aimed his floating gun in her direction. Madison did the only thing she could think of—she confused him. Or technically, she dazzled him. Inside his head, she created a blazing light show. The effect was instant.

William stumbled around, unable to see or think. He was very confused.

"What happened? What did you do to him?" asked Diego.

"I scrambled him," said Madison. "There's a light show going on in his head. I guess it makes it hard to concentrate."

William tripped and fell down.

"Or walk," said Kevin.

"Finish him," said Diego.

Kevin raised his gun.

A wave of vampires flew down the stairs.

44

VAMPIRE WAVES

The vampires launched themselves into the dark room. Their red eyes collected light and amplified it. Seeing in the dark was easy for them.

Kevin and Diego instinctively shoved the girls behind them. They were attacked first. Two vampires landed on Diego and pinned him to the floor. They struck his neck at the same time. Their fangs clanged against a custom-made titanium collar. He blasted them with silver tipped AK fire. They exploded into black smoke.

A flying vampire circled Kevin. He fired but missed. It lashed out with claws, but they sparked harmlessly off of his titanium collar. He made quick work of it with the sword and revolver.

Then the room was overrun with vampires. They were everywhere. Madison took her attention away from the light show in William's head to set off psychic grenades in the vampires. This time it worked.

Vampires exploded in black smoke. When they were done, Madison searched all over the room. William was gone. He had taken advantage of a moment of mental clarity and escaped. Madison went to the window, but she didn't see him. The dark street was empty.

"He's gone. He escaped," said Madison.

"Are you sure?" said Kevin.

"Yeah, I can't find his mind anywhere. I couldn't keep him confused and kill the vampires at the same time."

"You did amazing, honey," said Susan.

"Let's just find Faith," said Kevin.

"We can worry about him tomorrow," said Diego. "Let's go upstairs."

"Just what I didn't want to hear," said Susan. She heard a noise and turned.

One last wave of vampires came down the stairs. Susan was closest, so they attacked her. She struggled free and pulled out the twin .45's. She didn't have silver bullets, but she blasted away regardless. Diego and Kevin joined in and finished them off.

One last vampire came down the steps and Susan immediately blasted her twice in the chest, not taking any chances.

Kevin yelled out.

It was Faith.

45

___

SILVER SLIVER

William ran hard. He barely noticed the branches ripping at his clothing and skin. He didn't have time to notice it. He had one thought going through his mind: *Get off the mountain.* Unfortunately, he had nothing on him. Nothing. Not a gun, not a phone, no money, no weapon. Not even car keys. He would have to improvise.

He slowed down after a couple of minutes. He was still weak from all the blood loss. It didn't sound like they were coming after him. But he couldn't take any chances, so he kept up a quick walking pace. It was dark and cold out. William had no jacket, but his adrenaline was pumping, so he didn't notice.

What he needed was someone to rob and murder. No witnesses, no calling the police. The moon was only a silver sliver, so it threw very little light.

He stumbled through the woods until he came to a clearing. It was a log cabin. A shiny Land Cruiser was parked in the driveway. William stood still in the shadow of a tree for a few minutes. He listened carefully and got a lay of the land. Someone was in the house, but there were no neighbors. William picked up a big branch.

He crept up to the Land Cruiser and rammed his shoulder into the side. Then the alarm went off. William ran back behind the tree. A tall man came out of the house. He had car keys in one hand and a shiny pistol in the other. William wanted that weapon badly. He snuck behind and smashed him in the back of the head with the branch. The gun went flying. *Perfect*.

William went for the gun when he felt a sting on the back of his neck. "No! Not now, dammit. The gun and the car were mine." He fell to his knees and disappeared into the alien bridge.

46

WINTER COLD

"**G**et her on the couch," Kevin yelled. "And let's get some lights on."

"We're going to need some towels. Actually, a lot of towels. Chest wounds bleed a lot," said Diego. "I've studied field medicine."

They maneuvered Faith's body onto the couch.

"I didn't know it was her. I swear," said Susan. "It was dark; all I saw were vampires."

"It was an accident. Let's clean up the blood," said Diego.

They looked. There was no blood.

"Shouldn't she be bleeding?" asked Madison.

Kevin looked Faith over. He looked at her pale skin. He put his hand on her forehead. She was winter cold.

"Susan, I'm guessing the bullets in that .45 are regular. Not silver," said Kevin.

"Yeah, how d'you know?"

"Because if they were silver, Faith here would have exploded into black smoke."

"You're saying—" said Madison.

"No, no way, she can't be a vampire," said Susan.

"She is," said Kevin.

Faith sat up, and her eyes opened. They were red.

"I am," she said. And then she passed out.

Diego shoved the women behind him. He brought the AK-47 up and aimed it directly at Faith's face.

Kevin pushed the gun aside. "Not cool. Don't point that at her."

"But she's the undead. She could kill us all the minute she gets hungry," said Diego.

"She won't."

"How do you know?" asked Diego.

"I just do."

"Um, I'm going to have to agree with Diego. Have you ever dated a vampire before? What if her idea of a good night is turning you into a bloodsucker?" said Susan.

"I'll be honest, I'm just glad she isn't dead," said Kevin.

"But she is dead, actually," said Diego.

"You know what I mean. She's not all the way dead."

"Isn't dead all or nothing?" asked Madison.

"This is not the place to argue. Back to the house," said Kevin.

"Yeah, this place gives me the creeps. It smells like sulfur," said Susan.

They carried Faith outside and put her in the truck bed. Kevin got in with her. He laid her down and cradled her head in his lap. Everyone else piled into the front.

When they got to the house, they debated about where to keep Faith. Kevin voted for the living room. Everyone else voted to put her in the bedroom. And put a padlock on the door.

Diego clicked the big master lock closed.

"This is so not cool," said Kevin. "I should be in there with her."

"So you can get turned into a vampire? Not really great for us," said Susan.

"I don't think she would do that," said Kevin.

"But you don't know for sure, right?" said Susan.

"I guess not," said Kevin.

"Let's wait to see what happens. We can reload our weapons, eat some food, rest, and we'll see how she is in a couple of hours," said Diego.

Kevin looked out the window into the mountain blackness. "I was supposed to protect her. To keep her safe. Wow, did I fail. Not only did she die, now she's the undead. And it's all my fault."

"It's not your fault, man," said Diego.

"William took her to get to me. And it worked."

"Don't give up. Maybe she'll be okay," said Susan.

"I was going to ask her to marry me."

"Aww," said Susan.

"Yeah, imagine that now. Me and my vampire bride. I guess we would honeymoon in Transylvania."

"Or Hollywood," said Madison.

"Seriously, this has been one colossal failure. I lost my girl. Madison almost got hurt. I dragged all of you into danger. You know, I moved up here to find some peace and quiet. Someplace I could grow a couple of plants and write a couple of screenplays. Nice and simple. And look what I found instead. Hell Mountain."

"Don't give up on Faith. She's strong. She might survive this," said Madison.

"How do you know? You only met her tonight," said Kevin.

"I read her. She's tough."

"And what if she's not? What if she's a flying, rabid, murderous vampire? How can I destroy her?" said Kevin.

"Don't worry about it, dude. I'll do it for you. A stake through the heart. Quick and painless. She won't even know what hit her," said Diego.

"Thanks, but it's my responsibility. It's my fault. I'll have to do it. And then I'm getting the hell out of here. Too many memories of her here. Maybe I'll move to Alaska. Me and Inky in the tundra. I can't get into trouble in the middle of a snowy wasteland."

"I think you could," said Susan. "But we need food, right now. Calories will help us all feel better. My psychic powers tell me." Susan laughed. No one else laughed at her mom joke.

Kevin didn't eat, but everyone else had French bread pizza and crinkle fries. It wasn't great. Then they streamed a couple of classic episodes of *Fringe*, and everyone fell asleep. No one slept well, like they were waiting for something big to happen. And then it did.

Diego was the first to wake up, he thought they were under artillery attack. Kevin got up and then the girls. They were all awakened by a booming sound. It took them a second, but they realized at the same time—the sound was coming from the bedroom. It was the door being pounded. Faith wanted out.

Wham! The door flew off its hinges and smashed into the wall. Faith stepped into the hallway. When they brought her back to the house, she looked frail and sickly. All that had changed. Now she was strong and gorgeous. Her skin radiated glowing energy. She was paler than she had ever been, but it made her even prettier. Now she was dangerous and exotic. Her legs had grown thicker, and she was rounder now, more powerful. Her eyes were bigger, black pupils swimming in crimson. Her fangs poked out of her full, pink lips.

"I'm starving," said Faith. Her voice was deeper and raspier. She now had a touch of Lauren Bacall or Kathleen Turner. A syrupy sweetness backed by danger and sex. "All this regenerating and recuperating has taken a lot out of me. I need food." She stalked down the hallway like a leopard.

Kevin fought every instinct in his body not to aim his gun at her. He stood still as she walked by. She pinched his cheek.

"Don't look so serious. I would never hurt you, my love. I wouldn't hurt any of you. But I need food and there's a big forest out there."

Her fangs grew to the size of a saber-toothed tiger's. Her skin hardened and gleamed like marble.

She walked out, stepped off the porch, and flew into the dark sky.

47

BUCK TEETH

The sky was charcoal and freezing. But temperature no longer bothered Faith. She hardly felt it.

That's a cool new power, she thought.

The moon was low in the sky; the forest was a maze of shadows. It didn't matter to Faith. She could see as if it were daylight. She wondered if she could spot William from the sky. She knew the smell of his blood; it was imprinted in her mind. Somehow, she knew she could track him.

She saw it floating in front of her like a transparent rope, leading her down a long path. She followed it down a road, through a neighborhood. It went down through the trees, next to a cabin.

Faith landed and crouched down. He could be somewhere nearby, and he was still very dangerous. She listened carefully for two minutes and heard nothing. She reached out with all of her expanded senses. He was not there. But there was a body somewhere—she could smell the blood.

She circled the cabin and found a man face down in a pool of blood. The smell invaded her nose. It made her stomach rumble. She drooled. He was still alive. Barely.

She bent down to get closer to the puddle of deep crimson. She could see it was still liquid; it hadn't dried yet. *Maybe just get a small taste.* She could lick it up like a cat. Besides, he was already injured, so it wasn't like she was hurting him. The blood was already there.

She looked around and got down on the ground. She stopped herself. She would not be a human killer. Sucking his blood while he was still alive would most definitely kill him. No, she would not do it. Now, if she found William, it would be a different story.

His trail disappeared into thin air. Only one explanation she could think of. He had disappeared into another dimension. He was literally nowhere on Earth, and he had left behind another victim. Faith took her phone out and dialed emergency services. This man needed an ambulance. There was not much she could do for him. Her healing powers were gone, and she was so hungry she was ready to faint. *Time to find some food.*

Perhaps a walk in the woods, she thought.

She launched herself into the air, looking for a treeless patch, a meadow. Some place she could see the bunnies coming. Her super vision found a spot, and she landed. It wasn't long before she heard noises in the black woods. It sounded like hopping, only these were heavy footsteps. Like something a giant rabbit might make.

She saw their eyes in the tree line. "I'm right here."

She sat down in the middle of the field. They hopped closer, covering ground quickly with their long jumps. There were a dozen of them, and they were huge. Giant muscles bulged out of scaly pink skin. Tufts of white hair gave them a scraggly, ugly look. Their faces were set in a horrible sneer that showed off a mouthful of fangs fronted by two huge buck teeth. They were not pretty.

Faith waited, still seated. "Come a little closer. I'll make a good snack."

She waited. One more jump and they were on top of her. She could feel their scraggly fur—it felt like hay. And they smelled like a moldy old towel. She slipped between their legs, flew up into the air, and pounced on them. The mutant bunny men were very surprised at the turn of events. Now they were fending off an attack.

Faith would need strength to take out the whole pack. She devoured the first mutant bunny she got her claws on. The way she fed was not elegant or sexy like they portrayed in the movies. She ate him like a woodchipper. Her mouth was a school of piranha, thrashing with blood spray.

Before they counter attacked, half of his torso had disappeared. And now she was ready. She felt new strength pulsing through her body like a wave of electricity. Maybe she would play with her food. She grabbed a bunny man and flew up. She threw him as hard as her new muscles could. He soared for half a mile before crashing into a tree.

So, she could throw very far. *Good to know*, she thought. A bunny man jumped at her from behind. She heard him, turned, and kicked him while he was still in midair. He skidded across the grass for the entire length of the meadow. The bunny man stood up and shook his head. He looked up just as Faith landed on him. He was being eaten before he realized what was happening.

The mutants charged, and Faith ran at them.

48

HEART OF THE MOUNTAIN

When Faith walked back into the house, she had changed color from porcelain white to crimson red. Every inch of her was covered in blood, even the backs of her ears. Everyone had a weapon pointed at her, except for Kevin.

"Calm down, people, I'm full. The forest had plenty of food to offer."

"Are you hurt?" asked Kevin.

"No, none of this is mine. I get the feeling it would take a tank to hurt the new me."

"Or just a single silver bullet," said Diego, lowering his gun.

"He's got a point," said Susan. "Oh, hello, I'm Susan, by the way. I'm Madison's mom." She held her hand out and then took it back when she saw how much blood was on Faith.

"Hi, I'm Madison," the younger woman said. Except, Faith noticed, she didn't move her mouth when she spoke to her. "That's right, I'm psychic. I'm talking to you in your head. Let me fill you in on what has happened since you were kidnapped."

A bright flash filled Faith's mind, and then she simply knew everything that had happened. How the boys met Madison, how they escaped the werecoyotes, the fight at the big house, all of it, like she had been there.

"There is a lot I have to tell you about," said Faith, "but I'm still dripping over here. So I'm going to hop in the shower and then we will talk."

Faith stood under the hot water and took in the smell of her rose scented soap. She was happy to get the stench of the bunny men out of her nose. Her muscles were not sore. She thought for sure they would be, but they were fine. She flexed her forearms; it felt like she could crush bones with her bare hands. It was a good feeling.

She turned the water off and wrapped herself in an over-sized purple towel. She stuck her head out the bedroom door. "Kevin, could you help me with something for a second?"

"Sure, what's wrong?" He walked down the hall.

She pulled him into the room. She let her towel drop, showing off her taut, glowing body, and then she attacked him. She ripped his pants off and then she was on top of him before he realized what was happening. She flipped him on top and then levitated the two of them. Kevin reciprocated the passion and didn't even realize they had been floating until it was over, and they were wrapped in each other's arms, still in midair.

"Do you think they heard us?" asked Faith.

"No, we were quiet."

In the living room, Diego looked at Susan, who looked at Madison.

"Were they just—"

"Diego! Not in front of my daughter," said Susan.

"Mom, seriously! I'm almost eighteen; you think I've never heard people having sex before?"

"When did you—"

"Ugh, never mind! You're so embarrassing!" Madison stormed out of the house. Inky followed, guarding her.

An hour later, they were all sipping hot cocoa in front of a fire. Inky was curled up in its warmth.

"They took my healing ability," said Faith. "I'm not telling you this for sympathy. I'm telling you this because they used that power to go through a door."

"A door to what?" asked Diego.

"A door to here. It's an invasion. They are coming to feed."

"Feed?" said Susan.

"On us."

"On us?" said Kevin.

"Not the way I feed. Not flesh. They feed psychically. They are soul parasites. They feed off of our greatest fears and passions. If you live, they leave you an emotionless zombie."

"How do you know all this?" said Diego.

"William told me. And then I saw the machines they use when they removed my power. They have big plans for this mountain. And they are not good."

"How many are there?" asked Diego.

"They have brought one ship across. But with the energy they are going to harvest here, they will bring more," said Faith.

They sat in silence, absorbing the new information.

Kevin stood up. "Then we'll just have to stop them."

Diego stood up. "I was going to say the same thing, dammit."

"Why us?" asked Madison.

Diego puffed his chest out. "Because we crush monsters. It's what we do. How many vampires have we destroyed already? No offense, Faith. How many werecoyotes did Madison take out single-handedly?"

"Susan is deadly with those .45's. Diego has been killing monsters for years. I'm from Detroit, so nothing scares me. And Vampira here could take out an army. Who else can do it but us?" said Kevin.

"Yeah, I don't know how crazy I am about that nickname. I feel like it's kind of racist, or at least speciesist. I suspect it's offensive somehow. But I agree. I want to fight," said Faith.

"Then we need to know where they are," said Kevin.

"I think I might have a piece of the puzzle. Before I blasted William with a light show, I found a phrase that stood out above everything else. It was 'the heart of the mountain.' Does that mean anything to anyone here?" said Madison.

"No," said Diego.

"Not to me," said Susan.

Kevin rubbed his head. "Hold on, I've seen that somewhere." He went to a bookcase and came back holding a dusty book.

"I got this at the thrift store on the edge of town. It's called 'The History of Frazier Mountain.'" Kevin opened it and shook it. An old map fell out. He unfolded it and laid it out on the coffee table.

Scrawled at the top it said, "The Heart of the Mountain."

49

A LITTLE FAITH

The map was of an old mine that went deep into the middle of the mountain. The main shaft went a mile down into the rock.

"If this name was in William's mind, then this is where they are," said Kevin.

"It makes sense," said Diego. "It's a perfect place to hide and run an operation. There is no chance of them being accidentally discovered, and their position is easily defended with only one entrance. It's a deadly choke point. If they have suitable weapons, it will be next to impossible to get inside."

"But we have to stop them. Or this mountain will be overrun and lots of people will die. I love this place. I don't want it destroyed. This is where I raised Madison," said Susan.

"Mom," Madison whined.

"I'm allowed to say that I enjoyed raising you. Get over it," said Susan.

Kevin pointed on the map with a pencil. "We have to make our way up the steep slope to the entrance here. From there we go through a dark and narrow corridor to the heavy elevator. These notes say it's a long trip down to the bottom."

"Once we're down there, we will have no idea what or how many of what we will be facing," said Diego.

Faith bared her fangs. "That's why you have me."

"And me," said Madison. "You haven't seen my psychic grenades yet," she projected her voice into Faith's head.

"Ooh, something to look forward to," Faith replied.

"You know we might not all be coming back. This is practically a suicide mission," said Diego.

Kevin smiled. "You just need a little Faith."

Everyone booed his pun.

Faith looked out the window. The sky was getting lighter. Morning was here.

"And that's my cue to get to bed. Black-out curtains are a vampire's best friend. You coming?" Faith held out her hand to Kevin.

"All right, everyone sleep, get rested and prepared. We attack tonight," said Kevin.

"How about a day to go to the beach and get mentally ready," said Susan.

"If they're already here," said Diego, "they won't be taking time off to sightsee. We need to strike first."

Kevin and Faith retired to their bedroom. Madison and Susan curled up on the couch. Diego went to sleep on the floor, holding the AK-47.

50

TROPICAL ISLAND VAMPIRE

T he elevator bumped along slowly. It was really a moving platform. All the lights had long since burned out. William had a flashlight that he floated above his head, giving him as much light as he needed.

Light or dark, William wasn't worried about his safety. He was surrounded by stinking, hulking, reptilian body-guards. They stood at least a foot taller than him and were twice as wide. Nothing could get to William. Lam had explained that his kind were not meant for things like phys-ical labor or security. They contracted the reptilians to handle that.

When Lam pulled William into the bridge dimension, he was sure it was his time to be eliminated. It surprised him when Lam put him in charge of security. He knew William was acquainted with their enemy, so they thought he should be the one in charge of killing them all.

William was not happy at the idea of killing Faith, but he would get over it. He was really looking forward to murdering the girl that had scrambled his brain. He was going to strangle her with his bare hands until her eyes popped out. Then would he feel like things had been put right.

Although Lam was a sonofabitch, he was great at supplying weapons. Apparently, they had been stockpiling human weapons for decades. If William wanted a Soviet land mine from the 1980s, Lam would make a dozen crates appear. If he wanted his reptile troops to have modern FN SCAR rifles, Lam would manifest them with or without laser sights. William's choice. The only time Lam showed the slightest trace of happiness was when he was giving human weapons to humans. This did not escape William.

The elevator stopped at the top level, the ground floor. William led his squad through a long dark tunnel, which widened at the opening of the mine. Here he had a great view of the slope leading up the hill. It would be next to impossible for a team to make a frontal assault. Even if they made it through the minefield, they would get picked off by rifles before they got anywhere near the elevator.

William had asked Lam, "Why now? Why this moment in time in 2020 did you decide it was time for invasion? What changed? You could have done this any time in the last fifty years."

"It is because of your military."

"What do they have to do with anything?"

"Last year they publicly admitted that they don't know who is flying the advanced vehicles in the sky. How long before the public asks what should they do about it? They will demand weapons that can stop our observation drones. Eventually this will lead to war. We are going to preempt such actions. We will win the war before it is ever declared.

The time envelope for this event will close soon. Now we strike. We really have no choice if you model the probabilities. And we have."

This all made logical sense to William; he even liked the idea of the mountain descending into chaos. But there was another feeling. There was a sense of overwhelming dread. It was one thing to terrorize a town; it was another to enslave all of humanity. That didn't sit well in William's mind. He didn't like losing to anyone, and this would be one very big loss. He shoved the thought to the back of his mind, where he usually put things that concerned him.

The mines were ready. He had a hundred soldiers at his disposal, and all the weapons he wanted. Everything was in place. There would be an attack, and it would come at night. Faith was now a vampire; she could not maneuver during the daylight.

Faith. He was furious with her. She had gotten herself turned; she had endangered his plans, and she had gone back to her friends. He would have to kill her. For sure. She caused too many thoughts in his head. If he could just talk to her one last time. Tell her how much she disappointed him. And then he could kill her, or at least take her with him when he escaped. He did not plan on staying on the mountain after tonight; he was going to disappear. Probably to somewhere tropical, far off anyone's radar. Literally. And he would take Faith with him. She could stay inside during the day.

No, he would have to kill her. She was causing him to have stupid thoughts, like taking a vampire to a tropical island. Idiocy.

The sun was going down. He turned and went back inside. There were other things to take care of. No way anyone could make it past the perimeter and get inside the mountain. No way. But if they did... William was not stupid enough to neglect interior security. There would be troopers, motion activated machine guns, and even nerve gas. Nothing could survive that.

51

ONE VEST

Faith was last to wake up. She stretched and yawned and looked out the window. "I guess I won't be seeing any more sunsets or sunrises."

"That's true. But you can fly, so it's a pretty fair tradeoff," said Kevin.

"You have a good point."

Diego was dressed and checking over his weapons.

"Anyone here hungry?" asked Susan.

"No," they all answered simultaneously.

She raised her hands in surrender. "All right, I was just checking. I'm not hungry either."

Madison pulled her sweatshirt on. "Let's get this started." She headed for the door.

Diego stopped her. "Hold on, I got something for you." From his bag he removed a bulletproof vest.

"So, I'm the baby that needs protecting? What about everyone else?"

Diego blushed. "I only had one. I figured everyone would agree with me. Kevin and I are too cool for a vest,

Faith is the undead, and I'm pretty sure your mom would rather you have it than her. Anyone else disagree?"

"Why did you single me out?"

Diego looked away.

Susan stepped in, "Oh, just put it on and quit being difficult."

Diego held up his duffel bag. "There is something in here that is very explosive."

"What is it?" asked Susan.

"Explosives," he said, "so try not kick this bag, or shoot it or set it on fire."

They piled into the pickup, nervously.

"Maybe you should put the bag in the back of the truck instead of up front with us," said Kevin.

"I like that idea," said Susan.

Diego sighed. "Bunch of cowards."

Faith floated up. "I'm going to make sure there are no attacks from the air."

They drove up the mountain and turned onto a dirt road. There were tire tracks, but tall weeds were growing up the middle. No one had used the road for a long time. Faith followed them overhead. The moon wasn't full, but there was enough light that she could see far ahead. The road and sky were clear.

52

VAMPIRE MAGAZINE

Willam had a special magazine filled with twenty silver tipped .308 caliber bullets for his SCAR rifle. It would put an end to Faith for good. Then he could stop thinking about her.

He played with it in his hands, and then he slapped it into his weapon. He clicked the magazine release latch, and the mag came out. He put it on top of his desk in the surveillance command room. He put a regular magazine in the rifle. He thought about another security check he needed to do and left the office.

Later, after the attack, William would wonder about what had distracted him and made him forget where he put the special vampire-killing magazine. It would bother him that it was nothing he could remember. He had simply pulled out the magazine and left it.

He walked down the long hallway that led away from the ship. At both ends were motion activated machine guns. When the fun started, he would activate the sensors, and then anything that walked into the hallway would be ventilated.

"Sucks for them." He smirked.

Above him ran a mile of tubing attached to tanks of poison gas. Anything that survived the bullets would be painfully killed by the outlawed nerve gas Lam just happened to have lying around. The gas would eradicate anything in the tunnels fifteen minutes after the entrance was breached. He had to give them time to get down the elevators and into the tunnels before the gas was released. Then there would be no escape, and everyone would die.

This would only be necessary if they actually made it to the mine. William had some air defenses in place to stop them early. *What's the point of having access to vampires if you don't use them?* he thought.

53

DOG FIGHT

Faith kept pace with the truck for a few minutes, but then she started experimenting with her flying abilities. She learned that if she pulled her elbows back and raised her head up, she immediately slowed down, like she had air brakes. But if she straightened her body and tensed her shoulders and chest, she took off like a missile. She pointed her toes and fingers till they ached. She went even faster.

Faith pulled up and slowed down until she was hovering in place. The air was colder up there, and the wind was stronger. She could smell the sweet scent of the pine forest below. She looked around for the truck. She spotted it miles back, winding up the dirt road. She turned; in front there were a dozen small dark clouds. Maybe it was going to rain. But, Faith wondered, when were clouds so small?

The clouds started moving; they gravitated towards each other. They formed a line in front of Faith. These were not clouds, she realized.

"Vampires," her mind shouted. Her skin hardened, and

her fangs extended. She was ready. She aimed low and sped towards the ground. They immediately followed her.

Faith looked behind her. Good, they were coming after her. She would lead them away from the truck. Better that she handle them herself. She tucked her head, pointed her fingers and toes, and tensed her shoulders and arms. *Boom*, she took off. She angled her trajectory up. From there she got a good view of the forest. Faith spotted a thick area of trees. *Perfect*. She aimed at the green branches and disappeared in the cover.

The vampires struggled to keep up with her; she was faster than them, but they were determined. They followed her into the trees. Faith was hanging down from a branch as the vampires flew past her. She reached out with her death hardened talons and decapitated four of them before they realized what she had done.

She took off back into the sky. She tossed a head behind her for intimidation.

It was one thing for a human to kill a vampire. They had to stick to a couple of tools. Sunlight, silver, a wooden stake or a crucifix (garlic turned out to be total bullshit), but none of these tools were necessary for a vampire. They could just kill each other with no dramatics.

She flew in a loop and came down behind them. Faith attacked. She grabbed the closest vampire and kicked him in the chest. He flew backwards, smashing into another. They both careened out of control. And then she was on them, slashing and biting as they tried to pull out of their dive. They were extra dead before they hit the ground.

Faith flew up, ready for more. She turned to look, and they swarmed her, all of them. They were not waiting for her to attack again. They tumbled through the air, fighting, a pack of airborne wild animals.

She tried to shake them off of her, as the ground rushed up.

54

AN EASY DRIVE

Diego steered the truck over the dirt road. He kept an eye out for big holes and rocks. Kevin had his head out the window. He had seen Faith take off, but he hadn't seen her since. He kept watching the sky, which was too dark to see anything, but he kept trying. Madison and Susan were sandwiched between them.

"How much farther?" asked Susan.

Madison looked at her phone. "We have four more miles."

"All right, we'll be there in a few minutes. No problems so far. Maybe this will be easier than we thought," said Diego.

Wham! Faith and her vampire attackers crashed into the hood of the truck in a ball of fangs and claws. Diego swerved but kept on the dirt road.

Faith punched and kicked her attackers as they tried to take her all at once. She held them off. She was stronger and faster than they were, but they had numbers. One vampire turned and saw Madison through the windshield. He smashed his hand into the glass and grabbed her by the throat.

"Hell no." Susan pulled her twin .45s out and took aim.

"No, wait." Kevin grabbed her hand. "If you miss or the bullets go through, you could hit Faith and that will kill her for good."

Susan hesitated.

Madison closed her eyes and entered the monster's mind. It was all blood and screams. She focused the rage back on to itself. The vampire shot up and forward like a rag doll. He landed right in front of the truck. Diego happily ran it over with a loud pop.

Faith jumped over the cab and into the back of the pickup. There was more room to maneuver. The vampires stupidly followed. She slashed a neck and then pulled out a heart. It burst into a fist of black smoke. Only two vampires were left.

Faith crouched, ready to spring. Both vampires flew up and crumpled in mid-air. They hit the ground dead. Faith looked at Madison, who gave her a thumbs up. Faith returned the gesture.

The truck slowed down.

"Come on, man, give it some gas," said Kevin.

"It's not me. Something's wrong with the truck."

It jerked and stuttered a couple of times and then died.

"Of course. You had to say this would be easy," said Kevin.

"I said maybe it would be easy."

"Big difference." Kevin sighed. He picked up a backpack full of ammunition.

"We walk from here."

55

BLACK SMOKE

Stan was ready to go home. It had been a long day and a longer night. Hardly anyone came in for the last two hours. He sold a couple of lottery tickets, a 12-pack of beer, and a few gallons of gas. It wasn't really worth staying open for such small sales, but the locals depended on him, so he kept the gas station open until midnight.

That's why everyone in town liked Stan. Everywhere he went, people waved and smiled. He was everyone's "buddy." Actually, most people in town pissed him off, but he never showed it. They were cheap, they stole, they tried to trick him on change, but he just kept up his friendly demeanor and tried to ignore it.

Stan came over from Syria, and he was more than happy with the peace and quiet the mountain offered. It was a lot nicer than the civil war he had escaped from. He ran the gas station, went for walks in the woods, and enjoyed the Mexican restaurant near the freeway. All he wanted was a girlfriend, and now he had one. A pretty Persian girl named Samara. He was happy. In fact, he was rushing through closing down the store so he could get home sooner. She was waiting for him.

He finished zeroing out the register and grabbed a bottle of champagne on the way out. Why not start the evening off right? He stepped out into the night. The air was frosty, so he slipped on his flannel jacket. He looked over at his black Charger. It was the only car in the parking lot. It was waiting to take him home with its rumbly engine and plush interior. He locked the door and turned to walk to his car, but it was gone.

Stan spun around, looking for his car. This only happened once before. He knew what was coming next; it was from his recurring nightmare. He took off running down the street.

When Stan was a kid in his old neighborhood, bravery was a really big deal amongst all his friends. When they heard about a haunted, abandoned mansion on the outskirts of town, they all dared each other to go. Stan wanted to show how big and strong he had grown over the summer, so he volunteered. But there were two stipulations: he had to be alone, and it had to be at night.

Stan went that night with a bicycle, a flashlight, and a pounding heart. He parked the bike outside the big white house. He walked to the double front doors. Stan turned around and saw that his bike had disappeared. He was pretty sure one of his friends must have followed him and taken his bike to scare him. Stan would not give up that easily.

He boldly strode into the house, refusing to show fear. Right away he could tell something was wrong. The house was freezing. It was a scorching night in the desert, but somehow, with no power, the house was as cold as a tomb.

It was dead black, and with no power for the lights,

Stan's flashlight was the only source of illumination. Even the moon was dark. But he would not quit. Besides, his friends were probably outside watching him, so he was not about to act like a coward now.

The downstairs was big and empty. The ceilings were low, but the living room was big. The furniture was still intact. Paintings hung with no vandalism, and the large couches in the middle of the room were intact. Either Stan was the first to enter the house or people had been too superstitious to disturb anything.

He went up the marble stairs to the second floor. Somehow it was even darker up there. Stan made his way down a long hallway to the master bedroom. His plan was to grab a souvenir that he could show off to his friends, and then he would leave quickly, but not running. Forget staying all night.

He ran his flashlight along the walls. There were a couple of small statues, but they weren't impressive. He kept looking. Then in the middle of the room, on top of a circular table, he saw it—a big multi-colored glass bottle. It looked heavy, important, and expensive. This would be his trophy.

Stan looked around before taking it, like someone was going to catch him. He laughed at his silliness; there was no one around for miles. He went to grab it, and the bottle moved just slightly, enough to make Stan knock the cork stopper off. Stan's heart skipped a beat. This could only mean one thing.

Thick black smoke oozed out of the bottle and formed a gigantic creature that towered over Stan. Yellow, demonic eyes flashed open and looked down at him. It was a Djinni.

"Thank you for letting me out. For your reward, I will eat your soul."

Stan yelled a prayer to Allah and ran. He didn't wait to

see what would happen next. He barely touched the ground as he raced through the hallway and then threw himself down the stairs. The surrounding walls crumbled and burst into flames as he ran by.

He sprinted for his bike but remembered it was gone. He knew it had not been his friends that had made it disappear. He just kept running into the desert. He didn't care about the direction, as long as it was away from the house.

That's why when Stan saw his car in the parking lot had disappeared, he knew somehow that the Djinni had returned. And his only instinct was to run. He sprinted past the drugstore, the police station, he turned the corner, and headed towards the hardware store.

Maybe if he made it to the main road, he would be okay. He looked around but saw nothing. He did not slow down. In front of him, erupting out of the storm drain, a foul-smelling cloud formed into something large and evil.

Stan had been dreading this moment for twenty years. His reaction was to stumble backwards and fall down. His heart raced too fast. Suddenly Stan's chest became very heavy, and his breathing became much more difficult, like he was trying to suck air through a straw. The last thing Stan saw before his heart gave out was a pair of yellow eyes staring back at him with delight.

56

DOG MEN

Betty thought she heard a noise. She was pretty sure it wasn't one of her four cats, Millie, Sammy, Frazee, or Willie. She knew their noises back to front. This was something else. She was pretty sure it had come from outside.

She ran to the kitchen and got her water gun. If it was that damn dog again, she was gonna squirt him. Her stupid neighbors let their dog roam all over the neighborhood, leaving his doodie plops wherever he wanted. And somehow it was usually in her yard. She thought about calling security, but she decided she would take a picture and put it on Facebook. A good public shaming would do the trick and would also make her happy. She might have been seventy, but she would not be pushed around.

She crept to the window with her water gun in one hand and her phone in the other. Betty pulled the shade back. Sure enough, it was a dog. But as Betty's eyes focused, she saw it wasn't her neighbor's dog at all. Their dog was a light-colored Labrador.

This was something else entirely. Its yellow eyes stood out against the jet-black fur that stood up like spikes. And it was huge. It must have been five feet tall at the shoulder. Actually, thought Betty, it was a wolf. But there were supposed to be no wolves on this mountain. It looked around, sniffing at the air. It hadn't seen her. Then it stood up on its hind legs. It must have been seven feet tall.

Betty was already horrified. She had been afraid of dogs since a stray had attacked her when she was eight years old. But this was different. And then she saw three more dog men step out of the shadows.

Betty realized she still had her phone ready. A photo would prove there was something crazy in the woods. She would probably get her picture in the local paper. And it would look great on her Facebook page! She aimed and hit the button.

The flash lit up her yard. She had forgotten to turn it off.

She pulled back from the window. Had they seen her? She heard them growling to each other; they were communicating. This made her go cold.

Betty looked around for a place to hide. It was a one-bedroom house with no basement, and there was nowhere to go. Now she wished she had bought a gun when she had the chance. She ran to the bedroom and crawled under the bed. It was the best she could come up with.

She listened carefully. Screams came from a distance. Were her neighbors also being attacked? *Crunch*. Betty was sure the door had just been kicked in.

Her cats ran and hid under the bed next to her. Maybe she should have gotten dogs. Cowardly Cats! Her heart was racing faster than it had in the last twenty years. She could see their feet; they were in the room. Betty couldn't breathe anymore. Her thin lungs struggled for air, but her chest felt like a horse had kicked her.

They threw aside the mattress. She looked up, and the dog men were staring down at her. Her heart gave out just as they reached for her.

57

CRAZY HOUSE

The police station was looking like a crazy house. Officers were running around, grabbing equipment on their way to the parking lot. The phones would not stop ringing. Sirens were blaring.

Detective Mathew Frost picked up a jangling phone.

Someone was in big trouble. Tampering with the town's water supply was probably a federal offense. For sure they would be charged with a terrorist act. LSD in the reservoir was a new low, even for a maniac.

He checked his gun and headed for his car. Yet another insane report. Multiple people on Hale trail were reporting giant dog men going house to house, killing people. Frost eased himself into the big Dodge sedan. He knew there was no such thing as a mass hallucination, so the only explanation for the multiple witnesses had to be some kind of powerful drug. It was literally the only logical explanation. It's not like monsters were real.

He pulled out of the parking lot but suddenly hit the brakes. He watched Stan, the gas station owner, sprinting down the road. He was being chased by a black cloud with yellow eyes.

Dammit, I must have had some of the tainted water, he thought. *I'm going to kick someone's ass.*

58

MINEFIELD

Kevin and Diego led the way. Even though they didn't have a truck anymore, they still followed the dirt road. Faith flew overhead to give them a long-distance view of what might be coming.

Madison stumbled suddenly, holding her head.

Susan grabbed her. "What's wrong?"

"I felt something big. Like lots of people are dying, right now. I think the town is under attack."

"What is it?" Kevin called back.

"She thinks the town is under attack. She felt people dying," said Susan.

"The only way to stop that is to stop the invaders," said Diego.

Kevin started running. "Double time."

They followed him. Running with backpacks and weapons was difficult. They were all sucking wind when they came to the hill that led to the mine.

"Finally," said Susan.

Diego loaded his rifle. "Stick to the trees, stay in the shadows. Don't make it easy for them to spot you." They crept through the woods, everyone with their weapons ready. The tree line stopped, and the terrain became desert and scrub bushes. There was very little cover.

"What are we going to do?" asked Susan.

"I don't like it. This approach is out in the open. Feels like the perfect spot for an ambush," said Kevin.

"What other option do we have? We can't flank them and go through a back door. That's the only entrance," said Diego.

Kevin looked around. "It just feels like we're walking into a trap."

"Of course it's a trap. This whole thing is a trap," argued Diego.

Madison stepped out from the trees. "We don't have time for a discussion. The town is being attacked. Let's just keep moving forward."

Madison walked up the dirt trail. She stopped suddenly and froze. The others ran to her.

"What's wrong?" whispered Susan.

Madison held up her hands. "Stop right there. Don't come any closer. I'm pretty sure this is a minefield."

Kevin shook his head. "How would you know that?"

"Because I just stepped on one."

"Oh, no," said Diego and Susan at the same time. He ran to her and looked closely at her feet.

"That's an anti-personnel mine. It will kill you with shrapnel the minute you step off," said Diego.

Susan shook her head. "There has to be a way to get her off."

"It was literally designed to make that impossible," said Diego.

"Yes, but we have something no one counted on. A vampire." Kevin pulled out his phone and dialed a number.

Faith was floating fifty feet above them, keeping an eye out for any signs of an ambush. She was wondering why everyone had stopped moving when her phone buzzed in her pocket.

"Yeah?"

"Hey, we've run into a problem," said Kevin. "How fast can you fly?"

Kevin put the phone back in his pocket. "Okay, Madison, I'm going to need you to hold your hands up above your head."

"Why?"

"Just do it. You're not afraid of heights, are you?"

Faith came around in a long, high arc. She was about a mile behind Madison. First, she let gravity build up her speed by dropping from her high position. Then she leveled off with five hundred yards to go. She straightened her body, pointed her toes and fingers, then tensed her shoulders and put her head down. *Boom!* Her afterburners kicked in. She flew closer to the ground, almost skimming the bushes. Madison was rushing at her. Faith reached down and grabbed her hands just as she was passing overhead.

Madison saw Faith streaking at her like a missile. She held her hands up high and was yanked so hard off the ground she came out of her shoes—which were catapulted when the mine exploded.

"Hold on," yelled Faith.

Madison hugged her tight. They flew low, and then Faith took them high.

"Well, they definitely know we're here now."

And then rifles fired, and bullets zipped past them.

59

AIR DANCING

William heard the mine explode. He ran for the entrance, rifle in hand. He floated a flashlight over his head so he could see in the dark tunnel. When he looked out over the hill, he saw nothing but shadows. He pointed to one of the reptilians, who let off a flare gun. Now the hill was lit up with a pink glow.

He still saw nothing on the ground. So he turned his attention to the sky, and his heart skipped a beat. Faith was flying across the battlefield. His soldiers fired at her, but she spun and dove and then rose again, like she was dancing in the air.

William felt the excitement rising up his back. There she was. Was he happy? Could he kill her now that he found her again? Where did he put his vampire bullets? These questions infuriated him. And now he missed his chance to shoot her down. He was disgusted. He kicked the nearest soldier.

"Concentrate on the tree line! Look in the shadows. They're out there. Keep firing the flares."

Faith swooped down over the entrance. She was doing

recon. And she looked like she was holding on to someone. The reptilian soldiers fired at her again.

"Don't shoot, you'll never hit her. Stop wasting ammo. Concentrate on the ground over there." *What a stupid order*, he thought. *Good thing they don't ask questions*. He walked back to the elevator. There was no chance that they could get up the hill and into the mine. William went down and checked all the equipment again, just in case. Part of him wanted to stay there and watch Faith fly. He told that part of himself to shut the hell up and jump off a cliff.

60

SOFTENING IT UP

F aith brought Madison in for a gentle landing, since she had no shoes anymore. Susan grabbed Madison and hugged her for a long time. "No more running out in front." She looked at Madison's feet and started taking off her shoes. "Here, take mine."

Madison stopped her. "Mom, you know I can't fit into your shoes. They're too small. Don't worry, I'll be fine. The dirt is soft."

Another flare went off overhead. Kevin motioned at them. "Get back. Stick to the shadows."

Rifle fire smacked into the trees in front of them. Diego studied the landscape. "We're kind of pinned down over here. This is not good."

"We need to get up that hill, through the minefield, right?" asked Faith.

Kevin moved to a tree closer to her. "Yeah. What's your thought?"

"I'll clear the field."

"Sure, great idea. Why didn't I think of that." Kevin rolled his eyes.

Faith looked around and spotted a large trunk. She ran at it and smashed it with her shoulder. She did it again.

"Um. What are you doing?" asked Kevin.

"Softening it up." Faith flew ten feet in the air. She grabbed on to a pair of branches and flew as hard as she could. Slowly, the tree roots let go of the ground.

Faith picked up the immense tree and flew at the minefield. She launched it and flew up to get away from the blasts. The explosions were huge; they built on each other, creating an echo effect that was so loud it hurt. The entire group was thrown backwards.

Susan brushed leaves out of her hair. "Holy crap."

"That's an effective way to clear a minefield," said Diego.

Kevin shook his head. "I had no idea she was that strong."

Faith landed. "Just stick to the channel I gouged out and you should be fine." She flew up.

"Where are you going?" Kevin yelled.

"To get a look at the entrance to that mine."

61

HIDEOUS MONSTER

William was working on the nerve gas lines when he heard the chain of explosions. *Maybe the minefield got them all*, he thought. But he had a feeling he wouldn't be that lucky. Just in case his hunch was right, he walked over to a silver case. He couldn't remember where he put his vampire killer bullets, but this rifle was the next best thing.

William ran to the elevator. As usual, it took forever to get to the surface. When it stopped, he kicked the doors twice. Both times, he hurt his foot. He got to the entrance, sweating and out of breath. He shouldered his rifle and searched the sky. He looked through his three-thousand-dollar infrared scope.

He lined up his shot. She was only a hundred yards away. This would be easy. He led her, sucked in his breath, and—

Another flare exploded in the sky, washing out his image of her. "Dammit! Will you stop shooting those stupid fucking flares," he yelled. He looked for her against the dark sky. She was easy to spot with her beautiful glowing skin.

"Beautiful?" his mind screamed. "She's a hideous monster! The longer you let her live, the longer your weakness grows."

William had no choice. She was their best weapon, and she could not be allowed to destroy all their plans. They promised him power and money, and he would not throw all that away on a whim. That would be the dumbest thing he had ever done.

On the other hand, she was really pretty.

"Goddammit."

He pulled the trigger and felt some relief.

62

SPLATS

F aith dipped and rolled in the sky. With all the shooting and flares, she could not fly in a straight line. She aimed low and skimmed the ground. She counted at least fifty reptile creatures. She swooped back up. She studied the battlefield.

Even with the mines taken care of, her friends would be cut down by the lizard's superior position. She would even the odds right now. She dove and snatched a lizard man holding a rifle. She sped straight up into the sky, dragging the reptile by his claws.

When they were a hundred feet up, she looked at the creature. It was green and grey, it was covered in scales, and had the face of a giant crocodile. And it was slimy. Faith hated slimy! It sank its teeth into her arm.

"You know that might hurt, if I weren't already dead." She dropped him. He took a while to hit the ground. And then he splattered. Faith hovered and spotted more victims. She dove and came up with two more croc men.

"Later, fellas." Two more splats. She was putting some dents in their numbers. More splats.

There were rifle-toting crocs in the higher positions, there was a minefield they already cracked, but that was it. She saw no more defenses. That must mean that there were surprises waiting inside. Booby traps, ambush, whatever, it was waiting for them. She would fly back and tell them what she found. She turned to fly back when—

Bam, a big dart hit her in the neck. Faith pulled it out, went unconscious, and fell out of the sky.

63

ANGRY WORM

Kevin, Diego, Susan, and Madison watched Faith fall out of the sky.

"Oh, no," said Madison.

"What do we do?" asked Susan.

Diego looked at Kevin. "She should be fine. She's dead, remember? Falling out of the sky won't make her any more dead than she already is."

"Yes, but now they have her. I can't stand here and let that happen." Kevin loaded his AK and ran up the hill.

"Wait!" Diego yelled after him. "I guess this is when we charge." He ran after Kevin.

Susan and Madison followed.

"Stay behind me," Susan yelled.

Gunshots started coming.

"Get to that tree trunk. That's our cover," said Diego over his shoulder. "And stay low!"

They ran hard and fast. Madison felt the dirt under her toes. It felt good. It was cool and wet. They could hear the bullets whacking into the ground, getting closer.

Susan concentrated on not falling. The last thing she

wanted to do was embarrass Madison. She skidded across a slick spot in the dirt, but she stayed on her feet. Bullets kept streaking past them. She angled herself so that Madison was covered. Finally, she made it to the huge horizontal tree trunk. Diego and Kevin were shooting back, so she covered her ears.

Kevin pointed off to the right. "I saw her fall over there. We gotta get her before they do." Rifle fire kept coming in, but Kevin left the tree trunk and ran towards it.

"Dammit, that's fucking suicide." Diego ran after him, firing.

Susan and Madison watched them running up the hill. "Let's stay here," said Susan.

"If we stay, we die. They will blast this tree until we have no more hiding spot. Let's go with Diego," shouted Madison.

"It's safer here."

"We will not save this mountain by being safe. Come on." Madison stuck out her hand. Susan grabbed it and they ran together. They ran across the dirt, around rocks, and over brush. By the time they caught up to Kevin and Diego, they were winded. Another flare went off above them.

Kevin ran. "Let's go!"

They kept running, looking for any cover. They crouched behind a group of small, skinny trees.

"We gotta keep going; this cover sucks. This way." Diego pointed to a new spot by large boulders.

They stepped out and were immediately surrounded by reptiles with rifles.

"Crapola," said Diego.

The reptiles prepared to fire. Madison dove into a lizard head. She hopped from mind to mind, setting her psychic grenades as she went. Their heads snapped back, and they dropped dead. Instant aneurisms.

"She fell this way." Kevin ran faster.

They ran after him. They rounded a crop of big rocks and there she was—being picked up by William.

For a second Kevin was happy because William had his hands full carrying Faith, so they had the drop on him. He was about to shout commands at William when he noticed the floating SCAR rifle aimed right at him. He shoved Diego, and they dove behind the rocks.

The SCAR fired a .308 bullet that was heavier and longer than the AK's ammo. The boom was like thunder. It kept firing.

Madison and Susan hung back.

"We're pinned down," yelled Kevin.

Diego prepared to attack. "He's going to have to reload in a second. Get ready."

The shooting stopped. They ran from behind the rocks.

The rifle was floating in the air, clicking the trigger on an empty magazine. William was already gone.

"No! He's getting away." Kevin ran ahead without waiting.

"Again? Come on." Diego motioned to Madison and Susan.

They finally glimpsed the entrance to the mine. They were close now. They could see a dozen figures in silhouette, firing at them. Diego emptied his gun, returning fire. Three of them went down. Madison grabbed his arm and pulled him back.

"Get me closer to them," she said calmly in his mind.

They watched Kevin running ahead, almost getting shot.

"We gotta stop him," said Diego.

"Kevin!" Madison yelled in his head. "Stop running. Getting killed won't fix anything. Wait for us; if I can get close enough, I can end them all."

He slowed down and got low behind a ridge wall along the path to the entrance. If he stuck his head up, it would get shot off, but if he stayed low, they couldn't get to him without moving closer. The rest of the group caught up.

"We close enough now?" asked Diego.

"Almost," said Madison.

Diego reached into his backpack and pulled out a glass jar. "I didn't want to use this unless it was an emergency. I guess this qualifies."

"What the hell is that?" asked Susan.

"It's a baby worm. The Mongolian death worm."

"But it's tiny," she said.

"Until it gets mad. Then it grows, quickly."

"How do you make a death worm mad?" asked Madison.

"You smash the glass jar it's living in." Diego tossed the jar behind the reptilians.

The worm quickly rose to ten feet in height and roared. The reptilians looked around, confused. The worm attacked with streaks of lightning from the two antennas on its head. The reptilians exploded in a shower of green goo and white bones.

The fat pink worm barely moved, but half the troopers were now dead. The remainders ran backwards towards the ridge where Madison was waiting. The second they were close enough, she exploded their minds with her psychic grenades.

"Well, that was easy," said Madison.

The worm roared again and shot a bolt of lightning at her. She ducked.

"So, um, how are we supposed to get rid of the worm?" asked Madison.

Diego removed a small super soaker water gun from his

bag. He walked up the trail towards the worm. Everyone followed.

"So, it's like, um, allergic to water?" asked Kevin.

"Not exactly."

The death worm's antennae started glowing. Diego approached it, pumping the water gun, and pulled the trigger. The worm froze on the spot. "Liquid nitrogen," said Diego. "It hates being frozen. We can't stand around all day looking at the giant frozen death worm. We have an invasion to stop."

Madison pulled out her phone and took a quick selfie in front of the worm.

Kevin slapped a new magazine into his AK. "Something tells me this will not be easy."

They entered the mine.

64

DISPOSABLE

William carried Faith down the hallway. He could have floated her, but for some reason William liked holding her close to his body. He wasn't sure why.

He was half running and walking. He was not going to get caught in the hallway when the auto machine guns or the nerve gas went off. Not that he really thought the idiots would make it inside. Especially now that he had taken their vampire.

He could have taken her to the ship, but his secret plan did not involve Lam. The invasion was not his fight. In fact, it was the perfect opportunity to slip away. The tunnels leading to the ship were long and winding, like they had been laid out to confuse people. William walked the entire thing a couple of times. His excuse was he was inspecting the defenses, but really, he was looking for something.

William found what he was looking for, past an area that looked like it had caved in. He easily moved the rocks with his telekinetic ability. And there it was. He had a hunch;

something about the layout told him there had to be a side tunnel to an exit.

He imagined the temptation would have been too large. Some miner had gotten sick of handling gold every day but never taking any home with him.

William could picture it easily. Every day the miner had slipped away and dug a little more in his secret tunnel. Until he finally broke through the outside wall. How much did he take with him, William wondered? He obviously made it out because there was an exit. William stashed his stolen SUV right in front of the slim crack in the wall, behind a clump of trees and bushes. It was the perfect hiding spot.

He put Faith on his back in order to make it through the narrow exit. He laid her down in the passenger side of the vehicle. He looked in the back at the big black suitcase. It was his retirement fund. He had simply told Lam, "I need ten million dollars in hundred-dollar bills." An hour later, the suitcase showed up in his SUV. No questions, nothing.

William got into the driver's seat. He was about to turn the key, but something bothered him. It had been too easy. He wasn't worried that it was a trick; it was the opposite. Lam didn't care. It couldn't have been more obvious that he was going to take the money and slip away, and it didn't bother Lam one bit.

William felt very disposable.

Lam was done with him; he had gotten what he wanted out of William. Never mind the physical pain he had caused or the damage to his body. He was fairly certain that all the time he had spent on the space bridge had given him some sort of radiation poisoning. Whether it was fatal, William wasn't sure, but he was going to find out on a tropical island far away from the mountain.

He tried to put the key in the ignition. His heart sped up,

and sweat ran down his face. He stopped. His heart went back to normal. He tried to start the engine again, and his body started panicking again. He could not leave and live with himself.

Lam didn't care. Clearly William wasn't important to their operation or they wouldn't be letting him leave. And Lam certainly didn't care if he died like a dog on a floor somewhere.

"That's what Lam wants from me? A dog's death?" William said out loud. He took the key out of the ignition.

Fuck that.

William was not going to be disrespected like that. He picked up his rifle.

65

CHUPACABRA BITE

The mine entrance was really a cave that led to a man-made shaft that went almost half a mile underground. The mine was a confusing network of tunnels where a person could get lost for hours with only one known entrance and exit: the elevator.

In the middle of the maze was Lam's ship. It was very large. It was cylindrical and as long as a football field. It looked like a giant cigar.

Kevin knew all of this because he had memorized the map Madison had drawn. It even included Lam's ship. Her powers were amazing. Now, with Faith gone, she would have to be their star player.

He looked down at her feet in the ambient light from their flashlights. She was still shoeless. He would have found her replacements, but, of course, they were fighting reptilian aliens that didn't wear any shoes at all.

They walked deeper into the cave. "There will be a big industrial elevator up ahead. It will take us all the way down."

Gunshots blasted in front of them. Everyone dove. Kevin

fired back immediately. Madison hit them with psychic grenades. The reptilians were dead immediately. Madison thought she was well suited to close quarter combat.

Diego got up and brushed himself off. "Everyone okay?"

"Yeah," they all said.

It was cool outside, but in the cave, it was already hot. Sweat ran down Kevin's back. And it stank like the lizard house at the zoo. They made it to the elevator. It was a big hulking yellow thing. Huge doors stood closed in front of them, and a red light glowed above the door. The red glow and their flashlights were the only sources of light.

Kevin pressed the button on the elevator. "It's a long way to the bottom. It's going to take it a while to get up here."

"Great," said Susan. "Who doesn't want to hang out in a hot, dark, stinking tunnel, filled with reptile aliens and who knows what else."

They stood in silence. Finally, Diego spoke up. "All right, fine." He pulled up his sleeve. There were twin scars running the full length of his forearm. "Who wants to hear a story? This is from a chupacabra bite."

Everyone laughed.

"Yeah, right," said Madison.

"I'm serious. So, we used to have this old goat named Pedo. Cuz he smelled so bad. And every evening at sundown, Pedo would go to the garage and kick the door with his back legs. We couldn't tell if it offended him that the sun was leaving or what.

"One night we realized we hadn't heard our nightly Pedo. My dad told me to go outside and check on him. Now keep in mind I was like fourteen, so I must have weighed like a hundred pounds or something. I go outside and there's old Pedo being bitten by this weird creature I had never seen before.

"My dad had described it to me in the past, so I knew what it was. It was grey and wrinkled with super blue eyes. It was about the size of a large dog. It had weird humps on its hindquarters, and it had a long naked tail. It was a chupacabra, which literally means 'goat sucker.' And there it was, sucking our goat. It had its fangs in Pedo's neck and it was draining his blood.

"I had several options. I could run inside and grab a weapon, I could call for my dad, or I could run away and pretend I never saw a thing." Diego paused for effect.

Madison couldn't help herself. "So, what did you do?"

"I threw myself on top of it and knocked the goat out of his mouth. It sank its fangs into my arm instead. Next thing I know, my dad is pulling me by my feet. And that's when the fangs went down my arm. Oh, and then he shot it with a .357. I got a wicked scar for a stuffed chupacabra on the mantle. My dad always laughed about it, saying I almost lost my arm for an old pedo." Diego laughed.

No one else laughed.

"I forgot to mention that 'pedo' means fart in Spanish."

Still, no one laughed.

"Ah, I guess you had to be there."

Ding. The elevator arrived. The doors slid open. Five reptilians jumped out, guns firing.

But the humans were faster. They fired until all the reptilians were down.

"This is our elevator, lizard face," said Kevin.

They stepped over the bodies and got on the elevator.

66

HEAVY CHAIN

Willliam ran down the tunnel. If the attackers made it into the tunnel, the nerve gas would go off in fifteen minutes. He would have to make this quick. The SCAR rifle was heavy in his hands. He floated it in front of him using his telekinetic powers instead. He got the feeling that his radiation sickness or whatever they poisoned him with was getting worse every time he used his powers. But right now, he didn't care.

Lam had disrespected him, and he would have to rectify the situation before he could retire to his tropical island paradise. He could not enjoy a margarita on the sand if Lam was not thoroughly punished. Some humans might be disposable, but William was most certainly not.

William wasn't even bothered by the thought of an invasion. He didn't care if the entire planet became psychic food for Lam's species. As long as he had his little island, he would be fine. And with the hardware he had stolen, he could defend his slice of heaven for a long time. If anyone could even find it in the middle of the ocean.

And now he had Faith. He was going to bring her with

him. Eventually she would come to love him, as he loved her. Together they could watch humanity burn from the safety of their little world. They could survive on birds, fish, and whatever fruit they could find on the island. It would be enough. Faith. Her jet-black hair, her long legs, her alabaster skin—they would all be his. And she would be stuck on the island with no way off. Wait, he realized, she could fly. That would be a problem. Solution: he would stop at Home Depot and get a long, heavy chain and a padlock. Problem solved.

The tunnel was dark, and there were no lights; it was, after all, a secret escape tunnel. William used a small flashlight to illuminate the narrow passageway. He came to another, bigger tunnel. He took a step and then immediately jumped back when he remembered. The motion sensing machine gun went off, sending a burst of 5.56 ammunition whizzing right past William's face.

He waved his hand and clicked the safety on with his power. He left it on, in case he made the same mistake on his way back. The ship was deep into the tunnels and farther down. One tunnel sloped to a lower level where there was an underground lake. The ship was on the shore.

William froze; he heard voices. Far off, but they were human voices. It was them. He looked at his watch and calculated. Would he have time to kill them all and murder Lam, before the nerve gas went off? He had twelve minutes left.

He smiled. William loved a good challenge.

67

SHATTERED BONE

The elevator bumped along slowly. Diego slapped a new magazine into his AK. "You should all reload, check your weapons, all that good stuff."

Everyone looked at their weapons and reloaded.

Susan reached into her bag and pulled out a Gatorade. "Here." She tried to hand it to Madison.

"Mom!"

"It's hot, you're sweating, drink," said Susan.

Madison refused.

Diego looked at her. "We can't afford to have you pass out from the heat."

"You're right," said Madison as she took a big drink.

"I think they purposely made this the slowest elevator ever, so by the time we get down to the bottom, we will have died of old age," said Kevin.

Diego chuckled. "It is an eighty-year-old mine."

"We've got to find Faith. How many frickin' times am I going to lose her?"

"I'm not trying to sound like a movie cliche, but we should split up into two teams. You and Susan go after Faith, while Madison and I put an end to their invasion," said Diego.

Susan looked up. "How are you going to do that?"

"I'm going to turn their ship into a fine powder with all the dynamite in my backpack."

"Wait," said Susan. "You mean to tell me we went through that entire gun battle while you had that on your back?"

"Yep."

"One stray bullet would have blown us all up!" yelled Susan.

"True, it was a calculated risk. But what would be the point of getting all the way down here with nothing to stop them?"

"I see your point, but still."

"Be mad later," said Kevin. "We're here."

The elevator came to a low stop. With a loud creak, the doors opened. The maze of dark tunnels opened up in front of them.

"Wow, look at that," said Susan. "Echo, echo, echo!" she yelled.

"Shhhh! Don't announce to everyone that we're here," said Kevin.

Diego studied the hand-drawn map. "This main tunnel leads directly to the heart of the mountain. We all go this way. Let's go carefully."

"I don't have time for carefully. Madison, can you look for her with your mind?"

"Yeah, I can try."

He walked quickly out in front. Madison walked behind him. She closed her eyes and concentrated.

"Anything?" asked Kevin.

"There's good news and bad news. The good news is I

found a signal. She's still alive. The bad news is that she's far away and I think they drugged her."

"But you don't know where she is?"

"I know she's not nearby. That's all."

"Well, at least that's something. Let's pick up the pace, people." The tunnel was long, dark, and hot. The air felt thick. Kevin walked ahead, his flashlight lighting their path. He came to an intersection where two tunnels crossed.

"Come on, guys." Kevin walked through. The motion sensor was tripped, and the machine gun fired. Kevin was saved by the bullet that hit him. The shot was so powerful that it threw him backwards out of the line of fire. This stopped him from being hit multiple times and turned into a smoking corpse.

The one bullet that hit him did its damage and shattered his arm high up by the shoulder. Kevin rolled around on the floor. Flashes of light exploded behind his eyes. His arm crackled with invisible fire.

Diego ran, pulled his pack off, and took out a medical kit. He skidded on his knees next to Kevin. He held him down and bandaged the arm before Kevin realized what was happening.

"Here, take this." Diego put pills in Kevin's hand. He put a bottle of water in his other hand. "Drink."

Kevin took the pills and swallowed big gulps of water.

"This is going to help the pain," said Diego. "But you're going to be a little unsteady on your feet." He helped Kevin up. "Hold on. This is going to hurt, but it will hurt a lot more without it." He took the rest of the bandages and wrapped Kevin's arm tight to the side of his body, pinning his arm in place.

"We've got to get you to a hospital," said Susan.

"First, I've got to find Faith. And you have to stop an invasion."

"And how are we supposed to get past this machine gun?" asked Susan.

Madison dusted off her bare feet. "Maybe we can crawl under it?"

Diego picked up a rock and rolled it down the hall. The machine gun fired, following the rock with its bullets.

"Won't work," said Diego. "That thing is capable of motion tracking. We'll have to come up with something else."

"Can we shoot it?" asked Susan.

Diego peeked around the corner. The gun saw him and fired. He pulled back.

"No, there's a shield in front."

Kevin groaned. "How long until these pills kick in?"

"Probably ten minutes."

"Then I don't have any time to waste." Kevin picked up a rock and tossed it high in the air, misdirecting it. He ran under the stream of bullets. "Come on."

"I guess that'll work," said Diego.

They all did the same trick and kept walking. The cave split into three.

"Madison, can you point me in a direction of where she is?"

Madison closed her eyes. "I'm getting a faint thought from this direction." Madison pointed left.

"Then that's where we're going. Susan. Let's move." Kevin held a rifle in his good hand. Awkwardly.

68

I GET KNOCKED DOWN

William heard two voices getting closer. One of them, the man, kept mentioning Faith. So, he was either a devout Christian or he was Faith's boyfriend. Normally, he would have loved to wait until they passed by and then creep up behind them and knife them. First the boyfriend and then the woman. Usually a low stab between the ribs would puncture the kidneys, and then it was a painful and fatal wound.

He looked at his watch; he didn't have time for the old wait and stick. The nerve gas was set to go off in ten minutes. He would have to let these little fish go; he was after a whale. A whale named Lam, and he was going to slice him open, soup to nuts.

The voices were getting closer. If he was going to go, it would have to be now. He hurried across the tunnel and disappeared into the shadows. He had been practicing a way to trick Lam. All based on the horrible, worst song ever made, "I Get Knocked Down" by Chumbawamba from the late 90s. William figured that if he could just repeat the song over and over again, Lam would not be able to read his thoughts. The main thought being, *I'm going to murder Lam.* A rifle, a knife hidden in his boot, his bare hands—he would use something. He would have killed for a grenade.

Suddenly, he heard footsteps running towards him. A voice called out, "Don't move, dirtbag!" Gunshots.

69

MIND SCREAM

Kevin was looking over the map. "I will take William out. You get Faith and take her to safety. When we find her."

"If we find her," said Susan.

"No reason to be negative; we will find her."

"It's easy to get lost down here. There are tunnels everywhere."

"Yes, but we have a map," said Kevin.

"But that doesn't mean—"

"Shhh!" said Kevin. He thought he saw a shadow run across the tunnel. "I saw something. Or someone. Come on." He ran awkwardly with one arm bandaged to his body.

Susan ran behind him, both hands on her .45s.

"Sonofabitch, he's here." Kevin fired his gun. He missed by a mile.

William turned around, rifle aimed at Kevin. Kevin aimed his rifle at William. With one hand.

"Yeah, kid, you should get outta here before you get hurt some more."

"Go to hell, dirtbag. Where is Faith? What did you do to her?"

"Did it ever occur to you that maybe you don't deserve her? How many times have you lost her now?"

"The only thing keeping me from blowing your face off is that you know where she is."

"Listen, little guy, I gotta go. I don't have time for this," said William.

"Where are you going?" asked Susan.

"I'm going to go kill the thing in charge and put an end to this. Okay? So put your guns down and I'll be on my way."

"Where's Faith?" asked Kevin.

"She got away from me. She escaped the mine. She's probably on her way up the elevator right now. So, you go get her. I gotta split."

"What's your hurry?" said Susan.

"I'm a punctual guy," said William.

"Bullshit!" yelled Kevin.

"Fine. It's not going to matter, anyway. There's nerve gas set to go off in like ten minutes. You'll never get out in time. Hahaha. You two might as well start making out, cuz these are your last minutes on earth."

William was silently floating a knife behind Kevin. He suddenly struck with it. Susan saw the glint of metal out of the corner of her eye. She spun and fired. She knocked the knife out of the air.

They both turned and shot at William, but he was already running down the tunnel. He turned a corner and was gone.

"Should we go after him?" said Susan.

"No, we have to find Faith."

"Do you think there's really nerve gas?"

"Honestly?" said Kevin. "Yeah."

"Hold on." Susan closed her eyes.

"What are you doing?"

"Screaming in my head for Madison to hear me," said Susan.

"MADISON!" Susan thought.

"Yes, Mom?" Madison replied in her head.

"We just ran into William. He said there's nerve gas rigged to go off in around eight minutes. Where are you?" she thought.

"Diego and I are going to cut off the head of the snake. If we can kill their leadership, maybe we can end the invasion."

"What about the nerve gas?" asked Susan.

"We'll be fine. They will not have nerve gas on the ship."

"Good point. I'll come and help you. I don't want you fighting them alone," thought Susan.

"No, Mom. I can do this. You need to get out of the mine. Now. There's no time."

"Okay," thought Susan.

"Promise me, Mom."

"Okay, I promise to go."

"So?" asked Kevin. "Did you reach her?"

"Yeah. She asked me to come help her. You go find Faith; I'll find Madison."

"Makes sense to me. Good luck. See you outside." Kevin turned and ran.

70

SULFUR WATER

Madison was running hard. She sucked in foul, hot air that seemed too thick to breathe, but she kept going.

"My mom said nerve gas will go off in eight minutes."

Diego ran alongside of her. "Then we have to get to that ship. There won't be any nerve gas there."

"That's what I said." Her heart was racing faster now, but she was pretty sure it wasn't from the running.

They came to another fork. "It's this way," said Madison. The tunnel descended gradually. Then it became steep. There was a dark mass up ahead.

"What is that?" asked Madison.

"It's the underground lake. Good thing the dynamite is in a waterproof plastic bag. We don't have time to think it over or psych ourselves up. Come on." He ran and dove into the water with no hesitation. Madison followed his example.

Her body was immediately shocked. The water was warm, and it stank of sulfur. It was dark. She couldn't see what was underneath her feet. She did not like that, but she forced herself to concentrate on her swimming.

She caught up to Diego, who was using his flashlight to cut through the dark. "It's up ahead this way," she said.

"You're sure?"

"I can see it in my head," said Madison.

"Okay, let's do it. Wait. Hold on," said Diego.

"What's wrong?"

"I thought I heard something." He shined the light around them. All he saw was dark water.

"Maybe it was nothing," he said.

Suddenly Diego screamed out in pain and was dragged underwater.

71

QUICK DEATH

Kevin ran awkwardly. He was looking at the map, while holding a flashlight on it, while trying to hold a rifle with his broken arm. If he ran into any resistance, he would be in trouble. He had no backup and only one working arm. And it was really hard to shoot the AK-47 that way.

According to the map, there was a side tunnel that led to an exit. He would aim for that. If Faith was still in the tunnels, she would be fine; she could survive nerve gas. She wasn't alive, so she didn't need to breathe anything. Kevin, on the other hand, would die a painful, lung-scalded death. So he would make it to fresh air and then figure out his next move.

He turned right, down another long tunnel. He rushed; time was running out. He heard a noise and spun around with the flashlight. It slipped out of his hands and rolled across the ground, broken. The tunnel went pitch black.

Kevin heard footsteps getting closer. They had a wet, syrupy sound to them. He prepared his good arm with the rifle when he remembered something in his pack. He pulled out a road flare and snapped it open. He threw it in the middle of the tunnel.

In the red flickering light, he saw a half dozen reptilians making their way towards him. They had rifles and claws. Kevin didn't know how he was going to fight them. He was outnumbered and outgunned. He would shoot until he was out of bullets and then he would beat them with his one good hand.

Kevin heard noise behind him. There were more reptilians. He was totally surrounded. At least it would be over quickly.

72

EAT NOW

Madison floated, listening. She waited for Diego to surface. He didn't. It was too dark to see. She shined her light around and saw many pairs of yellow eyes on the surface, getting closer. Alligators!

"Diego!" she yelled.

The water was turning red.

Madison closed her eyes and reached out with her feelings. She read the creature that was trying to drag Diego down to the bottom of the lake. She got only one thought repeated over and over that translated to "eat now."

She tried to hit it with a psychic grenade, but it was too primitive of an animal. Its mind was not vulnerable to thoughts turned against itself. Its thoughts were too simple. She searched for another way, and she found it. Its mind was so simple that she was able to access the main controls. The five senses and main functions. She immediately stopped its heart.

The alligators coming at her were so close now that she could see bits of old meat sticking out between their fangs. They swam at her and attacked as a group.

The closest alligator opened its jaws, aiming for her head. Madison put up her forearm and jammed it in its mouth. Before it could chomp down and make her an amputee, she stopped its heart.

She silently raced through all of their heads, stopping their hearts as she jumped from mind to mind. She left dead alligators in her wake.

Diego resurfaced, drawing in a huge breath.

"He bit my leg."

"Can you make it to the shore?" she asked.

"Yes."

They swam. Diego took turns between the backstroke and the sidestroke. It was hard to swim with one good leg and all the equipment. Diego took the dynamite and a tourniquet out of his pack and put it in his cargo pocket. He let the pack go and sink into the dark water.

"You all right?" she asked.

"For sure." There was a trail of blood behind him.

Up ahead, there was an almost blinding shine. It was the ship. And it was massive.

73

KNIFE IN TEETH

Kevin opened fire, yelling something about stinking reptiles. By the red glow of the flare, the reptilians were staying back. And then he ran out of bullets. They pounced.

Kevin turned and ran. He threw his rifle aside. It was useless now. He made a right and then a left and kept sprinting with one arm tied to himself. He could hear them still chasing him. Getting closer.

He reached into his back pocket and found the small 9 millimeter. It was his backup. It was nothing compared to the AK, but he could easily shoot it with one hand. Maybe he had a fighting chance. If he couldn't outrun them, he could take out a couple with his handgun and maybe finish the rest with his knife. It was a big Bowie knife, and he could still feel it in his boot. He silently thanked the universe for keeping it there.

He turned again. He could lose them in the maze of tunnels. Though none of his moves had tricked them so far. *They can probably smell me*, he thought. They were still coming. He ran down another tunnel, no longer bothering with the map. He came to a rock wall. It was a dead end.

"Literally." Kevin laughed. This was where he would make his last stand. He racked his gun one handed against his belt loop. He put the Bowie knife in his teeth. When the 9 ran out, he would grab the knife and start slashing. He was taking them with him, if it was the last thing he ever did.

74

OPEN THE DOOR

Diego tried to walk, but all he could do was a kind of stiff leg limp that looked like Frankenstein's monster. He was leaving puddles of blood with every step.

"You have a tourniquet?" asked Madison.

"Yeah."

"Then lie down, or you're going to bleed to death before we stop them."

She took the tourniquet and tied it around his upper thigh. She turned it until the blood flow slowed down. Diego grimaced but refused to scream.

"You're going to have to stay here," she said.

"I'm not going to let you do this alone."

"You can't walk and you're losing a lot of blood. Unless your plan is to have them slip and fall down, you're going to have to stay here. Cover my back. Make sure no one comes up behind us."

Diego racked his AK. "I can do that."

"Be alive when I come back." Madison pulled him close

and kissed him passionately and deeply. Diego was surprised.

"Relax, I turn eighteen next month."

She let him go and walked to the ship's hull. It was smooth; there were no seams or rivets. She walked alongside it. She had to find a door or a ramp, some kind of opening. So far, she saw nothing. She kept walking. The ship was long. She couldn't see where it ended. She had to get inside —time was running out. She ran her finger along the ship. Suddenly a door opened, and a ramp slid down.

Oh, well, she thought, *there goes the element of surprise.* She walked up the ramp. The inside was the opposite of the tunnels; it was bright. The light was yellow, and it seemed to emanate from inside the walls of the ship. Madison reached out with her mind and found that Lam was waiting for her. He was on the bridge of the ship, in the front. She walked the length of the hull. It was a long walk.

She could hear movement around her. Other grey aliens, running the ship, working controls, overseeing the invasion. When they saw her, none of them were interested. In fact, they seemed to ignore her. Lam must have claimed her for himself. That was fine, she thought, it would be his death.

Madison came to the bridge. It was large with a ceiling that must have been fifty feet tall. The front face was entirely made of glass from floor to ceiling. Standing perfectly in the middle of the room, like some sort of statue, was Lam. He wore all white, which somehow emphasized the swollen bulbous shape of his head.

He was much shorter than she expected. In fact, he was inches shorter than Madison. For one crazy second, she considered the possibility of physically attacking him and beating him with her bare hands.

"Don't be ridiculous, my dear, you could never get close enough to touch me." Lam waved his hand and Madison was frozen where she stood. She strained to free herself, but it was like she was encased in cement, though she could breathe with no problem.

Then I will handle this a different way. It's grenade time, she thought. She closed her eyes.

"You really are quite silly," said Lam. "You can't enter my mind. I enter yours."

Madison suddenly found herself surrounded by blackness. Where was she? She realized she was still on the ship. Lam was manipulating what she was seeing. He had broken into her mind.

THREE PARTY

Diego lay on the ground, leaning against his pack. The AK was lying across his lap. The tourniquet was working. He scanned the lake for any movement; there was none. There was no noise either. All he had were his thoughts, and they were not happy. He did not like sitting on the sidelines while the action was happening in the ship. What if Madison needed him? Could she take on an invading alien overlord on her own? Yes, her powers were amazing, but still. He doubted anyone could do it alone.

Diego stood up. He got woozy for a second but leaned on his rifle like it was a cane. He took a couple of deep breaths —that helped. He could do this. He had to. How could he consider himself a man if he wasn't able to help out the beautiful seventeen-year-old girl who was fighting a monster alone?

He limped by the ship and came to the ramp. He pointed the AK in front of him, low, with his finger on the trigger. He would not get caught sleeping. Diego entered; it was brighter than he expected. There was a long white hallway that seemed to run the length of the entire ship. He walked quietly, looking for aliens or any sign of Faith. He spotted both almost immediately.

Going off into side rooms were grey aliens. He was sure that they could see him, but they didn't seem to care. Should he keep stalking quietly or just open fire and kill as many aliens as he could find?

Fuck it, he thought. *It's alien killing time.*

Then he saw the wet footprints on the floor. Faith had gone this way. He lowered his rifle and followed her tracks. He walked the entire hall until he came to the bridge. He crept carefully into the room. If he was quiet, maybe he could three party Lam. While he was fighting with Madison, Diego would take Lam out. It was his favorite Fortnite move: the three party.

Lam and Madison were frozen in place, clearly locked in some sort of psychic death match. The timing was perfect. He could light the fuse on the dynamite, grab Madison, and escape before Lam was even moving again.

Diego took the dynamite out of his cargo pouch and removed it from the plastic bags. He was ready. He opened up the silver zippo lighter.

"Do you really think I would be susceptible to a primitive technology that was discovered a hundred and fifty years ago? You might as well attack me with a sharpened stick," said Lam.

He waved his hand, and Diego was frozen in place, still holding the dynamite.

76

A SPARK

Six reptilians stalked into the tunnel. Kevin turned on the flashlight in his phone. He put it down on the ground to give him some light. It was very weak.

The lizards took their time sauntering towards him. Kevin figured they were trying to intimidate him. That was a mistake. Kevin leveled the handgun, snapped off two shots, and two reptilians went down. They learned quickly and fired their SCAR rifles, firing until they had to reload. The boom from the guns was amplified by the cave walls. Kevin's ears rang so loud he could hear nothing else.

He ran at them, figuring this was the last thing they were expecting. Kevin shot the closest lizard, grabbed him, and held him like a shield. He nailed another one. There were only three left now. He took another shot in the bad arm. Kevin went down on his knees.

He would have yelled, but there was a knife in his teeth. He fired until the gun ran out. He threw the empty pistol and pulled the knife out of his teeth. He slashed, and he stabbed anything that moved. Over and over, until he was panting and leaning up against the cave wall. He would be killed now, but at least he had given them hell.

He looked around when the end didn't come. All the lizards were dead on the ground. Kevin went into his pocket and pulled out the one stick of dynamite he took. It would have to do. He knew he had forgotten a lighter, so he picked up one of the dead lizards' rifles. He leaned the stick of dynamite against the back wall. Kevin walked to the entrance to the tunnel. He raised the rifle and aimed for the dynamite. He used the wall to steady himself.

Behind him, Kevin heard a hiss. He spun, ready to fire, but there was nothing there. The hiss seemed to come above the tunnel, near the ceiling. It had to be the poison gas. A slow fog of green smoke was creeping towards him. He was out of time.

Kevin held his breath and pulled the trigger.

The bullet missed the dynamite by less than an inch, but the bullet sparked when it hit the wall, which set it off perfectly. The explosion was powerful enough that if Kevin had stayed in the tunnel, he would have been vaporized. When the dust cleared, there was a big hole in the wall. Moonlight beamed through it. The gas was almost on top of him; he ran for the fresh air and made it.

He took deep breaths. The night air was so much better tasting than the foul, stank tunnel system. Kevin spotted a Jeep fifty yards away. He took off running. Maybe it was her; maybe she was somehow safe. He highly doubted any of that, but he ran anyway.

When he looked inside, he felt a shock of relief. Faith was in the Jeep, in the passenger seat, sleeping. Kevin reached in and grabbed her hand. He held it to his face and kissed it. He silently thanked god she was still alive. Or at least as much as a vampire could be alive.

Faith's eyes opened. She looked around. "What the hell?" She stretched. "Last thing I remember, I was flying."

"Yeah, William shot you out of the air."

"Why do I feel so slow?"

"He used a tranquilizer dart."

"That insane douche," she said, "I'm going to kill him."

Kevin opened the door and helped her out. He put an arm around her to steady her. "Wait, there's poison gas that was released in there. I don't know what's happened to the others. They may need help."

"You got it." Faith stood tall, ready to take off.

"Hold on," said Kevin. He pulled her close and kissed her. "Be careful. I love you."

"Took you long enough." She kissed him back and flew off.

77

DR. FOGLER

Madison was tied to a chair in a waiting room. It was an old waiting room. The furniture was all brown and beige. She knew right away; it was her childhood dentist's office. She was hit with a dread that rolled through her like a wave.

Her dentist had inherited his practice from his father, who had been there since the 70s. But Dr. Fogler was really cheap, so he had refused to update the furniture. The place was like a creepy time machine. He was also so cheap that he hated to use enough novocain. Which was why Madison dreaded going there. It was a painful time machine.

She heard a noise coming from the next room. It was thunderously quiet, so she could hear the tiniest of sounds. It was a skittering. Like tiny feet walking along a linoleum floor. *Of course*, she thought. *Insects*. She automatically pulled at her ropes. They did not give at all. *This is all in my mind. There aren't even any ropes. What was it Neo said? There is no spoon.* She imagined the ropes disappearing. She looked down. The ropes were still there.

"Fine." Madison yanked and kicked. She strained until a

vein stood out on her forehead. The ropes stayed intact, but now Madison was bleeding. The ropes had cut into her skin. She could tell that she was also bleeding in the real world, outside of the mental prison Lam had created. *Injury in here means injury out there*, she thought. *This is some bullshit.*

The skittering got louder. It had to be insects. Lam was doing a magnificent job of raiding her worst memories. Her fear of insects had started after a game of hide and seek when she was ten years old. She was excited that she had found an amazing new hiding place. One that guaranteed she would win the game and show all the girls who was the smartest.

Madison had stumbled on to it by accident. She discovered a blackberry bush and was eating happily; the berries were fatter and blacker than she had ever seen. And they were delicious. It was an explosion of juice and sugar every time she bit down. There was a break in the wall of bushes. She slipped through.

In the middle of the nest of thorns was a tree stump. At first it looked like a boring old tree stump, but when Madison got closer, she discovered a hollowed out little cave in the tree. It was a space just big enough for a ten-year-old girl to fit. Madison crawled in. She pulled her legs up against her chest and practically disappeared to the outside world.

It smelled like dirt and old wood. She thought it would be hard and splintery inside, but it was the opposite. The wood was soft; the splinters were like delicate hairs. She snuggled in. She knew sleep was getting ready to overtake her.

And that's when the biting began. At first, Madison thought she had an itch, but then the fire spread all over her body. She looked down and saw dozens of spiders all over her legs, crawling up her stomach.

They were all biting her. She tried to swipe them away, but they were everywhere. Then they fell out of the top of the stump and covered her hair. They ran into her ears and mouth.

She screamed, spitting out spiders, and ran as fast as she knew how, but she plowed right into the thorn bushes and got stuck. By the time she worked her way out of the thorns, she was bloody and in shock. Her friends found her face down in the dirt with a hundred cuts everywhere.

Madison woke up in the hospital with tubes coming out of her, hooked up to bags filled with antibiotics. The doctor explained to her that the spiders were not poisonous, but their mouths were full of bacteria. All of those bites overwhelmed her system and almost killed her. She was stuck in the hospital for two weeks with nothing but a flip phone.

She had hated all insects ever since. Of course Lam had conjured a whole order of horrible bugs to devour her while she was still alive and screaming.

Madison would have to figure a way out. If this waiting room was subject to the laws of physics, then the chair was too. It was forty years old and brittle. She raised up on her two legs and then smashed the chair down with all of her weight. It collapsed.

She got up, still holding on to a metal chair leg. She scanned the room for a weapon. A chair leg was just as good as anything else she could find.

She stood there, in her old dentist's office, holding a chair leg, listening for the pitter patter of insect feet. Then she heard it again. It was coming from Dr. Fogler's exam room. It sounded like two taps and then a scrape. Over and over in a maddening loop.

There was an exit door across from the exam room. Madison doubted the door was unlocked, but she could at least try it. Or she could see what was making that sound. "Only idiots in horror movies go to check what is making a creepy sound. Go to the left and check the exit door."

It made sense, that was logical, but she went to the right and opened the exam room door anyway. It surprised Madison to see there was not an army of horribly tiny, hungry insects. It was just one, and it was huge. It was around four feet in height and resembled a black praying mantis.

The noise she had heard was its feet, coupled with the dragging sound its front claws made. They were long and pointy, with sawtooth spikes running down their length.

Madison was trying to figure out what she was looking at when it attacked her. It came fast, faster than something that size should have been able to move. It brought its giant blade-like pincer right down on her foot.

She screamed and tried to move back, but she was pinned to the floor. Blood shot out of the top of her sneaker like a mini geyser.

She smashed its claw with the chair leg. It pulled back, releasing her foot. She backed up against the door and tried to punch it open. It was locked. Someone had locked her in. She got up and pushed against it; it wouldn't budge.

She kicked it. The mantis was about to attack again. Then she realized—the door was supposed to be pulled open. She had been pushing it.

Madison pulled it open just as the pincer came down again. She made it out, closing the door behind her. The mantis slammed into it and tried to push its way out, just as she had tried. It ate its way through the door instead.

Madison ran to the exit and turned the knob. It was

locked. She turned to face the giant praying mantis. She was still holding the chair leg. It smashed through and came at her.

The door opened up, and a hand grabbed her. "Come on!" said Susan.

"Mom!" Madison was pulled through the doorway.

"Run," shouted Susan.

They were in a dark brown dingy hallway. They ran. The praying mantis followed them.

There was a large window at the end of the hall with a fire escape. Susan made it to the window and threw it open. Madison jumped through and grabbed the ladder. Susan climbed ahead of her and made it to the roof. She reached her hand down.

"Grab it, I'll pull you up," she said.

Madison took her hand. Susan pulled her up with her right and then stabbed her in the stomach with her left. Madison looked up, shocked, blood flowing down her belly.

"I find humans' need to trust to be a genetic liability. Your trust is your weakness." Susan turned into Lam. "You won't have long to regret it." He shoved her off the roof.

Madison plummeted straight down.

78

SIDESTROKE

Susan followed William closely. She knew he would lead her to the ship. He knew these tunnels a lot better than she did.

"You can stop hiding back there. I know you're following me. We're going to the same place for the same reason. You might as well walk up here with me," said William.

"No, thanks, I'm fine back here." Susan leveled her guns at him. She was ready to fire if he made any funny moves. Her heart was pounding with anger and straight chemical adrenaline.

"Suit yourself." He kept walking quickly. William felt the weight of the switchblade in his pocket. If she got close enough, maybe he would cut her open just for fun.

You gotta have fun in your life, or why are we even here? he thought.

They walked down the sloping tunnel that led to the lake. Susan watched William jump in and swim. When she was sure it wasn't a trick, she jumped in too. She swam hard and almost crashed into William, who was slower. They made it to the shore at the same time. Together they walked along the ship and climbed up the entrance ramp.

The ship was brighter inside than they were expecting. William gave Susan hand signals to follow him. She walked behind him, guns ready for whatever might try to sneak up on them.

There were grey aliens everywhere. Susan was ready to shoot, but they seemed to ignore her. They weren't interested; they were busy with their own tasks.

"We're here," said William. "Get ready."

Susan nodded; she was ready. Madison needed her.

They entered the room; it was not what they were expecting. Lam, Diego, and Madison all seemed to be frozen. Susan could see the blood running down Madison's legs, covering her foot. Judging by the strain on her face, Susan knew she was mentally battling Lam. But it was killing her. There was so much blood.

Susan didn't wait; she immediately fired at Lam. And hit him repeatedly. It broke his psychic hold. Lam used his telekinetic power to push the bullets out of his body and seal the wounds.

Madison fell in a bloody puddle. Diego unfroze, still holding the dynamite.

"Give me those," said William. He took the sticks out of Diego's hands.

Susan pushed Diego towards Madison. "Take her!" she screamed. "Get her out of here!"

He picked her up and ran. There was an edge to Susan's voice that told him it was time to go, no arguments. He made it through the ship with Madison in his arms. They got to the lake. Diego put her on his hip and did the sidestroke. He struggled to stay above water, between the girl, the AK-47, and his boots.

79

ALL HIS

Willliam held up the dynamite and lit the fuse.

"Don't let him put it out," he yelled to Susan. "Keep him occupied."

She turned and fired again.

Lam tried to stop William, but Susan kept shooting. She walked towards him, firing, all fear thrown aside. It was working. Lam couldn't attack them while he was on defense. Her right pistol ran out, so she ejected the magazine and slapped in a new one.

That was all the time Lam needed. With a thought, he sent Susan and William flying. They smashed into the back wall and fell, bones broken.

The dynamite was still lying in the middle of the floor, fuse burning.

William smiled and gave Lam the finger.

Susan looked over at the dynamite just as it went off. She saw a searing white flash. She let out a long sigh. Madison was safe. That was all that mattered, nothing else.

William thought about a tropical island sunset with

Faith standing next to him. He had been so close. For a second, she had been all his. All his.

Boom.

80

SUPERSONIC HEADBUTT

Diego was still swimming when the explosion happened. He was looking right at the ship when it blew. The weird thing was, he was fairly sure he saw the ship disappear right before the dynamite went off. It was there and then it was gone, and then the explosion. There was a half second where the ship was gone, and in its place was burning dynamite.

The explosion shook the entire cave. Even the water was affected. The water was calm until the dynamite; now there were big waves. The ceiling of the cave came down. Big rocks splashed into the water. Diego watched overhead, trying to avoid getting squished.

He made it to the shore and picked up Madison. The cave was collapsing behind him. There was no going back. Up ahead, the tunnel sloped up. He walked slowly with Madison in his arms. His leg had gone numb.

Diego heard a hissing noise. He looked around but couldn't find the source.

"What now, snakes?"

In front of him was the creeping green fog. He knew

instantly what it was. He also knew they had no gas masks. Death was approaching. He fell on his knees and held Madison closer. If they had to go, at least it was together.

Diego was suddenly flying through the tunnel.

"Hold your breath!" yelled Faith. She held him by the collar of his vest. Diego covered Madison's mouth. They sped through the tunnels, Diego's feet barely skimming the ground. He would have screamed because they were going too fast, but he would have sucked down a chest full of poison.

They rocketed through the green mist. She turned down a smaller tunnel, flew past automatic machine guns, and found a side tunnel that stopped in a dead end.

Faith sped up. Diego closed his eyes. She lowered her head and smashed through the wall with a supersonic headbutt.

81

BAKERSFIELD HOSPITALS

Kevin was sitting in the Jeep when the ground rumbled. Some rocks started falling from the mountain next to him. He figured that the dynamite must have gone off. They were successful. But where was everyone?

The wall next to the Jeep exploded outwards. The Jeep was showered with chunks of dirt and rocks. It was Faith. She dropped Diego and Madison.

Diego immediately loaded Madison in the back. Everyone jumped in.

"Let's get out of here. We need to get Madison to a hospital," yelled Diego.

"You don't have to tell me twice." Kevin hit the gas.

They raced down the dirt road, a cloud of dust behind them.

Kevin looked in the back. "Where is Susan?"

"She didn't make it," said Diego.

"What do you mean?" asked Faith.

"She and William were on the ship when it blew. But I am not sure what happened to the ship itself."

"You're going to have to be more specific," said Kevin.

Rocks rained down on the hood of the Jeep. The mountain was crumbling.

"Oh, crap," said Kevin.

"When the dynamite exploded, I was watching the ship. It disappeared right before it blew up. I mean, right before. Like one second it was there, then it was gone, and boom. If I wasn't looking right at it, I never would have known."

Faith gritted her teeth. Her fangs gleamed in the moonlight. "So then Lam and William escaped."

"And they took Susan with them," said Kevin.

A huge boulder landed in front of them. Kevin jammed on the brakes and turned the wheel.

"Pull over," said Faith. "I'll take care of this."

Kevin sped up, and Faith flew in the air. She covered the Jeep with her body, letting rocks bounce off of her that would have smashed the Jeep. The bigger boulders she punched and turned into dust clouds. When they were out of danger, Kevin stopped the Jeep.

They all got out. Madison was still bleeding. Her color was turning grey.

Faith picked her up. "It's going to take an hour to drive to the nearest hospital. She doesn't have that kind of time. I'll fly her direct."

"What if someone sees you?" said Kevin.

"It's Bakersfield. Those hospitals see way crazier things than just a plain old vampire."

She kissed Kevin and took off in a blurry streak.

82

CRAWLING FEDS

It took three surgeries before Madison finally stabilized. Her feet were actually way worse than she had realized. They had to remove splinters, pebbles, and glass shards from her soles. She had been running around so amped up on adrenaline; she hadn't even realized.

Madison was in a coma for two days before she opened her eyes. Diego was sitting next to her bed, holding her hand, when it happened. The room smelled like Band-Aids and alcohol.

Madison blinked a couple of times while she got her bearings. Diego gave her some water in a paper cup. She sat up to drink.

"What happened? I don't remember what... did we, um, did we win?"

"I guess you could say that. We stopped the invasion. We turned them away. They're gone," said Diego.

"Well, that sounds like a win to me. Where's my mom?"

"Yeah, that's why we can't really call it a win."

"What do you mean?"

"She's kind of gone."

"You mean she's dead?" Madison's eyes grew swollen.

"No, I mean she's disappeared. No one can find her. I saw the explosion. The ship disappeared right before the dynamite exploded. She and William were on the ship when it went."

"Where did they go?" she asked.

"I don't know. I was hoping you could help with that. With your powers."

Madison closed her eyes and strained. She slumped back down.

"I can't right now. I'm too tired."

Diego got up and walked around the room, stretching his legs. "And what happened to you? How did you get so injured? They had to do a bunch of surgeries to fix you up."

"I was fighting Lam in my head. I had to battle a giant praying mantis. And then Lam pretended to be my mother. He stabbed me in the stomach and pushed me off a roof," she said.

"That sonofabitch. I'll break his face."

"First, we have to find him. And my mom. How the hell are we going to find a giant UFO and an alien overlord?"

Diego moved quickly to the open door and closed it.

"Shhh. Don't talk so loud about that. The nurses were very curious about how you got so injured. I told them you were robbed in Bakersfield. That's not such a stretch," said Diego.

"Why do I have to be quiet? I'm not afraid of telling the truth! I'll call *Dateline* right now!"

"Okay, calm down for a second. There have been some... developments."

"What do you—"

"There have been government agents crawling all over

the mountain. I don't know what they're looking for, but they are mighty curious. They questioned Kevin and me for hours."

"Why?"

"They found my car by the collapsed mine. I convinced them we were just a couple of amateur treasure hunters. When we heard the mine collapsed, we showed up hoping to find some gold."

"They bought that?" she asked.

"I think so. I'm not sure. Would be helpful if I could read minds."

She didn't laugh.

"What am I supposed to do now? With my mom being gone. Legally. Do I have to go live in a foster home or something?"

Diego laughed. "Don't be silly. You turn eighteen in a month. You will be a legal adult. Live at home. Finish school. Be you."

"I guess that makes sense. Though I've never lived alone before."

"Don't worry. I'm a phone call away if you need something or you suspect there's a monster lurking outside."

"Bakersfield is too far away. I'm going to need you to be a lot closer. You're going to have to visit. A bunch." She took his hand.

"I can do that. Besides, we have a new mission."

"Finding my mom."

"Exactly."

83

MONSTER CHASERS

The house was a complete disaster. The front door was missing. Inky had been using the open doorway to go outside to relieve herself. Then she would go back inside and wait for her family to return.

When Kevin and Faith walked in, she launched herself and stood on her hind legs to lick them both. Her tail was wagging so hard she almost knocked herself over.

"Damn, this place is a mess," said Kevin.

"I'm not trying to stick you with all the cleaning, but the sun is almost up, and I need to get to a dark place."

While Faith was passed out, Kevin began the cleaning process. He started with the grow room. Almost all the plants had died. Out of twelve buckets, only two survived. The rest had died from neglect. They ran out of water a week ago, but Kevin had been too busy fighting aliens and monsters to notice.

He chopped the old dead plants and stuffed them in a black plastic bag. The viable plants he harvested. He cut them down, trimmed the big leaves, and hung them up to dry. Kevin's dreams of making thousands off this harvest went out the window. He would barely have enough to make $2,000 if he were lucky. That covered the rent for just two months. Hardly a windfall.

Kevin went through the house, throwing out trash left behind from their nights preparing for the epic battle. Pizza boxes, soda bottles, and candy wrappers were everywhere.

Inky followed him closely, her tail wagging the entire time. She was thrilled to have everyone back home.

When Kevin had three full bags of garbage, he loaded up the hatchback and drove to the dump. He usually hated taking out the trash, but today mundane tasks felt like a victory. Life would eventually return to normal.

Next, he drove to a little building by the post office. The sign above the door read "Library." He chatted with the friendly librarian, who looked a lot like Suzy from *Curb Your Enthusiasm*.

Kevin walked back to his car with a couple of books. He took time to pull over and watch the sunset. On the drive back home, Kevin stopped at the corner store. He picked up some drinks and a bag of ice. At the counter was a young kid with a shaggy haircut.

"Hey, man, how's it going?"

"Good, and you?" said Kevin.

"Oh, you know, things have been crazy."

"Yeah, since the mine collapse," said Kevin.

"No, man, the video."

"What video?"

Kevin's heart skipped a beat. Had someone caught them on video attacking the mine?

"You haven't seen it yet? It's all over the socials. I'll show you." He whipped out his phone. Luckily, there was no one else in the store.

Kevin watched the video as a grainy figure, a large hairy thing, walked across an empty field.

"Yeah, man. That was taken like ten minutes from here. From a car passing by. Right along the Five freeway."

"Hmmm," said Kevin.

"Damn right, hmmm. That makes this entire area Bigfoot country."

"I guess it does." Kevin picked up his snacks and left.

Faith was awake and sitting in the living room when Kevin got back home.

"Good evening, beautiful," he said.

"I think if I were still alive, I would be really sore. Never mind that psycho drugging me and knocking me out of the sky. I have the worst hangover ever."

Kevin went to the kitchen and came back with a big bottle of orange juice.

"I don't know much about vampire anatomy, but I'm pretty sure a cool drink will help."

Faith guzzled it down.

"It's a start," she said. "I'm sorry about your plants. It doesn't look like it's going to be much of a harvest. But knowing you, you will just stubbornly redouble your efforts and have a much better outcome next time." She looked over the grow room. It was mostly empty now, with a couple of plants hanging up to dry. It was far from impressive.

"Yeah, actually, about that. I've been thinking. Maybe we should combine our talents."

"What do you mean?"

"While you were sleeping, I've been doing some research. I went online. I went to the library. I talked to some people."

"What did you find?" she asked.

"This place has been haunted long before Lam got here.

Maybe that's why the mountain was an easy target for him. People have been seeing cryptids and ghosts for at least a hundred years."

"So, you want to move? I like the fresh air up here. So does Inky."

"No, I don't want to move. The opposite. I think we should talk to Diego and form a sort of company. Monster Chasers or something. Like if someone is having trouble with their chickens being eaten by a chupacabra or were-coyotes. Or if someone is being repeatedly abducted by outside entities. I mean, there are services people will need, and where are they going to go?"

"Right."

"And we don't just have to rely on being hired. We could hunt for creatures and get them on video. Then we put it on our YouTube channel and rake in the advertising money when it goes viral and we get millions of views."

"I could see that happening," said Faith. "What about Madison? Shouldn't we include her? She has some really powerful abilities."

"She's a kid. And she almost just died. She's still in the hospital. I don't want to be responsible for her getting hurt again. Besides, she's dealing with her mom being kidnapped somewhere across the galaxy," said Kevin.

84

A SNEAKER

Johnson's first instinct was to inspect the scene from the highest ground he could find. He drove the black Buick as far as the road went until it ended in boulders.

He got out. Black suit, black shoes, and black coat. Black man. Johnson scaled the rocks easily. He found the trail that led to the entrance of the now collapsed mine. There were shells everywhere. There had been a big battle here.

And then Johnson found the bodies. Dead, scaly reptilians. Dozens of them. He hated reptilians. They stank like rotten meat. Always. The road was being blocked off by CHP, but it wouldn't take long for some adventurous kid on a dirt bike to find a way up there.

A video or pictures could be uploaded in a minute. *My god, things were easier in the past. No internet, no phones. Oh, for the days of analog.*

He was going to call in unit 442 to clean up the scene and remove the bodies. He put on his black sunglasses. In the lenses, the words appeared: ACTIVATE 442 IMMEDIATE AIR REMOVAL NEEDED ON MY LOCATION.

Johnson made it up to a ridge and scanned the area. Besides bodies and shell casings, he still found no clues. The information was out there; he just had to find it.

He studied the sloping hill. By the tree line. That's where they had been. He should have been looking down there. He blinked his eyes for a full second, and the magnification in his glasses increased by a hundred times. Now it was like he was down there in person.

Johnson looked left and blinked rapidly. An image from an overhead satellite came into his left lens. He zoomed in with two more blinks. And there it was, just what he was hoping for: a single sneaker. *Perfect.*

Johnson pulled into the hospital parking lot an hour later. It was the second one he had tried. He would try them all if he had to. Methodical was not a problem for Special Agent Johnson.

The sun was sickeningly bright. It was a relief when he walked through the entrance area without a problem. He was broadcasting mental static. It made people ignore him and shy away. They wouldn't remember he had been there.

He found a nurse and asked her if there had been a young girl admitted with severe foot damage. Most likely barefoot. She told him everything he needed before she opened her mouth. Johnson had to remind himself to wait for her to speak or it would be obvious he had read her mind.

85

PIZZA TRADE

Madison left her mother's room the way it was. She was going to find her and bring her back, so there was no point in changing anything. Madison was firm on that; nothing would move her.

Diego had a duffel bag full of clothes in one corner of her living room. He also had a suitcase full of weapons in another, but they were both happier that way. After dealing with vampires, aliens, werecoyotes, and an all-star team of weirdo creatures, heavy firepower was something they wanted close by.

Madison felt the same way about Diego. With her mother gone, the house was silent; it made Madison nervous. With Diego clomping around the house, she felt a little more at ease. That he was an experienced monster killer also made her feel a lot better. It had nothing to do with his chiseled jaw, or the way his smell made her heart pound so loud she was afraid he would hear it.

She noticed him in the bathroom, doing something to the toilet.

"What are you doing?" she asked.

He had the lid off and was looking in the tank. "Hiding places. I have a small revolver I'm putting in a Tupperware case. I'm going to leave it here for an emergency. If someone or something tries to take you hostage. Tell them you have to go to the bathroom."

A year ago, she would have called him insane and kicked him out. Now she just replied with a "Good idea."

"How does a pepperoni pie, chicken wings, and some fried raviolis sound? I'll drive to Mike's Pizza."

"That would sound really good, if your hands weren't in a toilet."

"Oh, right. Haha. Listen, I've been thinking about this: I think we should watch *Fringe* all the way from the first episode. I know you haven't seen it, and it's totally worth it. It's like a different monster every time. Some of them are accurate, some of them are way off, but it's a good place to start."

"I am so ready for some binging," said Madison.

"Me too."

"I believe you said something about getting pizza? I'll make you a deal. You go get it, and I'll be on the couch waiting to snuggle up to you when you get back. Maybe I will even start a fire."

"Sounds like a really sweet trade. I'm coming out ahead, but whatever."

Diego slipped a 9 millimeter in his breast pocket. It was filled with silver tip bullets. Vampires, weremonsters, who knew what was out there. Silver seemed like a good idea.

"I'll be right back. Don't miss me too much. It's not healthy."

She threw an orange couch pillow at him.

Diego opened the door and jumped back. An African American man in a black suit was standing at the bottom of the stairs, holding up a dirty sneaker like it was a golden talisman.

"Diego Gonzales. Is Madison home?" said Johnson.

"Why, hello, creepy guy I've never met that somehow knows who I am. None of your business."

Johnson held up his badge.

"You're going to have to be more specific," said Diego.

"I'm with a special homeland security task force."

"Of course you are."

"Is Madison home? I have something that belongs to her. It also proves you were at the scene of the invasion and mine collapse. I'm guessing some of those were your shell casings we found. No, don't worry, we are fingerprinting them as we speak."

Johnson walked up the stairs and brushed past Diego, using his mental static trick.

"Madison, there you are. I've been looking for you all day. It's nice to finally meet you," he said, none of this with his mouth. "Have you been missing this?" He gave her the sneaker.

"What do you want?"

"No, no, you don't understand. I'm not an enemy. In fact, we are going to become best friends. I'm here to help you. After everything that you went through at the mine, I'm the only one on this planet that can help you."

"How do you possibly know what happened? You weren't there. No one knows what happened."

"But it's like I was there. I saw everything you saw. Because I got it all out of your head just now," said Johnson.

"That fast?"

"I can teach you how to do that. And other things."

"Is that how you got past Diego without him punching your face off?" she asked.

"Exactly. It's a trick I use to walk past people without them noticing me. I call it mental static."

Diego was standing there watching them. "Why are you guys just staring at each other without talking? You look like a Spaghetti Western."

"We're talking in our heads," said Madison.

"Oh. That's pretty weird. And rude."

"He's right," said Madison out loud. "Why are you here?"

"I'm here to help."

"That's very generic," interjected Diego.

"I think we can help each other. You give me what I want, and I can help you with what you want."

"And that is?"

"You are obviously very powerful, but you lack the training that could make you into something truly spectacular. Come and train with us."

"No way. I will not be some jack-booted government thug who oppresses people."

"That's not what I do."

"Wait, you said you would help me. Help me how?"

"I can help you get your mother back."

"What? How? She's somewhere across the universe. Wait, who do you work for?"

"Space Force."

86

CHAMPAGNE TIME

I t took a week before Kevin and Faith could get the house back to normal. Kevin found the door and attached it to the entrance again. They scrubbed the vampire blood out of the carpet and cleaned up William's blood in the attic where he had kidnapped Faith.

Inky was happy to be back to her routine—a long walk in the woods in the morning and a dark crisp walk at night through the neighborhood. She had hamburgers for a couple of nights in a row. They felt bad about leaving her alone for so long.

Faith went back to work at the hospital in Bakersfield. But she switched her schedule to night shift only. Her commute used to take an hour; now it took only ten minutes. Her coworkers thought her boyfriend must have been dropping her off and picking her up because they never saw her car in the parking lot.

Kevin tied up another bag of garbage. "This is the last load going to the dump. This place is actually clean now. I think it's cleaner then when we moved in."

Faith looked around and nodded. "That's cuz we're awesome."

She flew across the room and kissed Kevin.

"Who doesn't love a kiss delivered by airmail," he said. "Listen, we should think about saving up so that we can put a down payment on a house."

"Really?"

"We're just wasting money on rent right now. And I don't see us splitting up anytime soon," said Kevin.

"Me neither."

"All right, cool, now we have a goal to work towards. When I get back from the trash, we should open that bottle of champagne I was going to open for the end of the harvest."

When Kevin returned from the dump, Diego's truck was in the driveway.

"Hey, man, just came by to say hi. Madison's house isn't that far from here," said Diego as they shook hands. Diego was not a hugger. "This place is looking good."

"Thanks, it took a couple of days, but we got it done," said Kevin.

"I wanted to talk to you guys about something," said Diego.

"We wanted to talk to you about something too," said Faith.

"I was thinking we could join up and form—" said Diego.

"Some sort of monster hunting team," said Kevin.

"For hire," said Diego.

"Exactly," said Faith and Kevin at the same time.

"We should set up a website, a YouTube channel for our videos," said Faith.

"Twitter, Insta," added Diego.

Kevin went to the kitchen and pulled out the bottle of champagne.

"This feels like the right time for this." He came back. "So, there's a video of a Bigfoot just a few miles from here. It's gone viral. Let's get some of our own footage for our new channel," said Kevin.

"Sure, a few million views is a great way to start off," said Diego.

"Faith, can you do some flyovers and see if you can find it?"

"That would be easy. Wait, what about Madison? Shouldn't we bring her in on this? Her powers would be really helpful."

"Yeah, she's a little busy right now. New classes. She's going to school."

87

SCHOOL

Madison pulled into a plain strip mall on the outskirts of Edwards Air Force Base. She got out and checked her surroundings. She slung a duffel bag over her shoulder. There was a liquor store, an abandoned tire place, and tucked in the corner was a dingy tax office. That's where she walked.

She unfolded the piece of paper in her hand and read the instructions. She entered and looked around—there was no one there. The front desk was literally dusty, and the waiting room was empty.

She sat and looked at the clock on the wall. When five minutes passed, she walked to the door marked "Staff Only." There was a keypad. Madison remembered the code they gave her and punched it in. The door unlocked and swung open.

A plain white hallway led to a set of shiny elevator doors. She put her eye up to the panel. There was a green flash, and the doors dinged open. *More elevators*, she thought.

The trip down might have been three minutes, but it seemed like half an hour. The elevator came to a stop and then started moving sideways. After a ten-minute horizontal ride, the doors opened and agent Johnson was standing there in a black suit, waiting. Smiling.

"You look like it's the first day of school and you're nervous," he said.

"Well, isn't it?"

They walked down a corridor, passing soldiers with no identifying patches.

"I wouldn't call it school; it's more like, well... All right, yeah, it's school. But there's no reason to be nervous. You're the most powerful student in the class."

"Really?"

The ground shook underneath them. The lights overhead swung back and forth. Soldiers looked around nervously.

"No, not really, but it's close. It's hard to quantify between different abilities," said Johnson. "Just remember why you're here."

"To find my mother."

"To protect your country in ways very few people can." He stopped talking and said into her mind directly, "If you want them to send you into space, you should stick with my answer."

"Right," she replied silently.

They came to the training room. Johnson waved his hand by a sensor and the door opened up. The room was mostly dark, but Madison heard what she was pretty sure was a quiet explosion. She could see shadows running around, fighting.

The room suddenly got really cold, and something wet landed on her shoulder. She looked at it.

"What the hell? Is it snowing in here?" she asked.

"Don't worry about it. You'll do fine." Johnson shoved her into the room.

The door slid shut. Madison heard it lock behind her.

~

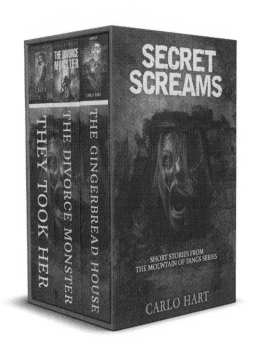

Get your FREE box set of terrifying novellas!
Go to **carlohart.com**

Grab the horrific sequel to Mountain Of Fangs!
<u>TENTACLES OF DEATH</u>

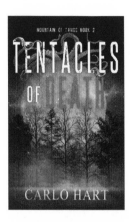

Book 2 - Kevin, Diego and Faith must fight a black witch who is terrorizing Frazier Mountain. Can they stop her from opening a doorway to an invasion of evil? Can Madison use her powers to stop a deadly monster on the moon?

Get yours today!

REVIEWS

If you enjoyed this book, please consider leaving a review. I would really appreciate it! Reviews really help new authors. Thank you! Horror readers are the best!!

CARLO HART

A former comedy writer for the TV show <u>American Dad</u>, when Carlo isn't painting or hiking with his dogs, he is writing horror stories, in a cabin at the top of a mountain. Surrounded by monsters.

f

Made in the USA
Middletown, DE
13 November 2021

51788665R00201